TWD II

TROUBLE WITH A DREAM II
VICTIMS?

Predators and Killers; A Fight for Justice

by Penelope Wells

A tale based on the life and times of the artist Penelope Wells

GALVANIZED GROUP INC.

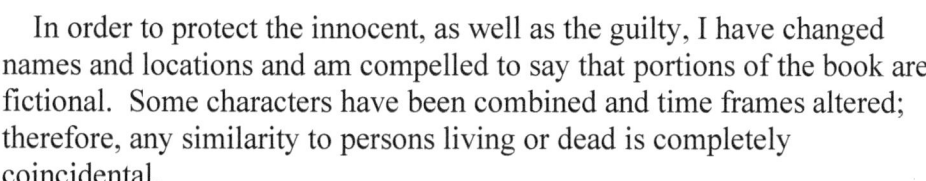

This is my story, written in my own words. I'm not what you'd call a professional writer, but I have been asked to recount the tales of my adventures to captivated friends and acquaintances ever since I was a tot.

After I was offered a movie deal and told that Hollywood was desperate for me, I decided that it was time to put pen to paper and this is it... my story....

THE LETTER

Dear Pat,

    I'm writing to let you know that I'm on the run. I've shot four men, members of an outlaw motorcycle club, it was self-defense, but I doubt that the truth matters much right now. Things are chaotic, I'm certain that a hit man is on my trail and probably the FBI as well.

    I'm headed for a safe place; you know that I can survive. I'll see you when it's over.

              Love,

              Sissy

TABLE OF CONTENTS

OLD FRIENDS, NEW ENEMIES

I was now separated from my husband, and no one in my family gave me any grief about it as I had expected they would. They just didn't talk about it; that is no one but Aunt Helen, Uncle Henry's wife. When she heard that I was at Pat's she came right over and invited herself in. "I heard about you and Larry," she said, "and I want you to know that a woman's place is with her husband. You've made your bed and now you're just going to have to lay in it. You married him, and it's too late for you to do anything about it now. Penelope, I know what I'm talking about; I know that it isn't always easy. There were many times through the years that I would have liked to leave your Uncle Henry, but I did the right thing and I stayed with him."

Then she brought up God, just like I knew she would. "You know that the Lord is against divorce and it says in the word that you are supposed to submit to your husband. I happen to know that Larry still loves you and wants you back. Now stop this nonsense, you do the right thing, like I did, and go home to your husband where you belong."

She had obviously talked to Larry, and was actually on his side! Yes, it was a sad situation; she had no caring or sympathy for me. There I sat battered and broken with the fresh blood of my baby on my heart, dead at the hands of its father. My animals also murdered, and I had barely escaped with my own life. And here sat my Aunt, pious and proper in her expensive clothes and jewelry, her fancy car waiting to take her back to her stately home. Yes, she knew all about it, the self-appointed judge and jury, giving me advice directly from, "The Throne of God."

Returning to Larry was a death sentence, a sentence that she had imposed on me with no trial or evidence. I didn't defend myself; I would do nothing to try to change her mind. No one but Pat ever knew what had really happened that day and I could trust her to keep the secret.

As for myself, I didn't think that God would want me to ruin my whole life because I had made a mistake. I was moving ahead no matter what anyone tried to do to stop me.

I think that I remember reading something about that in the Bible, something about not judging others.

Yes it was true, I had made a big mistake, if I hadn't married Larry I wouldn't have gone through any of this pain and heartache. I didn't even know that people as vile as him existed. I was hurt and confused; I needed guidance to make right decisions in the future. I remembered a sermon that our pastor had once preached; "In times of trouble don't reach for alcohol, don't reach for drugs, don't reach for sex to ease the pain, reach for God." It sounded like good advice. What did God have to say about this? I wanted to find out. The next Sunday morning, I dressed up and went to church.

It had been a long while since I had been to the church. When I pulled into the parking lot and got out of the truck, I heard some loud clamoring. What was that annoying noise? When I entered the church building I was surprised to find that it was music. It was horrible, loud banging drums and songs that rambled on and on, repeating the same thing over and over again, with no real melody.

Heading the song service was a woman screeching at the top of her lungs; drowning out all of the other instruments except the drums. It was like being in a gymnasium at a basketball game, the ball furiously bouncing and the announcer yelling over the loud-speaker. I sat down at the back of the church and was soon suffering from a headache.

What had happened to the good old songs that had a pleasing melody and a meaningful powerful message? How did these people sit through this? Was it possible that they actually enjoyed it? I wanted to leave, but decided to stick it out; things could only get better from here.

At long last, the song service was over and the pastor began to preach. I was hoping to hear something that would help to give me direction. But I was having a difficult time listening to the sermon; some of the women in the congregation were pointing at me and I could hear them whispering. I sat uncomfortably through the service and after it was over, a deacon of the church began to chat with me. We were politely passing the time of day when his wife came out of nowhere and rudely jerked him away. She gave me a filthy look and said, "This is my husband!"

"Well good for you," I retorted, "I'm real happy for ya."

I tried not to let it get me down. After all, I couldn't let this nonsense stop me from reaching out in the right direction, reaching out to God. I still made an effort, but I was shunned by them all. Did these old biddies actually think that I was after their husbands? They most certainly did, and they were taking a stand against me.

I realized that I no longer met their requirements and they let me know that I wasn't welcome anymore.

I was on my way out the door, when I actually heard a woman refer to me as damaged goods, making very sure that I heard it. She was surrounded by friends and when I turned to look at them, they began to laugh nervously. Had I become a joke? I didn't say a word and just kept moving toward the door; I had to get out of there!

I had already walked through the gravel parking lot and was climbing into my truck when the pastor caught up to me. Here was a "great man of God." I thought that he must have seen what had happened and was rushing to my aide. Now maybe I would get a kind word, something, anything, to help ease my pain.

The pastor was on a mission and there was no lead-in. "Penelope, I appreciate your difficulty, but I have to inform you that your church membership has been revoked. We don't allow divorced people to be members of this church and as a custodian of the church I have to follow all of the rules, not just the ones that I choose. Now you can still come and worship, but you will no longer be a church member."

I couldn't believe my ears! When I needed "God's people" the most, they were actually kicking me out! I hadn't asked for anything, I had just hoped for a good sermon and maybe some polite conversation. Was that too much to hope for? Apparently it was! I started to tell him how I felt about it when he interrupted me. "Now don't misunderstand me, I never said that you couldn't attend the church, just that you can no longer be a member."

I had seen the church help homeless people and drug addicts. They ran to the aid of anyone who was ill, people that were complete strangers. I was a member, but it seems that I was caught in a loophole, care for people, love people… except for me.

This was not the God that I had learned about; God clearly wasn't in this place! They called themselves Christians, but it couldn't have been further from the truth. These people were an example of everything that Jesus had stood against! I was glad to know that they were a bunch of phonies and that I was best rid of them!

"Sir," I addressed the pastor, "you and your church are doing the work of the devil much more effectively than any Satan worshipper could ever hope to! Satan is sitting right in the front row of your congregation, and you are supporting and promoting him. You, as the pastor and spiritual leader, are responsible before the Lord for what you have created here!"

I was angry when I drove away and I hit the gas petal a little hard. The gravel in the parking lot went flying and sprayed the pastor. "Oh no! I didn't mean to do that!" Then I had a quick thought; he was the ring leader of this lynch mob and I decided to open fire, so I hit the gas petal and blasted him. Dust and gravel flew everywhere, I spun the truck to the right, then to the left. The pastor was coughing and yelling at me, trying to get out of the way. I was terrorizing him, but he deserved it.

The other church members came pouring out of the building to see what was going on. I pulled out onto the street and burned a patch of rubber that ran the full length of the church. I glanced back seeing the cruel hypocrites left coughing in a cloud of black smoke. The cars in the parking lot were covered with dirt and gravel. "Let them sue me, I don't care anymore!" I roared down the road in my big truck.

I went straight home and sat on the sofa, trying to calm down; then I got on my knees and prayed. I realized that I was in good company; it was the religious leaders who had given Jesus the most grief. They were the ones who had actually fought to crucify him.

I cannot compare myself to Jesus, of course; obviously He would have handled it better than me. But, I felt that He at least knew what I was going through.

Weeks went by; I was getting stronger every day and actually beginning to feel like my old self again. I called the Interior Designer that I worked for and told her that I would soon be ready to return.

"Perfect timing!" she exclaimed, "I've got a couple of big jobs coming up in a week or two and I could really use you." It was nice to know that I had a job to go back to.

Pat had taken a week off of work, and her childhood friend, Tiffany, was visiting. Tiffany and Pat, had been friends their whole lives and they managed to spend time together every summer.

Tiffany had already been there a few days when I got a call from my old childhood friend, Skip. Skip and I had somehow managed to keep in touch. He had a huge ranch far up in the mountains and asked me for a favor. Every year, Skip and most of the ranchers in his town went to compete in the rodeo and they didn't have anyone to do the evening feed while they were away. I was happy to do him the favor. Skip was coming down the mountain for supplies and planned to pick me up the next day.

That evening, I was packing my things, getting ready for the trip when, Pat and Tiffany, came back from the movies. "Whatcha packing for? Planning to escape from us?" Pat jokingly asked.

"Skip's going to compete in the rodeo again this year and I'm gonna do the evening feed for him and his neighbors."

"You're going to Skip's place? I love it up there! Do you think he'd mind if Tiffany and I came with you?"

"Of course not, I'm sure he'd be happy to have you and Tiffany. I'll call and let him know that you're coming along. It'll be more fun for me that way too, I'd like the company."

Pat and Tiffany, were in the other room packing when I heard Pat say, "Hey Sissy, don't let me forget to bring the guns and the big ammo box. We can get in some good target practice in while we're up there."

Just as I was starting to answer my sister, Tiffany screeched, "I'm not going if you two are bringing guns! I don't even want to be in the same house with a gun! Guns are evil and they kill. Returning violence for violence takes you right down to the criminal's level and it never solves anything. People just need to be kind and reason with each other to solve their differences. Soon guns will be outlawed, then only the police will have them, and we can put an end to all the senseless killing."

Wow! Where did that come from? What was Tiffany's problem? I had never heard her talk like that before.

Pat shouted right back at her, "Disarming the citizens is going to stop all the senseless killing? Tiffany, you've lost your mind if you think that outlawing guns is going to disarm criminals. The only ones who will have guns will be the criminals, and they'll know that us good, law-abiding citizens won't have protection. We'll be defenseless against them and none of us will be safe in our own homes! Guns kill? A gun never killed anyone, it's merely a tool. How can you say such a thing? You may as well blame a pencil for misspelling a word as to blame a gun for killing. People are the ones who do the killing and if they don't use guns they'll kill with something else."

I could see that the argument was about to escalate and I needed to intervene, so I called Pat, "Come here, I want to talk to you for a minute."

Pat came angrily stomping into the room to see what I wanted. "I've had all I can stand of that Tiffany," she said. "Since she's been going to college she's driving me up the wall with her superior know-it-all attitude.

All she's done from the minute she got here is belittle me. She's been my friend my whole life, but I'd just as soon send her packing and never see her again."

"Pat, you know that I'll back you up, whatever you decide, but think it over before you do something that you might regret later. Tiffany's one of those people that's been over-protected all of her life. She's never had anything bad happen to her and I hope for her sake, that she'll be able to continue to live in her ignorant bliss. You have to realize that she just doesn't know any better."

"Yeah, I guess I can suffer through with her for a few more days. But it's gonna cost us some good target practice."

"That's okay, we can practice another time."

I knew better than to go up into the mountains without a gun, Skip's place was so isolated that the bears walked right down the middle of the streets. But, to keep the peace, we left the guns behind. I thought that I was doing the right thing, trying to salvage, Pat and Tiffany's, long term friendship.

The next day, Skip picked us up and I was thrilled to see my old friend again. We reminisced and laughed about all the fun that we had had together as children, and by the time we reached the ranch, I was feeling better and looking forward to taking a dip in the swimming hole again.

When we pulled through the gate, Skip was surprised to see his wife and friends standing in the driveway, ready to leave for the rodeo. As soon as Pat, Tiffany and I got out of the truck, they climbed right in. The dogs piled in on top of them and they drove down the driveway waving goodbye.

Because of his sudden departure, Skip had forgotten to leave us the keys to the car and we had no way to travel the long distance from ranch to ranch, when it was time to feed. Luckily, they hadn't taken all of the horses to the rodeo; there were three geldings in the pasture near the house. I knew the horses and had ridden them before. When we went into the tack room we found that all the bridles and saddles for the horses were there. "Well it looks like we're going to be riding-horseback," I announced.

"That's okay with me," Pat said happily. "Now, let's get the groceries put away, get out to the swimming hole and start having some fun!"

We quickly packed a lunch and hiked out to go swimming and lay in the

11

sun. What a wonderful time we had; it was a lovely sunny day and the water was crystal clear. Skip had the tire swing up and the girls were having a ball, swinging and jumping into the refreshing water. I was still a little banged up, so I passed on the rough stuff and took it easy.

Time flies by when you're having fun, and it didn't take long before the sun had passed over and it was time to feed. It was hard to leave, so we pushed it to the very last minute and stayed as long as we possibly could.

The three of us hiked back to the house and when we got there, we realized that we didn't have time to change our clothes, so we quickly pulled our cutoffs on over our bathing suits, saddled up the horses and rode off.

Skip's horses were nice well-trained animals and a pleasure to ride. We stopped at each ranch and fed the dogs, cats, chickens and horses. Things went smoothly; it was a big job but we finished in a few hours, and started the long ride back to Skip's place.

We were trotting along in single file, on the shoulder of the country road, when I heard Tiffany start in again. "You know Pat, I consider this animal cruelty, riding a horse with a heavy saddle and a bit in its mouth, forcing it go against its will. Horses are living beings and they have just as many rights as we do. How would you like someone riding on your back?"

"I do have someone on my back… you! If you feel that way, get off and walk," Pat snapped.

"I consider myself a kind person and that's just exactly what I will do," Tiffany said indignantly. "Someone has to be an example to you two barbarians." Then she dismounted and started walking, leading the horse down the road. Pat and I stopped trotting; we slowed the horses down so that Tiffany could keep up with us.

I had thought that leaving the guns behind would have pacified Tiffany. I was hoping that we could have all gotten along and enjoyed ourselves, but at that point I knew that she had an agenda, and that it was going to continue to be difficult to deal with her.

At the rate that we were moving, we wouldn't make it back to the ranch before dark… not a good idea. I was trying to decide how to handle Tiffany when she began to preach to Pat and me about animal cruelty; as though we were guilty of the atrocity.

I wasn't going to go at a snail's pace for Tiffany's benefit and then listen to her insult me any longer. "Tiffany either get back on the horse or give him to me, I'm heading to the ranch as fast as I can get there. I'm not going to get stuck out here on the road after dark with the horses because of you and your nonsense. You want to walk, you go right ahead and walk, but don't expect Pat and me to cater to you any longer, I've had enough!" then I reached down and took the reins from her.

At that moment, I noticed a beat-up dusty car slowly moving toward us. Three disgusting men pulled up alongside and started trying to pick us up.

"Go bother someone else!" Pat sharply told them.

"Get lost creeps," I chimed in, and the weirdo's started to drive away.

"Pat, there's no need to be rude," Tiffany scolded, and then waved for the car to come back. "Maybe they need directions or something."

It was clear to see that Tiffany was asking for trouble and I didn't want any part of it, "You're on your own Tiffany," I sternly told her. Pat and I were fed up and we trotted down the road together ponying Tiffany's horse alongside.

The car quickly backed up to Tiffany, and Pat and I slowed down a bit and looked back. Tiffany walked up to the car and was leaning in the window with her cleavage hanging out of her bathing suit top, talking to the disgusting men. We were still close enough to hear the beginning of what she was saying, and the idiot was actually apologizing for our behavior!

Pat looked at me aghast, "What if she gets in the car with those creeps?"

"If she does, there's nothing we can do about it." What was I supposed to do? Go back, scold her, and tell her to come with us? She had already made it perfectly clear that she wouldn't have listened to anything that we, the ignorant uneducated hillbillies, had to say.

Minutes later, here came Tiffany running down the road after us, her face was red, and she was all shook up. The despicable men in the car were driving along side of her, laughing and taunting. When they got closer, Pat and I demanded that they leave her alone. The men called us lesbians and made a terrible scene. Things were soon out of control and they started to get out of the car. Pat and I prepared for it to come to blows, but when we showed no fear, the men got back in their car, shouting and calling us filthy names as they headed down the road.

We tried to beat it to the ranch, but noticed that the creeps were sneakily trying to follow us. We rode down one of the side roads, trying to avoid them, with Tiffany stubbornly still on foot. Then, we hid with the horses behind some big oleander bushes and watched as the car past us by.

"Let's wait a while longer until we're sure they're gone," I said. "If they saw us turn in here, hopefully they'll think that we're staying at one of the spreads down this road. Nobody down here is at the rodeo and the dogs will be on 'em in a split second."

When enough time had passed, we started to head back to the ranch, carefully watching for the car with the horrid men. It was nearly dark, and Pat and I weren't poking along waiting for Tiffany. She soon got tired of running, trying to keep up, and eventually got back on the horse.

There was no sign of the beat-up car, I was certain that the men hadn't followed us and we had arrived safely at the ranch.

Pat and I tried to be gracious. We didn't embarrass Tiffany by pointing out how stupid she had been and neither of us mentioned anything about what had happened on the road. I was hoping that she had learned a lesson and would get off of her high horse.

Unfortunately, that was too much to ask for; we were brushing the horses down when that blasted Tiffany started in again. I couldn't believe it; she just wouldn't let it drop! "It wouldn't have hurt you two to show a little kindness. Just because those men were uneducated and unattractive was no reason for you to be so rude to them. You said some horrible things and started all the trouble. After all, they are human beings and you really hurt their feelings. It's no wonder that they reacted the way they did!"

It was hard to believe, but Tiffany was actually blaming Pat and me for the whole incident! "Tiffany, cut the crap," I said, "we all know what happened back there, why don't you just admit that you were wrong? What'd they do, try to pull you into their car?"

Tiffany looked at me indignantly, "They did no such thing, what happened was not their fault, they were just hurt and angry because of the way that you treated them. Those unfortunate men didn't know how to react properly, they just lack the benefit of a decent education."

"Yeah, I could tell… uneducated."

Who did she think she was fooling? It was pathetic. Now I knew what Pat had been going through the past few days. I wished that I hadn't stuck my big nose into it and stopped Pat from sending Tiffany home. We would have been having a great time if she hadn't been there.

I tried to keep my cool and when we finished grooming the horses we all went inside the house. We had no sooner closed the door, when Tiffany started in about gun control again; going on and on about guns killing people. We tried to ignore her, but she just wouldn't stop.

Talking to two country girls about gun control, what was she angling for, a pop in the nose? Was that what it was going to take to her shut up?

I interrupted her, "Let's start dinner now," I suggested and was relieved that the distraction had worked. Tiffany actually shut up for a minute and we all went into the kitchen to start cooking.

Pat was still fuming. She was preparing to cut bell peppers and reached into a drawer and pulled out a big kitchen knife. She held it up in front of her face, "See this knife Tiffany? Maybe you should outlaw it too. You know, I did hear tale of someone getting murdered by a kitchen knife. The knife just jumped up, all by itself, and rammed itself right into a man's heart. Knives are evil and dangerous and they kill."

Pat was screaming, her eyes were blazing she was so mad. For a split second I thought that Tiffany had pushed her over the edge, and I was afraid that Pat might go after her with the knife. I was happy to see that I was wrong, when Pat quickly went on, "And don't forget all the other senseless killings Tiffany, you can't just focus on guns and overlook everything else, why you have to stop them all if you really want to get the job done right. Let's see, cars kill, and people have been hung with rope, then there's poison, drug overdose, and baseball bats. People have also been pushed off of bridges and been killed, and don't forget cliffs, oh yes and razor blades. There are so many ways to kill, should I go on? Why, Penelope herself had a boyfriend killed by a beer bottle, surely you should go on a campaign to outlaw "them." I can see the slogan now, 'No more beer bottles, beer bottles kill!' And you have documented proof of an actual senseless killing. You and those highfaluting people at that school you've been going to, have your work cut out for you, trying to stop all the senseless killing in the world … Tiffany! You're ridiculous!"

"Stay on the subject at hand Pat, the subject is guns, not all this other nonsense that you're babbling about. You don't need a gun, no one does. What do you think the police are for? To protect you of course! If I ever have a problem with someone, I'll just be kind and reason with them. I certainly won't be like you and Penelope and step down to their level and threaten them with violence like you shamefully did today. Your ridiculous cruel performances; with those poor ignorant men on the road was a perfect example. Of course, I'm not foolish enough to believe that every person can be reasoned with, but on the slight chance that I encounter someone so primitive that they can't grasp the basics of common human decency, I'll simply call the police and allow them to solve the problem for me. It's all very pedestrian, Pat, and if you had half a brain you could grasp it. The police are properly trained and they know how to handle a dangerous situation better than you ever could. That's why you should leave it to a trained professional who, unlike you, actually knows how to use a gun properly. It's the only way that we can all be truly safe."

"Oh, I get it now," Pat answered, "you believe in fairy tales, the police are super hero's that can appear on the scene within seconds and save the day. Is that what you honestly think? The police are only people, just like you and me; by the time they get the call and make the trip to help you… it's already over…..you're dead or whatever, just another statistic."

Before Tiffany could answer, I had to get them stopped; I didn't think that Pat could take much more. The way that things were going, Tiffany was about to have a firsthand experience with violence very shortly.

I took hold of Pat's arm, "Pat, just drop it, please," I begged, "she's an idiot and there's no reasoning with her." Pat took a deep breath and held herself together.

Despite the disagreement with Tiffany, we somehow managed to have a nice meal; then we watched scary movies and stayed up late.

Skip had a big place and there were plenty of bedrooms for all of us, but when it was time to hit the sack, Pat and I bunked together and Tiffany stayed in the next room. I left the bedroom window open as I always did, for fresh air. When we turned out the lights, Pat and I stayed up and talked and joked about Tiffany for a while. What an "educated" fool she was!

When we finally unwound and started to settled down enough to go to sleep, we heard a strange noise, "Did you hear that?" I asked Pat.

"Sure did. What was it?"

"It might be the mule banging into the shed…… Oh no, I hope it's not a bear!"

"No, I think it's a raccoon, it's too close to the house." Then we heard it again. "Oh God please don't let it be a bear!!!"

"Hush, listen…. It's Tiffany!" I said. The noise was definitely coming from Tiffany's room. "It sounds like she's trying to pry the screen off the window."

"What next?" Pat said disgustedly. "She's probably taking off the screen because she thinks that we're persecuting the damn mosquitoes. Mosquitoes gotta eat too, you know."

I started laughing, "Feeding the mosquitoes sounds crazy, but who knows how far she'll take her screwball morality? Maybe that is what she's doing; I wouldn't be surprised." I got out of bed and walked toward the door, "I'll go check and see what's going on; she should have been asleep a long time ago."

I opened the door to Tiffany's room and the room was dark. "Tiffany, are you awake?" I asked. She didn't answer. Then I heard the noise again and turned on the light. There was Tiffany lying in bed with the covers pulled up around her neck, her eyes as big as saucers. "What are you doing in here? What's that noise?"

Tiffany tried to talk, but had a hard time getting the words out and she very quietly whispered, "Some…one ….is....tr…..ying   t.t.t.t.t.to open…the…..wi….wi…win..dow."

"Is the window locked?" I asked. She nodded her head, yes, and I believed that it was locked or they would have already gotten in the house.

Pat was right in the next room and I knew for certain that that window was open. I left Tiffany, rushed into the other bedroom and slammed the window closed and locked it. "Get out of here!" I yelled.

"Pat, someone's outside trying to get in Tiffany's window, probably burglars. It's well known that Skip competes in the rodeo every year; it's a perfect set-up for a burglar. Burglars don't like to go in when someone's home, now that they know that the house is occupied, they'll probably go away. We better check and make sure that all the doors and windows are locked, just in case."

Then I shouted to Tiffany, "Tiffany get up and call the sheriff, the phone's in the kitchen!"

I went to the kitchen and took three big butcher knives from the drawer. I kept one and gave one to each of the girls. Then Pat and I went through the big house; we turned out all the lights inside, and turned on all the outside lights as we checked the doors and windows. When we finished, we went to the kitchen to see what the sheriff had said. Tiffany was holding the receiver in her hand and still hadn't placed the call. I took the phone from her, handed it to Pat, and Pat called the Sheriff while I stood guard.

We waited for the sheriff; sitting in the middle of the house in the dark, between the back and front doors. "If they're burglars they're gone, but just in case, this is the plan; if they come in through the front, we run out the back, and if they get in the back, we run out the front." I didn't want to get cornered. If it were the men that we had seen on the road, I knew that there were at least three of them. There was a chance that they could be at both doors at the same time, but with all three of us, I was hoping that we could fight our way outside with the knives and get lost in the darkness. All we had to do was hold out long enough for the sheriff to show up.

We sat in the dark, waiting. "Turn on the lights," Tiffany cried, "I want to see."

Pat sternly responded, "Shhh, Tiffany be quiet, we have to leave the lights off, we don't want to be seen. This way they won't know what we're doing, where we are, or that we have the knives; just shut up and do what you're told."

"Tiffany, the darkness is your friend," I confirmed.

We could hear the prowlers going from window to window and door to door, jiggling the knobs and trying to force the windows open. I wondered how much longer it would be before they broke a window and came inside. There was no doubt that they knew that someone was in the house. Our situation became very clear to me, and that's when I got deathly afraid, these men weren't burglars, they were after us! I could only pray that the sheriff would make it in time.

We were trapped in the house and all we could do was wait. Wait for whatever was coming; rape, murder? Who knew what these villains had in mind for us? Who knew if we could escape?

We waited and waited. Where was the blasted sheriff?! We could hear the men outside, stomping and banging against the house. What were they doing now? How much longer would it be before we were fighting for our lives? My heart was pounding so loudly, I was certain that Pat and Tiffany could hear it.

If I had my gun I wouldn't be sitting here in the dark, scared and defenseless. At the first sign of trouble, I would have run the scumbags off. "Oh why did I let myself in for this?! I knew better than to come up here unarmed!" Trying to keep the peace with Tiffany could prove to be our violent end!

The phone rang, it was the sheriff's dispatcher, "We're having trouble finding the place. Where did you say you were? We don't have any record of that street on our map."

"We're between the Haskel and the Farber ranches on Skip Road. Hurry please! They're still out there banging against the house!"

"Okay, we're on our way."

More time went by, the prowlers hadn't come in the house yet and we saw the headlights of the sheriff's car coming down the road. "Thank God, they're here!"

We told the sheriff what had happened and he wasn't at all concerned. He stood on the porch and halfheartedly flashed his flashlight up and down the front yard, "Looks like your prowler's gone now. You girls keep the lights on, that's all you need to do to be safe. Quit worrying and please, just go to sleep. I don't have time for this nonsense, we're very busy tonight."

The sheriff was there and gone in less than five minutes. He hadn't done much, but at least I figured that he had chased the prowlers away. But Pat and I decided that we had better stay up, just in case. We kept the lights inside the house turned off, and we quietly sat in the dark and waited and listened.

Tiffany started to reach for the light switch again, "The sheriff told us to keep the lights on, we better do as he said. He's the trained professional and he knows what he's talking about!"

Pat grabbed Tiffany's hand and stopped her from turning on the light. "Tiffany, are you really that stupid? That sheriff thinks that we're just a bunch of hysterical females. He also said for us to go to sleep." She then raised her fist, "Do I have to knock you out and put you to sleep? Or are you gonna shut up and be quiet?"

I was looking at the clock, it had been exactly ten minutes since the sheriff had left when we heard, BANG, BANG… BANG, BANG, then the grating screech of the big garage door being raised. One minute later, the knob of the door leading into the kitchen from the garage was rattling and then someone started slamming into it, trying to kick it in; the door bowing from the force.

Pat and I jumped to our feet and positioned ourselves on each side of the door; the big butcher knives, clenched tightly in our hands.

"Pat, the second they come through, start hacking! Tiffany, get on the phone and get the sheriff back out here!"

"I can't, I can't!" Tiffany cried, "I'm too scared, I can't move!"

"Tiffany get over it, Pat and I have to do the fighting, just make the blasted call!"

BAM, BAM, the door was buckling. "Tiffany call the sheriff!"

Reality had set in and Tiffany finally got it, she screamed at the top of her lungs, "I TOLD THEM WHERE WE WERE STAYING!"

"Tiffany we already figured that out….it doesn't matter now, please… just call the sheriff!"

Pat and I were ready, the fight for our lives was about to begin. But were we bringing knives to a gunfight? Even if that were the case, we hoped to catch the enemy off guard, and take them out when they came bursting through the door.

"Sissy, Skip has to have a gun around here someplace!"

"He does," I answered, "but he told me that the guns were all locked in the gun safe."

BAM, BAM! The door was beginning to give way, when it occurred to me that Skip most likely had a gun in his desk drawer. "Pat, retreat to the den!" I ordered.

We began running and stumbling down the dark hallway, but Tiffany didn't follow. "Tiffany, come on!" Pat shouted.

Pat and I made it to the den. BAM! BAM! BAM! I could hear the crazy men pounding.

"Pat, help me push the desk against the door! The two of us began to push Skip's heavy desk across the huge room. But where was Tiffany? "Pat, keep pushing the desk, I'll go see what happened to Tiffany."

I ran down the hall and back to the kitchen, there was Tiffany still standing near the kitchen counter holding the phone in her hand. The invaders were coming into the house, the first one was half way through the broken door when I took the phone from Tiffany and put it to my ear; it was dead, they had cut the phone line!

I took hold of Tiffany's arm, she was stiff and sluggish and it was hard for me to drag her along, but we disappeared into the dark hallway.

I could hear the invaders close behind us, "Come on pretty girls, don't be afraid, we're not going to hurt you." Then they laughed a hideous insane laughter that echoed through the halls.

The invaders didn't know the layout of the house and they were having trouble finding their way in the dark. It gave me the edge that I needed, and I managed to push Tiffany into the den before they could catch us. I shut the door and immediately Pat rammed the desk against it.

Seconds later, the attackers began slamming into the den door, BAM! BAM! BAM! The sheriff wasn't coming this time, we were on our own. If we lived or died, it was up to us to defend ourselves.

"Pat, Skip must keep a gun in his desk, force open the drawers!" Pat and I used the butcher knives and began trying to pry open the locked desk drawers. "If we don't find a gun, we'll bail out the window and take our chances!"

The intruders were viciously trying to get at us, the desk moved every time they violently rammed against the door, and Pat and I slammed it right back. BAM! BAM! The sound of them wildly pounding was terrifying!

Pat and I were prying madly at the drawers, chipping at the strong solid oak struggling to get them open while we slammed the desk back against the door over and over again, as the madmen fought to get into the room.

Suddenly, Pat's voice rose over all the other noise; "HEY, WAIT A MINUTE BAD GUYS, LISTEN TO ME! WE'RE SENDING A PROFESSIONAL OUT TO REASON WITH YOU!"

Pat turned to Tiffany. "Come on Tiffany go, get on out there and reason with them. Go on! Really get out there! This is the perfect time for you to prove your theory. You show us ignorant hillbillies the proper way to handle these poor disturbed gentlemen. I'm sure that if you just explain to them that violence never solved anything, they'll be happy to stop what they're doing. And while you're at it, maybe you can find out just what their intensions are. It would be nice to be informed of the exact situation that we may encounter. I hope you're happy that we didn't bring our guns, I certainly am; I'm so glad that I listened to you. And I'm relieved that you're here with us Tiffany, you've been such a big help because you're so well educated in this field. You said that you would first try to reason with people, Tiffany… GO ON, GET OUT THERE AND REASON WITH THEM!! Tiffany, because of you and your stupid ignorant ideas, we might all die here together tonight!"

Tiffany just stood there unresponsive, and frozen with fear.

I had chipped away a big hunk of the drawer; it finally broke open, and inside was a revolver, a .44 Magnum with a long barrel. I pulled it out and at that moment, it was the most beautiful thing that I had ever seen. "Pat, look, a .44, now if it's only loaded."

"You bet Skip's got it loaded," Pat assured me.

I checked the cylinder; it was fully loaded with hollow points! "This gun's like a cannon, it'll blow a hole right through them!" I celebrated.

"Yee hah! Let's get 'em Sissy!"

There was some light shining in through the den window and I could see just enough to do what I had to do. I stood with the gun pointed at the door, "Okay let 'em in," I said in a determined voice.

Pat stood beside me, and Tiffany was behind, holding onto me tightly. I figured that she felt safer there, or needed me to hold her up.

I let out a yell, "IF YOU'RE COMING IN, COME IN NOW! I'M READY FOR YA!"

Suddenly, it was silent and I stood ready to fire. Then the men slammed against the door a few more times, the desk moved away, but we didn't push it back this time. The door was open enough for them to make it through, and the stupid fools were coming in! It would be the last thing that they would ever do!

I saw a shoulder slowly moving in through the doorway, I drew-down, my finger was twitchin' on the trigger; I was ready to take 'em out. He stepped behind the desk, all the way into the room and the second man was coming in right behind him. I figured that I could get two of them if I shot the second man first and blocked the doorway with his body. That would give me time to get off another shot and take out the first man before he could climb over his friend and get out of the room.

The second man entered the room and I took careful aim, in that split second, I pulled the trigger and Tiffany screamed, jumped against me and knocked me forward. "I missed him! Damn it, Tiffany get off me!" I pushed her away and raised the gun to get off another shot, but it was too late, the intruders were already running down the hallway.

I was going after them, I tried to rush for the door, but stupid Tiffany had a death grip on me like a drowning man, "Get off of me!"

"Let go of her you idiot!" Pat screamed. "They're getting away!"

Tiffany still wouldn't loosen her grip on me. Pat grabbed hold of her and tried to pry her loose, but I ended up kicking her before I could finally get free. The second I broke away, Pat and I bolted over the desk and went racing down the hall. When we got outside, the bad guys were hightailing it over the fence, they jumped into a car that was waiting for them, and raced off. It was impossible for us to catch up and they were too far away for us to even get the license plate number.

Pat and I stopped in the yard, panting and catching our breath, "We almost… had 'em," we said at the same time.

Just then, Tiffany came running out of the house, "Shoot them! Shoot them!" she screamed, waving her arms wildly. "Shoot…..shoot.. shoot…….shoot………shoot!" She fell to the ground sobbing.

"Shoot 'em yourself Tiffany." I dropped the gun next to her and Pat and I turned and walked back toward the house.

"Come on Pat, let her get acquainted with her new friend."

Tiffany had been saved by the very thing that she thought she despised, a gun. She had been protected by Pat and me, the very people that she had belittled and tried to convert to her beliefs. When reality hit, Tiffany wasn't prepared to handle it; it wasn't at all the way that she had been taught it would be. The enemy couldn't be reasoned with, and the police weren't the super heroes that she had counted on.

Tiffany had been influenced by a group of people who knew nothing of the real world. People who have lived their whole lives enjoying the peace and freedom that the warrior fought to give them.

Fighting and violence are never a pleasant thing; it's easy to turn your nose up and condemn, but without the warrior there can be no peace for anyone.

After the incident, Pat and I couldn't get away from Tiffany fast enough. We had nearly lost our lives because of her, and Skip's house had been damaged. I sent her away in a cab and we never spoke to her again.

Pat and I finished out the week at Skip's, with no fear. We cared for the animals and without our tormentor there, we had a wonderful time.

I was able to return to work the following week, and as soon as I had saved enough money, I looked for a new home. I found a charming house in town with an option to buy. The payments were high, but I could swing it.

I decided to leave the horses at Byron's ranch; he had grown attached to them and gave them loving attention every day. My spoiled horses had a full hundred acres of wild oats all to themselves. Standing in the pasture, the oats grew up past their chests and they simply nipped off the tender tips and munched them down. They were truly in a horse's paradise.

I knew that Larry would eventually find me, but if the horses weren't with me, he would have no way of tracking them down and harming them.

Unfortunately, showing Chief Joseph was out of the question as Larry was familiar with all of the horse shows. I was concerned that if he knew where we were going to be, he would have the time to devise murderous plans.

I told Carl that I had decided not to show Chief Joseph. He was disappointed and, I think, relieved at the same time. I'm certain that the shows didn't matter to Chief as he was living a stress-free, happy life in an ideal place.

I moved into my new home as soon as possible. It was located in a pristine neighborhood, surrounded by Victorian mansions that had been built by the town's founding fathers. I loved the house. It was over a hundred years old, with tall, intricately carved ceilings and spacious rooms with huge marble fireplaces in every one of them. The grounds were rundown and overgrown, but the house had been restored to its original beauty.

I hadn't been able to get many of my belongings when I left Larry, so moving in was quick work. That night, I spread a blanket on the bedroom floor and lit a fire in the fireplace. I lay down and pulled a fluffy quilt up around my neck. I watched as the luminous flames flickered and warmed the room. Lying on the floor of the big old, empty house, I felt a loneliness hovering over me, but still, I smiled as I drifted off to sleep.

As the weeks passed, I gradually bought furniture and decorated, filling my home with lovely things. When I got up the courage, I began the enormous job of landscaping. I started by watering the hedges, plants and trees that were miraculously still alive, and then I started pulling up the massive weeds and brush that overwhelmed the property. I pulled and chopped and tugged and discovered a croquet mallet and some balls that had been buried beneath the debris for many years.

I began to imagine what the garden must have been like back then, when the croquet game had been played; a lovely garden in full glorious bloom. I thought about bright sunny days and elegant lawn parties, so many years ago. Real ladies dressed in stylish softly-colored, summer dresses with big brimmed hats adorned with bows and flowers, and the gentlemen, so sophisticated and charming.

Could I make the garden just as lovely as it had been back then? I decided to give it a try, and tackled the toughest job of all, removing an enormous old, dead bush with long prickly thorns. I struggled with the twisted weathered limbs, chopping and cutting. The monstrous old bush seemed as though it was made of steel; it just wouldn't give way and I was beginning to get frustrated. I angrily grabbed hold of one of the thickest branches and began to pull with all my might. I pulled and cussed and pulled and cussed and suddenly found myself on my back holding a huge gnarly ball of root in my hands and a chunk of dirt in my mouth. I spit out the dirt and slowly got to my feet.

I had been working for hours and I hadn't even made a dent in the huge labyrinth of tangled weeds and twisted bushes and vines. I stood looking at the overwhelming work still ahead and was feeling a bit buried when something shiny caught my eye. I began to dig and pull back the curtain of leaves and loose dirt where I had unearthed the bush, and uncovered a jeweled rock fishpond with a cascading waterfall. I had discovered a treasure and immediately stopped working on everything else. I cleared the debris away and assessed the situation, then quickly ran to the hardware store to collect the materials needed to repair the broken old relic.

It took several days, but I finally managed the repairs and even though it seemed foolish, with the rest of the yard still in such a state of disarray, I filled the pond with goldfish, cute little water frogs and bright green turtles. When I had finished, I pulled up an old weathered chair and sat in the middle of the chaotic mess and watched the beautiful waterfall. The shimmering rushing water tumbled over and down into the glistening pool and I listened to its soothing sound.

The water creatures were soon enjoying their new surroundings and eating the delicious flies and bugs that I had bought for them. The fish flipped their long lacey tails and fins and the turtles slowly paddled about. The frogs were all very active, but there was one in particular who was a true adventurer. He climbed up the slippery stones to the top of the water fall and when the current caught him, it pushed him over the falls. I was concerned at first, but as soon as he hit the water at the bottom, he climbed back up and did it all over again. On one of his daring trips, he went over the top with his legs splayed as he flew through the air. I could hardly believe the wild entertainment.

I had a lot of fun watching my new pets, and that night, I sat on the balcony and sipped brandy while the little creatures continued their amusing show.

In the weeks to come, I did more work in the yard and I soon discovered that the fishpond wasn't the only secret that the backyard had been keeping. Buried beneath the many years of overgrowth was an old swimming pool that was also adorned with the beautiful jeweled rock, and just yards away from it, a pool house. They were both so old and broken, it seemed like an impossible task to even begin the repairs, but I persevered and got the swimming pool running and the pool house painted and furnished.

Though I dreaded the day that Larry would find the place, every night I looked forward to coming home to my beautiful castle.

Weeks after I had married Larry, my friend Kurt quit the local police force and moved to Los Angeles. He was working as a bodyguard for the owner of "the girlie magazine." This magazine owner was hated by so many people that he couldn't go anywhere without security, and the mansion where he lived was heavily guarded.

As a body guard, Kurt got to hob knob with celebrities and go to exotic locations on photo shoots to protect the beautiful models.

It took a while for the news to reach him, but when Kurt heard that Larry and I were separated, he surprised me and came to town. I was happy to see him and visit with a friend, but Kurt was in a very serious mood. When I asked him what was on his mind, he abruptly asked me to marry him. I couldn't help but laugh; Kurt always wanted the woman that he couldn't have, and he had never had me. I was certain that this was just another angle that he was using to try and get me into bed.

Even though I knew that Kurt wasn't at all sincere, I still couldn't help but be flattered. Here he was surrounded by world class beauties who modeled for the magazine, and he was still chasing after me.

I was curious, so I asked him, "Why do you want to marry me when you have so many opportunities with worldly beautiful women?"

Kurt said that the models were superficial and immoral and that they would do anything for money. "Some of them have had to have breast surgery done three times because the "breasts" get hard. It's mutilation;

let's be honest and call it what it really is! I don't want a woman like that, they're shallow and uncaring, and besides, a rack of bones with water balloons for breasts just doesn't appeal to me. You're different Penelope; you're a real woman, strong, wholesome and good. Every time I think of you, my mind goes back to the day that I saw you on horseback galloping toward me. You had on a white cotton blouse and your long hair was flying in the wind; it was as though you were gliding on air. It was by far the most beautiful thing that I have ever seen and I can't get the image out of my mind."

I wondered, "Did other girls really fall for this crap?" Even so, the fact was that Kurt really had cheered me up and I always felt safe when I was with him; first a police officer and now a bodyguard, trained to protect.

My current situation was tense; even though Larry hadn't found me yet, I was on guard, worried about what he would do when he did. I thought that it would be nice to get away someplace safe; to have a break from the stress of constantly looking over my shoulder, if even for just a little while, and I agreed to go to L.A. for a visit.

As soon as I could get the time off work, I flew into LAX. When Kurt picked me up, he explained that he had unexpectedly been called in to work. He didn't want me to spend the evening alone at a hotel, so he insisted that I go with him.

"There's a movie premiere and party at the mansion tonight and I'm sure that no one will mind if I bring along another pretty girl," he said with a smile. "You'll have fun; there'll be a lot of celebrities there."

Kurt and I stopped at his place first and I met his roommate. The roommate was friendly and Kurt seemed jealous that I had a brief conversation with him. When I told Kurt that his roommate seemed nice, he grimaced, "He's an asshole."

Kurt and I changed into more suitable clothes for the evening; Kurt into his starchy bodyguard suit and me, into a summer party dress.

When we arrived at the mansion, it was still early and Kurt decided to take me on a tour of the elaborate estate. He took pictures of me posing on the leopard skin couch and in other settings where the models usually had their photos taken.

After that, we walked the property and I saw that there was a menagerie of exotic animals that lived at the mansion. As we walked the grounds, a peacock started following me with his tail feathers fanned out in an impressive display. I was laughing, everywhere I went, there he was, that crazy bird, and he wouldn't go away.

Kurt took several pictures of me with the bird. "No one can ever get that peacock to fan his feathers and here he is, following you around with his tail feathers fanned the whole time! I just can't believe it! What makes you so special?"

It wasn't what Kurt had said, it was his tone, it was strange because he almost seemed angry about the bird's special attention of me, so much so, that I felt the need to say something about it to play it down. "Oh Kurt, he just knows that I love animals."

"Well other people love animals too; you're not the only one."

I changed the subject and on we went to the monkey house. Kurt called it a habitat; it was a huge cage full of natural trees and surroundings for the monkeys to enjoy. The monkeys were cute little guys, but nasty. When I got close they jumped on the fence, jerking off and trying to squirt me with it. Luckily I noticed what they were doing and quickly got out of the way.

After that, we toured the rest of the property and ended at the koi pond. Kurt snapped pictures of me feeding the fish until the party guests began to arrive.

I thought that I would feel uncomfortable around the high-profile guests attending the party that night, and expected that I would probably spend the entire evening awkwardly beside Kurt. But, as the night went on, I started to feel better and I wandered off on my own, to the buffet table. The table was full of decadent delicious smelling food and I decided to experiment and taste each of the exotic treats.

I was still eating when it was announced that the movie was about to begin; the lights went dim and the mansion filled with exciting loud music like a movie theatre. A gentleman directed me to a comfy chair and I ate caviar and drank champagne while I watched the premiere of a new movie that was about to be released. "This is excellent!" I smiled to myself.

The film was action adventure; I thoroughly enjoyed it and clapped vigorously when it ended.

As soon as the lights came back on, some of the party guests wanted to go swimming. They all left the room in rambunctious excitement and I got caught in the middle and ended up going outside with them.

I was just at this party to visit a friend; I didn't want to go swimming with these people who were involved with a steamy sex magazine. I thought, and probably expected that they would all swim nude, but when I saw that everyone had put on a bathing suit I decided to join in, (it must have been the champagne).

I went into the dressing room and found a modest one piece, bathing suit, and as I was putting it on, I had second thoughts. "Who do you think you are? Why you're nothing special, you'll just embarrass yourself wearing a bathing suit in front of these important men and gorgeous models." But then, I realized that unlike the other women attending the party that night, I had nothing to prove. I didn't need to impress and I really didn't care what anyone thought of me, so I decided to have a good time and take a refreshing swim.

The pool looked like a steamy mysterious cave; I swam a few slow lazy laps and then decided to go in the spa. I had never been in a spa before, the bubbling water was inviting and I cautiously stepped in.

There were already people sitting in the bubbling hot water, gorgeous girls and rich men. But later, when I looked more closely at these women, even in the dim light, I noticed the plastic surgery scares on their faces and bodies. I found that without all the pomp, proper lighting and retouch, the dream girls weren't all that spectacular, and I didn't feel self-conscious any more.

The girls in the spa weren't very pleasant to be around, they talked about crude things, things much better left in private. They were having a good time making fun of the other women who weren't within earshot.

The ringleader, Candy, was so cruel that when a young waitress mistakenly tried to give her the wrong drink, she brought the girl to tears and continued shouting and making fun of her as she dropped her tray and ran away. What a bitch she was!

These women were a vicious group, and they didn't like me. Candy, in particular, she kept giving me the evil eye, but I didn't let her drive me off.

Candy had a plan to make a joke of me; she stood up and turned, like she was going to get out of the spa, but then she pretended to slip and she threw herself against me pushing her humongous breasts right in my face. I gently pushed her away; there were no other options for me, but to push on the huge, out of proportion mounds, (they felt much more like beach balls than human flesh).

I wasn't going to let Candy get over on me and once I had her off of me,

I exclaimed, "Must be hard to keep your balance with those things!" and I laughed at her, loud and hard.

When Candy saw that she hadn't thrown me a curve and embarrassed me the way that she had planned to, she made a rude comment about my much smaller breasts and how Kurt must have a problem handling a "real woman."

Now I knew what her problem was, Kurt. Tall and muscular with wavy dark hair, a sparkling smile and chiseled features, Kurt may not have been the richest man there, but he was by far the strongest and the best looking. It was now obvious that Candy was merely jealous.

I decided to play it cool and I didn't say much, but my sideshow encounter with the behemoth breasted Candy had gotten the attention of a very distinguished man, and he asked me who I was.

"Oh, I'm nobody special," I answered.

My evasive answer further sparked his interest and also the interest of his movie producer friend who moved across the spa to sit next to me. The movie producer began to get very friendly and before I knew it, he told me that I was definitely star material and had promised me a part in his next major motion picture.

I just laughed; even though I knew that he was the real deal and could actually put me in a movie; I also knew that the only thing I could count on for certain, was a fling for the night with a drunken man.

"No thank you," I said with a giggle. (After all, it was still flattering).

"Oh, bigger fish to fry," he responded deeply thinking.

I didn't know it at the time, but I had spoken the magic words, "No thank you." The fact that a woman had turned down this famous man seemed to act like an aphrodisiac or a challenge to him and he worked harder to impress me.

As the night went on, his special treatment of me attracted even more attention. People must have thought that I was someone of great importance, for this famous talented man to be making such a big deal out of me, and before I knew it I was surrounded by admirers. I was having a great time laughing and teasing and simply saying "no."

At one point, I had to use the ladies room, so I excused myself and found the lavish powder room. I was checking my face in the mirror when Candy burst in and closed the door behind her. "Give it up bitch," she angrily spouted off, "it's a hopeless cause trying to fix that ugly face of yours."

I just ignored her and tried to leave, but when I reached for the doorknob, she grabbed my arm and tightly squeezed it. "Listen, Pee Pee, or whatever your name is, Garry's mine, and so is the part in that movie. You stay away from him or you'll live to regret it!"

I jerked my arm away, "Look, I'm not interested in Garry, the movie, or anything else; I'm just here to have a good time. Now, step aside."

Candy didn't budge; she took a threatening stance and glared at me. She had imprisoned me, assaulted and threatened me. I'm certain that at that point she expected to slice me into ribbons with her tongue; making cutting remarks about my smudged mascara and choice of nail color, in a vicious cruel attempt to destroy my womanhood by making me feel unfashionable.

But I had never learned the feminine technique of verbal sparring, and I wasn't going to put up with this raunchy bitch any longer. I gave her a hard shove and swept her feet out from under her.

I'll never forget the shocked look on her face as she was sitting there on the floor; it still makes me laugh to this day.

I put my hand on the doorknob and hesitated for a moment, "Hey Candy, I have a suggestion for ya, why don't you strap some counterweights on your back; it might help you with that balancing problem."

As I walked away, I could heard her scream, "You're gonna pay for this Penelope, if it takes me the rest of my life, I'll get you!"

"At least she got my name right that time."

As far as I was concerned, Candy, was just a drunken bimbo and I never gave her a second thought.

When I returned to the spa, Garry, and the group, were still waiting for me. I couldn't imagine who the heck they thought I was, but with all of the special attention I was getting I felt the need to entertain and I began to tell stories of my adventures, tales of the dangerous wild beasts who live in the treacherous mountains.

None of these boys had ever been out of the city and they were fascinated hearing the tall country tales.

When I finished the first story, they asked me to tell another and I began a new adventure. "I was riding my horse with the Sheriff's Posse, high in the mountains searching for a ten year old boy who had been lost while on a family hiking trip. We were combing the area desperately trying to find the youngster before darkness fell."

"It was getting late and it looked as though the boy wouldn't be found in time and would have to spend the night alone in the dangerous wilderness. There were mountain lions in the area and his chances of survival were slim."

"We were at a very high altitude and deep in the tall trees, when the call came through on the radio… the boy had been found!"

"We celebrated the victory for a moment, but then realized that we couldn't make it back before dark ourselves, and we decided to set up camp. We had plenty of food and water, and after a hearty campfire meal we laid out our sleeping bags and settled down for the night. The night creatures were stirring, a-croaking and a-singing, and the owls and bats flew over our heads."

"After the long hard day of searching, we were quickly sound asleep and the campfire died down to red glowing embers. Suddenly, I was startled awake by heavy footsteps and the sound of tree branches breaking; a gigantic animal was tromping through the woods toward camp! All the men were deep in slumber and there was no time to stir them awake. I reached for my rifle and had barely put my hand on it when a menacing dark shadow came into view above my head. I felt the breath of an enormous beast blowing in my face."

All eyes were on me waiting to hear what would happen next, when suddenly, someone reached down, grabbed hold of me and pulled me up and out of the spa.

It was Kurt; his shift had ended. "Party's over," he loudly announced to the men with a disapproving glare.

"What happened next?" my new friends hurriedly asked with a shout.

"I got a bearskin rug, of course! Good-bye!" I waved as Kurt carried me off.

I heard Candy in the distance, "Don't forget what I told you!"

As soon as we were out of view, Kurt put me down and told me that he was hungry. "Let's go get something to eat." He shoved my bag to me, "Put your dress back on!"

Kurt didn't say much in the car, I could tell that he was angry. He always wanted to be seen as the big shot and probably expected me to be awed by him, and him alone. I'm certain that he didn't expect a backward little hick like me to mix with the big city highfaluters.

Even though Kurt was angry, he took me to a fancy restaurant. It was located on a cliff overlooking the twinkling lights of the city, and we sat at the best table.

Kurt immediately ordered two drinks for himself and explained that he couldn't believe how nervous he was. We had been friends for years and I wondered what could be making him so nervous?

I wasn't very hungry and ordered a small dessert. Kurt had steak and potatoes, while downing one drink, after another. I was hoping that the meal would combat the alcohol, but I knew that he was drinking too much, too fast.

After dinner was over, there was just no dealing with Kurt. We had a scuffle in the parking lot when I tried to take the keys from him and drive the car. He opened the passenger door for me and insisted that he was fine.

I know that I shouldn't have gone along with him, but my other choice was to call a cab and I didn't know Kurt's address or have any idea of how to get there. "Maybe he is fine," I fooled myself, "Kurt's a big man, he can probably handle his alcohol." And I allowed him to bully me into the car.

It was a dangerous winding road from the restaurant and Kurt raced recklessly down the hill, screeching the tires at every turn. I uncomfortably sat in the passenger seat, quiet and tense, hoping and praying for the best.

Just short of a miracle, Kurt somehow managed to arrive at his house without getting in an accident. I was relieved when we got there, or more truthfully, thankful to be alive, and I wasn't about to get back in the car with him to go to a hotel.

I tried to figure out what to do; after paying for my airfare, I was broke. With the enormous expenses of refurbishing my new home, I didn't have any extra money to play with. Kurt had promised to pay for a hotel room for me, but when I asked him about it, he just put me off.

Kurt and his roommate lived outside the city limits and unfortunately, I hadn't seen a hotel anywhere in the area. I simply didn't have the money to pay for cab fare all of the way back into the city, and then for a hotel room as well; I was trapped. I would have to tough it out at Kurt's and deal with the drunken buffoon until morning, when he sobered up enough to take me to the airport.

Kurt and I decided to watch a movie that we had both been looking forward to seeing. Unfortunately, Kurt's roommate was monopolizing the television set in the family room, so we had to watch the movie in Kurt's bedroom, on the smaller screen.

We both went into the kitchen to make popcorn, but first, Kurt mixed himself another strong cocktail. I tried to stop him, to no avail, and then we went to watch the movie.

Kurt got even drunker and it wasn't long before he started groping me, "Penelope it's you, it's always been you! You're the only woman that I've ever loved!"

Kurt was incredibly strong, he was being rough and heavy-handed and he was hurting me. I realized that he was drunk, so I tried not to be offended, and gently push him off of me. But when I resisted him, Kurt grabbed my arms, pinned me down and grunted, "I'm the boss." He forced himself on me and then passed out while he was still on top of me.

Kurt was a big man, his chest was covering my face and he was so heavy that I was having a hard time breathing. I tried to call to the roommate for help, but I couldn't get enough air to cry out loud enough for him to hear me above the television. Trapped beneath this ugly beast, I felt like I would die if I didn't get him off of me. I was only able to take in short little breaths; it was a terrible claustrophobic feeling. With all my strength I pushed him and he tumbled to the floor, still snoring; it was a disgusting sight.

Not sure what to do, I gathered my belongings and decided to get the hell out of there. I spoke to the roommate, and after I threatened to call the police, he took me to the airport.

What had just happened? Kurt was my friend. Had I actually been raped? Was he going to use the fact that he was drunk to try to get away with it? Would that be his excuse? Was it my fault for going into the bedroom with him? Had I dressed too seductively? A dress with no stockings had made it easy for him.

What was I going to do about it? Report him to the police? Come back later and get my revenge?

Kurt hadn't beaten me and I had no proof that a rape had taken place, only that I had had sex with him. There was nothing that I could do legally, but make a fool of myself. With Kurt's high profile employer, I was certain that the case would be plastered all over the tabloids and I didn't need that kind of publicity. Even though I had been violated, I ended up blaming myself and didn't feel justified enough to ruin Kurt's good name and career.

Kurt had finally conquered me and he could carve another notch in his bedpost. I wondered if it mattered to him that he had to force himself on me to do it. And what did he mean, "I'm the boss?" Was it simply neurotic jealousy or had he been holding a grudge against me? Being a tough guy meant a lot to Kurt and Lucky Loop had made a fool out of him, a horse that he had just seen me ride. Was it too much of a blow to his ego for a woman show him up? I wondered if he felt like a big strong man now, now that he was, "the boss." He had knocked me down a few notches, he sure showed me.

If Kurt hadn't have been someone that I trusted, he would have never gotten away with it. Because I considered him a friend and didn't want to hurt him, he had gotten the jump on me. I felt stupid and ashamed.

I remembered what Grandpa Wells told me when I was a child, "You can protect yourself from your enemies, but you can't protect yourself from your friends."

Sometimes in life, you have to take your beating, and right or wrong, I believed that this was one of those times. And that's what I did, I sucked it up and I took my beating. I was so hardened by this time that it seemed like no big deal.

PENELOPE P.I.

When I returned home I was a little shaken up, but like I said, no big deal. I went back to work only to find out that the interior design business was shutting down. The owners were getting divorced and in the process, unbeknown to me, had bankrupted the company. I couldn't collect on any of the jobs that I had pending. I was in a bad spot as I had been working under the designer's license. I didn't have years to spend in school studying, I had bills to pay. I had to get to work right away, so I took some piecework, painting and hanging wallpaper for a construction company, just to get through until I could find a steady job.

It was a difficult time, work was scarce, and the construction crews working on the job sites were always cruel to me. They believed that I was taking work away from men who needed it to support their families.

"I've got to eat too," I told them, and toughed it out. Every day, it was a fight against the whole crew.

I was alone and struggling financially, but somehow I always managed to scrape up enough money to pay my bills and the board for my horses.

With all that had happened to me, I sometimes felt like I was ready to break; then I would drive out to the ranch and spend time with my horses. By the time I left them, I always felt like I was on top of the world.

It was difficult for people to understand how I would do without things for myself to keep such expensive pets. Truth was, that no matter how bad things got, I always felt an indescribable peace when I was with my horses. I didn't take care of them; it was they who took care of me. My horses were how I made it through the tough times.

After a few months of searching, I found a well-paying job working for a private investigator named Ray. He was a former police officer and a no-nonsense sort of a guy. Ray hired me to run the front office, set appointments and deal with clients. It was a long drive just to get there, but to have the steady paycheck, it was well worth it.

Working in an office was far from my dream job and I hoped for something better in the future, but I was very happy just to be making a decent living.

Months passed, and I had learned the businesses well. It was a Friday, well after closing time; I was finishing up and preparing to go home when a man walked into the office. I was tempted to tell him that we were closed and to come back another time, but he was adorable, a good humored grandpa type, wearing a tee shirt with a picture on the front of an old hound dog. The man had an endearing smile and cute pink cheeks like Santa Claus. He jokingly introduced himself to me as Slippery Sammy.

I laughed and shook his hand, "Nice lookin' hound dog," I commented about the picture on his shirt.

"Yeah, he's my mascot. Wait here a minute," he said, and then went to his car. When he came back inside, he handed me a tee shirt, like the one that he was wearing, with a hat to match. "There you go Darlin' hope you enjoy it," he said with a smile.

This was a sweet generous man and I wondered why he had come to see a private investigator, there was obviously something troubling him. I offered him a seat, "Well Slippery Sammy, what can I do for ya today?"

"Nobody really calls me that," he chuckled, "you can just call me Sam." Sam took a tense breath and then began to tell me his story; he had invested his life savings in a friendly neighborhood bar. Business seemed good and Sam couldn't understand why he was losing money. "If you can't help me, Miss, I won't last another month, I'll lose everything."

"Well Sam, I'm certain that we'll be able to solve this problem," and I suggested an employee theft investigation (bar shop). Sam was desperate and I felt sorry for him, so I scheduled it for that very night and gave him a discount. "Don't tell anyone what we have planned," I advised, "it could jeopardize the investigation."

"Alright Darlin', I'm sure you know you're business, I won't mention it to anyone."

He waved good-bye and quickly walked out the door. There was a spring in his step that I hadn't seen there before and I could tell that I had given him hope.

It had been a long hard week at work, and after fighting the traffic home, I was worn out. "Thank God it's finally over," I said as I dropped my keys on the table and flopped down on the sofa. I had just closed my eyes when the phone rang. I didn't want to answer it; but what if it was an emergency? I grumpily got up and answered.

It was Bruce, the operative which had been assigned the employee theft investigation that night at Sam's bar. "My partner's been in a fender bender and he can't make it tonight," he told me. "Would you please come and do the bar shop with me?"

"Look Bruce, I'm dog tired, and besides that, I've never done an employee theft investigation. This isn't just a routine job, this man is being driven out of business and it's very important that we have someone good on the case. There must be another operative available, someone who at least knows what they're doing."

"There is no one else; why do you think I'm asking you? If you don't go with me, Ray will cancel the investigation and I can't afford to lose the work. Come on Penelope, if my car gets repossessed it'll be your fault," he whined. "The job doesn't start until nine o'clock, you'll have some time to relax before you have to leave."

That was a laugh, if the bar shop started at nine, by the time I got in the shower, got my hair and make-up done and drove to the office... I was already late! I wanted to say no, but tired as I was, my heart got the best of me. I couldn't just stand by and let Sam go under. "I guess I'm better than nothing," I grimaced. I hung up the phone, rushed to get ready and then drove the long drive back to the office.

Bruce was waiting for me there. "Get in the car, I'll brief you on the way," he hurriedly told me and I climbed in and went over the paperwork.

When we arrived on site, I entered the building ahead of Bruce and sat at the bar, to shop the bartender and cocktail waitresses.

There was a band playing that night, and a cover charged at the door. Bruce took a position close to the door where he could count the people entering the bar, keep an eye on me, and have an overall view of the place.

I felt a bit lost when I first sat down; not being an observant person by nature it wasn't easy for me, and because of that, I knew that I had to try harder. I ran everything over in my mind. Did they pour the right amount of alcohol? Did they charge the correct prices and put the cash in the register? Did they make accurate change? Were they attentive and professional to the customers? Where they giving away free drinks? Did they follow health and safety codes? Was there anyone drinking on the job? Find out why this man was losing his business!

There were long checklists on the report that I was to write: the description of each employee, how long they worked, what hours, their breaks, what time and how long? If there was an infraction, when did it occur? I couldn't make notes, I had to remember it all and be accurate, perfectly accurate. This was a big responsibility and there was no room for mistakes, Sam's business was on the line and so were the jobs of the employees!

I was sitting on the barstool watching everything, trying not to look obvious when suddenly I felt paranoid; it was as though all eyes were on me. "Everyone must know what I'm doing!" I was so uncomfortable that I wanted to leave, but I managed to stick it out until the feeling passed and I regained my composure.

Once I felt more comfortable, I acted as though I was having a terrific time. I tipped big and tried to be friendly and it wasn't long before the bartender and the head cocktail waitress began to get chummy with me. We talked and joked for a while, and much to my surprise, the bartender bent over and whispered to me that the bar was being investigated that night.

I was shocked, how did they know this? And if they knew about the investigation, did they also know that I was the operative? "That blasted Sam, he wasn't supposed to say anything!"

It looked as though I had been made and that the investigation was over before it had even begun. I thought about chucking the whole thing and going home, but I decided to stick it out. I kept my cool and talked more with the cocktail waitress and the bartender, I even asked questions about the investigation. It didn't seem like they suspected me, but I couldn't be positive.

The cocktail waitress began to make fun of Sam, "That stupid old man doesn't have enough sense to come in out of the rain!" she sneered. "How dare he have us investigated!"

That of course pissed me off, but I chimed in, "He probably doesn't pay you enough anyway and the tightwad deserves to get ripped off!" I laughed. "Give me another drink!" I raised my glass.

It wasn't much longer before the bartender asked me who I thought the investigator might be. I was a bit thrown by the question; were these people merely toying with me? If they were, they were, and I had nothing to lose, so I decided to play along. I discretely pointed out a man in a suit, who was sitting alone at the far end of the bar. "I'm sure it's him," I said, "it has to be." They looked at the man and then agreed; the man at the end of the bar was indeed the investigator.

"Too bad sucker," I mocked him, "you're just wasting your time, we're hip to you!" I raised my glass again, "Pour me another one, bartender!" I was relieved; I now knew that I hadn't been made!

I decided to push a little to get more information and I asked the head waitress how they had come to find out about the investigation. I was shocked again when she actually told me! It was Sam's brother-in-law, the club manager, he had warned all of the employees to be on their best behavior! Seems that he got a cut of the stolen loot and didn't want his cohorts to be found out.

I was making ground and gaining confidence, even if the employees did know that they were being investigated, it was looking like I could still get to the bottom of things! Sam was depending on me, he needed my help, and I wanted to nail every single one of the scumbags who were stealing from the sweet trusting, old man. Sam wasn't going to lose everything if there was something that I could do about it!

I kept talking and having "fun" with the bartender and the cocktail waitress and soon more of the cocktail waitresses began standing around us at the bar. They seemed to be waiting for instructions or something.

"She's cool," the bartender told them, referring to me. Then he glanced at the "investigator," to make sure that he wasn't watching, and we all took a free shot, "cheers!"

As the night progressed, so did the shenanigans and the bartender recruited me to stand guard. I kept an eye on the "investigator" while the foolish employees stole right in front of me. The stolen money was placed into a purse that was kept under the bar, and before long it was packed solid with cash. The bartender was struggling to force the bills inside and he looked up and smiled at me, "We'll have to get a bigger purse."

I couldn't believe that it was actually happening, but it surely was. For whatever reason these criminals felt completely comfortable with me and catching them was incredibly easy. I just kept playing along, and even asked for a cut of the loot. (Just to keep my cover, of course.)

After the "investigator" left, Bruce caught the doorman and the bouncers pocketing admission fees as people came into the bar. And before the shop was over, we found that every one of the employees, working at the bar that night, were involved in the crime ring. CASE SOLVED!

When Bruce and I left the club that night, he was thrilled. "I don't want to work with anyone else but you Penelope! I've been on so many of these cases, and when the employees know about the investigation, we usually just put in our time and leave, but you just wouldn't give up! It was incredible the way you played those thieves!"

"Oh, it was no big deal," I responded, trying to be modest and play the whole thing down, but in reality I was very proud of myself. Even though the deck had been stacked against me, the night had been a complete success. It was the best feeling in the world to have been able to help Sam and now he would have a fighting chance.

The next morning, I gave him the verbal report, and he fired the thieves who were stealing him into bankruptcy. Soon the club began to show a profit; Sam wouldn't lose his investment after all! He of course was overjoyed, and asked that we shop his bar once every month, so that things would never get out of hand again.

When Ray got wind of the case, I no longer worked in the office; he assigned me exclusively to employee theft investigations and said that I was a natural.

The employee theft investigations meant added stress and late night hours, but I was making more money and had escaped the nine to five grind. I felt good about my work and I was making a difference, not just by exposing the thieves and criminals, but I also had the opportunity to do something nice by writing positive reports, commending the honest hardworking employees and recommending them for promotion.

I had an excellent success record for catching the bad guys. If a client had thieves working for him, the foolish employees continued to commit their crimes right in front of me.

I had only been working the employee theft investigations for a few months when Ray landed a big account in Las Vegas. I was surprised when he assigned me to the first bar shop in the Vegas casino.

The Las Vegas job was a big deal and it created a lot of jealousy between me and the other employees who were more experienced and had been on the job longer than I. There was one woman in particular named Joann, she despised me, insinuating that I must have been doing sexual favors for the boss in order to get the promotion so quickly. I never had to work with her, so I didn't let it bother me much; I just hoped that she didn't somehow hurt my reputation.

The Las Vegas casino was a difficult challenging assignment with a grueling schedule. After the flight, I was on the job the minute I hit the ground. I worked three days, Friday, Saturday and Sunday, and was only allowed to sleep four hours in a twenty-four hour period; two hours at a time, at the end of each ten hour shift.

I felt pressure to make good and I wasn't confident in my abilities. I had attributed my success to the stupidity of the thieves and I wondered if the Las Vegas thieves would be just as arrogant and sloppy. If they weren't, I might be in trouble, and I was plenty nervous about it.

I gambled from time to time to keep my cover, but sitting at the bar talking to the employees was the best way to find out information.

Things were more complicated in Vegas, with free drinks to gamblers, drink tokens and such; the scams were sophisticated, but it wasn't long before the thieves began to talk and commit their crimes right in front of me. I must admit that without the foolish criminals explaining to me how they did it, it would have taken me much longer to figure out their system.

Thanks once again, to the arrogance of the offenders that first weekend, I busted a whole ring of thieves. I was pleased that my "talent" had worked in Las Vegas as well.

After that first bar shop, profits at the casino bars increased by over thirty percent, it was phenomenal! Casino management was greatly impressed, and from that point on I was in Las Vegas working every other weekend.

I worked hard; the casino kept getting good results and began to use me in more creative ways. I was no longer just shopping the bars; I worked throughout the whole casino.

Ray partnered me with Bruce, he was a good poker player, and I posed as his girlfriend. We handled a lot of cash, it was a big responsibility and we were both under pressure to perform, but most of the pressure landed squarely on my shoulders.

Posing as the girlfriend, I had the freedom to move around. I could act dumb, get friendly with the right people, ask intruding, "stupid" or personal questions, and hopefully collect the information that I needed to catch the crooks and con-artists. There were times when I was in completely over my head, but somehow I always managed to come through.

By eliminating theft, the casino's profits kept climbing and they became more generous with me. I stayed in luxurious suites, wore designer clothes and donned sparkling jewels, but sadly there wasn't time for me to enjoy any of it.

To other people, I'm certain that it all seemed very glamorous; that is, as long as they didn't look closely enough to see the dark circles under my eyes. But my life wasn't at all what it appeared to be; I wasn't living the highlife, no far from it. I was on the outside looking in, working ungodly hours on assignments that were both dangerous and high pressure.

The owner of the casino where I had been working, referred his brother to us for an employee theft investigation at his strip club; also in Vegas. The man lived across the country, and didn't have a clue as to what was going on in his own club. I was assigned the new account, and once again, Joann was passed over.

The job at the strip club was different than the usual employee theft investigation; I was to pose as a cocktail waitress and the twist was, that I had to get the job on my own. There was concern that if the owner recommended me, it would create immediate suspicion.

Could I land a job as a cocktail waitress in a sleazy strip club? The thought of it made me cringe, but on the bright side, I could keep all of my tips.

The next day, I went into the club just as it was opening and filled out an application using the name of Stacey Allen. All of my information was fake of course, but reliable in case someone called to verify.

It was a relaxed atmosphere and I got an interview with the manager, Sal, right away. I presented myself as being new in town and managed to mention that I had no relatives or friends in the area, and most importantly, that I desperately needed the job.

Sal seemed to like me and I was confident that I would get the position, but then a week went by and still no call from Sal. Ray was about to give up and try another operative when Sal finally called... I had the job! "I knew you could pull it off Penelope," Ray said proudly.

I was to start the following week on Monday; it was a slow day, so I doubted that I would see much action. Sal said that he wanted me to have the time to familiarize myself with the job when there was less pressure. While that was probably true, I was also certain that no one else wanted to work the slow days and that the new girls got stuck with them. I was hoping that it wouldn't prolong the investigation, I didn't want to be in a strip club any longer than I had to be.

When I showed up for work the first day, I was given a uniform, it was revealing, but not as bad as I had expected it would be. The strippers on stage didn't want the girls on the floor, serving drinks, stealing attention from their show.

I started the case optimistically, but soon found that the people who worked at the club were very closed-mouthed, so much so that it was unnatural, like they were afraid or hiding something. That first day, I didn't see anything illegal, but could sense that there was something terribly wrong.

The job was full time; I had worked a forty hour week and had learned nothing. I hated the assignment, being in the unsavory atmosphere was already beginning to wear me down, the loud music and the flashing lights were hard on the senses. Between the dense smoke and having to shout above the noise to take drink orders, my voice was already beginning to sound raspy.

Putting up with the slobbering drunken men was the worst, they watched the strippers performing on stage, and then in a flurry of clumsy sexual excitement tried to grope me. I had to tolerate a degree of their depravity and flirt for tips, I had to, to play the part and fit in, but it really went against my grain.

I had never seen men in such a negative light before, and I soon understood why the women who worked at the club were so calloused and hard. These women degraded themselves for money, they flirted and made foolish men believe that they found them attractive, and even that they were interested in them. But in the back room, the truth came out and there wasn't a woman working there who didn't hate and resent the men who came into the club.

The next week, I got lucky and was able to work the weekend, and that's when the case began to come together. I was slowly being accepted and the other employees were beginning to get less guarded around me.

I had a customer that Saturday night named Earl. He was a friendly older man who told me that he was in town on business. When I brought him his drink, he reached into his pocket and pulled out a wad of bills. "I have to pay in cash," he told me, "don't want the wife finding out."

After I had served Earl his drink, the bartender signaled for me. When I went to see what he wanted, he changed my station and assigned another waitress to Earl's table. This was obviously a red light and I waited to see what would happen next.

It wasn't long before I noticed the bartender pouring something from a "special bottle" into Earl's next drink. After drinking it, Earl was "out of it," slumping over and slurring.

With a girl under each arm, he was escorted into a private room for a lap dance. Minutes later, one of the girls came out of the room and inconspicuously handed Earl's credit cards to the bartender. The bartender ran Earl's cards on a different credit card machine than the one that he used for the club. It was obvious that he had a separate account set up for himself and his cohorts.

One girl after another went into the room with Earl; sometimes four at a time and I doubted if he was even aware of what was happening. I was certain that all of his cash was gone, his credit cards maxed out and more than likely, his identity stolen.

The club was packed that night; it was wild and the men were drunk, staring at the girls and hooting and hollering. Not a one of them noticed that there were choice men being taken from the crowd and escorted into the private rooms…. men that never came back out again.

I was trying find out where the men were being taken when I noticed Sal, the manager, watching me, and for the moment, my hands were tied.

The next night, about half way through my shift, Sal called me into his office. He offered me a chair in front of his desk and I sat down. "Stacey," he said, "I've noticed that you seem distracted."

"I'm sorry, I've got a lot on my mind, but don't worry, I'll pick it up a little." I had been careful and didn't think that he suspected me, but I guessed that my disgust for the job was showing through. "He probably just wants me to be more friendly and cheerful," I thought, but it wasn't long before I could tell that Sal was digging for something much more disturbing.

Sal got a concerned look on his face and his voice changed to a gentler, milder tone, "You know if you're having some kind of a problem Stacey, I would certainly be willing to help you."

When he said that, I knew what he wanted and I gave it to him; I acted weak and needy like someone who could be easily taken advantage of. "I've got a lot to deal with," I spouted off, "I'll be careful not to bring it to work with me." Then I pretended to break down and said sobbing, "Please don't fire me! I need this job, I have fines and court costs and if I don't pay them off right away, I'll go to jail! I swear Sal, I'll try harder; I just couldn't handle going to jail again! You'll see; I can be better!"

"Oh, a little trouble with the law, huh?" Sal said with a smile on his face.

Because I had presented myself as having problems with the police, Sal knew that I couldn't go to them for help and I had now become fair game.

"That's okay Stacey, don't worry, I won't let you go to jail."

Now Sal had a steely look in his eye, he thought that he was getting his way, that I was his next victim and he began to move in on me. He slowly stood up from his desk and then walked around behind me.

I was never comfortable with someone behind me, I normally would have never allowed it, but I managed to keep in character. I held my breath; I wasn't sure what he was going to do next.

Sal moved closer and pressed something hard up against me, then he chuckled a bit and pulled a gun from his pants. He went back to his desk and placed the gun on top of it, carefully positioning it clearly in my view. Then Sal stood in front of me, leaning back on his desk with his fingers laced together. "We're like family here," he said in a sinister voice. "I don't want to fire you, I want to help you Stacey; in fact, I want you to look at me like a big brother, a brother that can help you with all of your problems."

Sal walked slowly behind me again and began to massage my shoulders; he ran his fingers up and down the curve of my neck. "You're so tense Stacey, just relax, there are ways that a pretty girl like you can make a lot of extra dough. That's always the bottom line, isn't it Stacey… money?"

The conversation went on and Sal quickly came to the point, prostitution, it was no surprise.

My voice was shaky, "Well…I don't know… I do need money badly, but I don't know if I could do something like that."

That wasn't what Sal wanted to hear and he moved his hands slowly around my throat. For a minute, I thought that he might try to strangle me, but then he released his tight grip, but didn't let loose of my neck.

"Oh now, you're just being silly Stacey, all the girls are doing it and making a good living on the side, it's perfectly safe." He leaned over and whispered in my ear, "I'd only hook you up with my very best friends."

"I'll think about it," I said, and I started to get up. I didn't want things to go too far and have Sal wanting a sample or something.

Sal moved his hands to my shoulders and pushed me back down in the chair. "That's fine Stacey, you think about it, but don't take too long, and just a word of advice… I don't like to be disappointed. You talk to some of the other girls and see what they have to say. They all made the right decision and they'll tell you how happy they are." Then Sal released me, but paused for a moment, "Before you go back on the floor, have a little pick-me-up."

Sal wasn't being nice or generous when he made the offer, he was giving an order. He walked back behind his desk, reached into the drawer and pulled out a mirror. I knew that this was a test.

"Oh, Sal, just what I needed, get me lined up and I'll be right back." I grabbed my purse and ran into the Ladies room.

Sal had exposed his hand and I knew that if I didn't snort cocaine with him, I wouldn't be allowed to leave the club that night. I was at a loss and wasn't sure what to do. Should I make a run for it? Act sick and try to get out of it? Then I remembered something that Joe, one of our operatives, had told me. He said that putting petroleum jelly in your nose would stop snorted drugs from entering your system. I sometimes carried a small tube of petroleum jelly in my purse to use on my hands and elbows. Did I have it with me tonight? I dug wildly through my purse looking for it. "Oh, please let me find it!" I pulled out the old lint covered tube, quickly opened it and put some in my nose. I checked my face to make sure that none of it was visible and went back into the office.

By the time I returned, Sal had the lines of cocaine ready and he was standing sternly over his desk staring at me. This was it; I was so scared that I was shaking, I had never done any drugs, I didn't even like to take an aspirin.

Sal noticed my hand shaking. "I'm so excited, I haven't had a treat like this in a long time. This stuff is expensive!" I exclaimed, trying to cover up.

"Okay, here goes," I said to myself, "I hope you're right Joe!" and I snorted up a line of the dangerous drug.

"Thanks Sal, that was great! Now I'm ready to get back to work, let me at 'em," I said enthusiastically, and hurriedly left the office.

"I've got deep pockets baby, come back again any time," Sal said chuckling.

I ran out of sight and blew my nose, ridding it of the powdery drug. "Thanks Joe," I whispered and I went back on the floor.

I had encountered drugs many times at the nightclubs that I shopped, it wasn't new to me. I simply reported it and the perpetrator was fired. But this was far worse, forcing drugs and prostitution on employees.

I couldn't wait for the night to be over; I wanted to get out of there. I was just an employee theft investigator, I didn't want to be involved in this. It was far too dangerous and definitely not worth the money that I was being paid.

When I returned to my hotel that morning, I pulled off my false eyelashes and removed the heavy makeup from my face. I took a long hot shower and waited until eight o'clock to call Ray. I reached him on his personal line. "Ray, it's Penelope, I'm way over my head on this job!"

"Penelope, what's going on? First... are your safe?"

"Yes, I'm safe, I'm at the hotel, everything's fine, it's just that this is far more than employee theft." I proceeded to tell Ray about the prostitution and the drugging of the out-of-town customers.

Ray was silent for a moment, "I'll inform the client and call you back later, get some sleep."

I hung up the phone and crawled under the covers.

A few hours later, Ray called me back, "Penelope, I got in touch with the client and he is furious, he wants to get rid of the whole bunch and clean the place up, but he can't fire anyone without proof. He's also concerned that the police will revoke his license and shut the business down if they get wind of it. He's asked us to continue discretely working the case and has offered twice the usual fee, plus there's a sizeable bonus in it for you if you agree to continue. Do you think that you can stall this Sal guy on the prostitution long enough to get things wrapped up? If you think you can, I'll send Joe out to work with you."

Joe was retired law enforcement and had worked the narcotics division on the toughest streets in New York City. He had already done me one good turn by telling me about the petroleum jelly trick. Joe knew his stuff and if there was anyone that had my confidence, it was he, so I agreed to stay on the case.

I didn't have to return to the strip club for two days, Joe flew in and we went over our strategy. He would pose as a customer and be at the club with me. I felt much better about the whole thing, having Joe there was great, now I had backup and I felt much safer and more confident.

Joe and I worked together the next week; unlike me, Joe was free to leave the property to investigate. He managed to tail the henchmen when they took the drugged customers from the club. He found that they were dropped at a sleazy motel where the motel manager took photos of them with horrid-looking prostitutes.

The next morning, the disoriented victims went to the motel management for help, where things only got worse for them. Guilty and afraid of being arrested, they usually called a friend who paid off the manager and then went home, disgraced.

Joe and I continued to work, and it became clear that the people that we had encountered at the club were working for someone else; we didn't want to close the case until we had caught the kingpin.

Now that Sal had given the word, the other waitresses were free to talk to me and more information was revealed each night. I found that Sal had a stranglehold on every one of the girls working there, and each of them warned me that it wasn't safe to "disappoint" him.

As the case developed further, I found that Sal's girlfriend Layla Lace, (an obvious alias) was the one who gave the orders; Sal ran the club and Layla ran Sal.

The girls told me that Layla Lace was a stripper and that she danced occasionally at the club to get attention. It drove Sal crazy, and Layla loved to do it, just to keep him in line and remind him who was boss.

I had to find out who this woman was, and I hadn't even gotten a look at her. All I needed was Layla Lace to complete the report and the case was closed. I could only hope that she would feel the need to make Sal jealous and show up at the club to do a striptease one night. All of the girls figured that she was about due to show up.

Joe and I finished out the week, I had been able to avoid Sal and stall his prostitution plans for me, but it was getting more difficult every day and I knew that I wouldn't be able to stave him off much longer.

We had the next two days off, and Joe flew home to be with his expectant wife. I stayed in the city and went to a show, anything to try and relax. How bad was this assignment going to get? I was worried, things didn't feel right. I only hoped that Layla Lace would make an appearance soon. I just wanted to get the information that I needed and be done with it, but somehow I knew that it wouldn't be that easy.

The two days passed, Joe hadn't shown up and I couldn't reach him by phone. It was nearly time for me to leave for the club, so I called Ray to see if he knew anything. Ray found out that Joe's wife had suddenly developed complications with her pregnancy, she was in the hospital and Joe needed to stay by her side. Ray said that he would fly Bruce out just as soon as he could.

Between the shuttles, wait time at the airport, and the flight, I knew that it would be a long while before Bruce would arrive. I would have to work the strip club alone.

I got to the club and suffered through the night, trying to dodge Sal, and I almost succeeded too, but toward the end of my shift he caught up with me. Apparently one of the regular customers had requested to have sex with me and Sal expected me to go with him, right then.

I was trying to get out of it when one of the girls overheard our conversation. She was angry that Sal was trying to set me up with this particular man. "He's my client," she complained.

Then another girl happened by, and when she realized what was going on, she was angry too. "You wish he was your client bitch, I was with George just last week. Don't listen to her Sal, she doesn't know what she's talking about, he's my client."

Then one of the girls shoved the other and they both started screaming at each other, and at Sal. I backed away to see what would happen; maybe this would be my way out.

Sal was in the middle, and I wondered what he would do. Would he still try to bring me into the equation? "Work it out amongst yourselves," he said, then stepped into his office and shut the door.

I walked away, the girls kept fighting and eventually settled it. Apparently this client was something very special.

It was as weird as weird ever gets, but at that moment, in a strange way I almost felt grateful to Sal; he was trying to do what he had promised me he would, and give me his best client.

The case was really getting to me; time was running out and I still hadn't seen or heard anything of Layla Lace. I was discouraged, and at the end of my shift, I considered calling it quits, "Maybe I should just go with the information that I have."

I went into the dressing room to change into my street clothes when one of the girls came in. "You better be on your best behavior tomorrow night, the infamous Layla Lace is planning an appearance."

The news was encouraging, Bruce would be here by then and we could finally wrap it up!

I was happy when I returned to my hotel room that night, but when I opened the door, much to my dismay, I saw Joann sitting on my bed with a smirk planted firmly on her face.

This bitch would love nothing more than to see me fail, or better yet, to show me up. I couldn't possibly allow her into the club, it would be dangerous having someone there, pretending to be my backup, but who actually wished me harm.

"Oh, hi Joann," I greeted her. "What happened to Bruce?"

"I was in the office when Ray got your call and I volunteered, so Ray agreed to let me come in his place."

"Oh how nice of you," I said sarcastically and wondered how she had managed to convince Ray to let her come.

After working all night in high heels, this was the last thing that I needed. How was I going to get rid of this bitch? I took my shower and went to sleep, expecting the answer would come to me when I wasn't so angry and tired.

I slept until it was nearly time for me to leave for the club. Joann started to get ready to go with me and I stopped her, "Joann, there's no way that you can work inside the club, a woman coming in alone will attract too much attention, you could never blend in. You're here to help me and it would help much more if you just stayed here in the room and worked on the file. I'm behind on the paperwork."

At that point, I could see the hatred in Joann's eyes; she started screaming at me, but I refused to get in an argument with her. It was my case and there was nothing that she could do about it.

Joann was fuming mad, but I tried not to let it bother me. I had to get on with the job and I needed all of my concentration and wit, I couldn't let this jealous shrew throw me off my game.

I had rented a little sports car, and as I angrily shifted through the gears I knew that I was making a big mistake working alone at the club that night, but I had to go through with it. With the pressure on from Sal, the case was quickly drawing to its end; I was desperate to wrap it up and get the hell out, before it blew up in my face. This would be my first and only chance to catch Layla Lace; it was now or never, and I was facing it completely alone.

Once I arrived at the club, I punched in and started serving drinks. It didn't take long before I heard a loud argument coming from Sal's office.

"Sounds like Sal's having trouble with his ol' lady again," the bartender laughed.

The arguing got louder and Layla stormed out of the office and went into her private dressing room. One of the girls whispered to me, "Looks like you're going to see the great Layla Lace perform."

I quickly devised a plan; I would sneak into Layla's dressing room while she was on stage and try to uncover her true identity. I was hopeful that I might find other pertinent information as well. I expected that no one would notice me during the distraction of her performance.

Layla was preparing and everyone seemed excited and tense; this appeared to be a big event. Layla was announced and she stepped out on the stage. I watched to try and get a description of her, but when she appeared, she was wearing a big feathered mask as part of her act. I decided to search her dressing room first and then catch the end of the act, after she had removed the mask and get her description. I figured with her prancing around naked it would be a pretty thorough description.

I could feel my heart pounding in my chest, but I tried to act casual and work my way across the club, toward Layla's dressing room. I had no lookout so I knew that I could easily be caught. I was afraid of what Sal would do to me if I was found rummaging around in Layla's things. Without Joe, I had no protection, but I had to make my move; this was my only opportunity and I had to take it.

I took one last look around the club to make sure that no one was watching, and just before I ducked into the hallway… Joann came bursting through the front entrance of the club, wearing a business suit and looking like an FBI agent. She had her hair pulled back in a tight bun, a pencil resting on top of her ear and was carrying a briefcase in one hand and a clipboard in the other. She looked around the room, referred to her clipboard and then approached the bartender.

I could tell that the crazy bitch was actually asking the bartender for me. I couldn't believe it! The bartender began to look around the room searching for me, and then he told one of the waitresses to find me for her.

Joann had successfully blown the whole thing sky high! I pushed my way through the crowd to get to her as quickly as I could. She was making such a spectacle of herself that some of the less drunken customers had made a run for the door, thinking that it was a bust.

I thought that maybe I could somehow salvage the case if I got her out of the club quickly and made up a good enough cover story, but no explanation came to mind. Who the heck could I possibly say she was?

As Joann walked through the club, the men cleared out of her way. She stopped at the end of the stage runway and stood there watching Layla dance. It couldn't have been any worse; Joann was deliberately trying everything that she could think of to sabotage the case for me and she was doing an excellent job of it!

"Joann, get the hell out of here!" I said when I got close to her.

Joann simply looked at me with that same smirk on her face and said, "I need some information to complete the report!"

"I don't care what you need; get the hell out of here, right now! I don't have time for this!" Layla's dance would soon be over and so would my window of opportunity.

Joann wouldn't budge and she started to argue with me while Layla was shaking her ass and bouncing her huge breasts on the stage. She twirled around and danced down the runway; she stopped when she got to the end and bent down looking at the both of us arguing there.

Layla removed her large feathered mask with a swoosh, and said in a loud clear voice, "Hello, Penelope!"

Penelope? I looked closely at her face, it took me a minute to figure out who she was, but it came to me soon enough… it was Candy, the top-heavy bitch who had given me trouble at the mansion! My cover had been blown! I had to get out of there before Candy finished her dance and told Sal that I wasn't Stacey Allen!

"Joann, you've blown my cover, we've got to get out of here! Now! It's not safe!"

"That's fine with me if you're a quitter," Joann said arrogantly. "I'll stay here and wrap up the case myself, I've read the file and I know what's going on."

"No Joann, you don't know what you're doing, it's not safe for either one of us to be here another minute. Get out now, while you have the chance!"

Joann wouldn't budge, she had her feet planted firmly on the ground. Short of knocking her out and dragging her from the building, there was nothing that I could do to persuade her to leave. "You want to stay here? You stay here at your own risk and suffer the consequences, I won't be responsible."

"You… won't be responsible for me?" she snickered. "That's a laugh; I'm ten times the investigator that you are!"

"Fine, have it your way." I had to give up and leave her there.

Candy had sworn revenge on me the last time that I had seen her, and now was her perfect opportunity and I wasn't going to stick around for it. I made a dash for my locker, grabbed my bag with my car keys and I beat it out the back door!

I drove to my hotel and no one followed me; I was home free. As I walked up to my room, I wondered what would happen to Joann. If she had really read the file, she did know what she was dealing with. What could she possibly be thinking? What was her plan? I felt like I should do something about her, but there really wasn't anything that I could do and I couldn't reach Ray.

After I barricaded the door, I threw back a couple shots of brandy, took my shower and turned on an old movie. It wasn't long before the old black and white mystery had peacefully put me to sleep.

Ring… ring … ring … I could hear something in the distance. Was I dreaming? It became louder and I finally woke up and realized that it was the phone. "Confound it, can't I ever get any sleep!" I answered the phone in a sleepy voice, "Hello."

"HELP! HELP!" I heard a woman scream. It startled me awake, it was Joann. "My car's been vandalized, I'm in the parking lot at a payphone, please come and get me!"

"What parking lot?" I asked.

"At the strip club, of course, where else would I be? They're after me, Penelope!"

I wondered why Joann hadn't at least run out of the parking lot and tried to get away before stopping to make a phone call. Some great investigator! "Okay, I'll come and get you Joann."

"Hurry, Penelope, they're going to take me out in the…NO! NO!" I heard Joann scream. There was a struggle and then the phone went dead… they had her.

"Damn it! Why is it always up to me? That stupid bitch!"

I threw on my jeans and cowboy boots and ran out to the car. I knew that there was no sense in calling the police, they would merely go to the club to ask questions, and that would go nowhere. By the time anything could be done, it would be too late and Joann would probably never be seen again.

I didn't like Joann, but I surely wasn't going to stand by and let her be murdered. I had to try to save her and I raced back to the strip club. Thinking that she was gone by now, the only hope that I had of finding her was to get to the boss, Candy, A.K.A. Layla Lace.

I parked a block away and stayed in the shadows as I snuck up to the club. First, I had to know who was there. I watched the building and could see that there were only two bouncers left. That was bad news for Joann, it meant that I was right, the other two men had taken her off the property.

It was always smoky in the club, so when the waitresses were on break they propped open the back door. I waited and it was only minutes before the door was left open, and I slipped inside without being seen.

I spotted Layla as she was coming out of her dressing room. I rushed her, pushed her back inside and closed the door. "Listen Layla, or whatever your name is, you tell me what you've done with Joann."

"Who the hell is Joann?" she laughed and then mocked me, by turning her back on me. When she turned, she spun around like she was performing; the sheer silk robe fluttered and sparkled. Layla was wearing stripper pasties on the nipples of her behemoth breasts and thong panties that stuck up her butt crack.

"I have no idea what you're talking about," she arrogantly said and then sat her bare ass down, with a plop, at her vanity and began to look in the mirror, admiring herself.

I wasn't playing games this time, this skank was going to tell me where Joann was, and that was the way it was going to be. "Come back to reality, you screwball, you're not impressing me. I'm not one of your demented fans! Now listen to me, because I'm only going to ask you nicely, just one more time. What have you done with Joann?"

For once in my life, I wasn't outnumbered or outclassed. Except for her tits, Layla and I were the same weight and size. "This is no contest," I thought … "it's just one on one."

Layla turned around on her pink puffy stool and looked at me indignantly. "You're the one who better listen; you're in my house now and you don't stand a chance in hell. All I have to do is let out a peep and you'll never get out of here alive."

With that, I lunged for her, grabbing her by the throat with my left hand, I pushed her head back cracking it against the vanity, and held her there. "Okay bitch, make a peep." I tightened my grip and she couldn't speak. Layla couldn't make a sound, she was motionless, frozen by fear, I could see it in her eyes and I didn't allow her take in a breath.

I pulled out my knife, the one that I had carried since childhood. I flipped it open with my right hand and flashed the blade in Layla's face so that she could clearly see it. "I'm not playing games with you Layla, I don't know how big you think you are, but right now, you're my bitch!"

I took the knife and pressed it into one of her enormous tits, a drop of blood dripped to the floor. "How attached are you to these things?" I asked, "I don't imagine that they'd be very hard to pop."

I waited until her face began to change color and I let her take a breath, then I tightened my grip again. "Are you ready to tell me what I want to know?" Layla nodded her head. "I'm going to let you breathe, but I'm warning you, you make one wrong move and you can kiss this tit good-bye." I released her neck, but kept the knife pressed firmly into the soft tissue. Layla coughed for a moment and then caught her breath. "Okay now… you tell me… Where is Joann?"

"She's being driven into the desert. You don't understand, she knows too much, I couldn't just let her leave!" (It was obvious that Joann had been flapping her jaw.)

"Well, you better figure out a way to stop this from going any further," I said as I poked the knife deeper.

"Okay, okay, I have a radio, I can reach them."

"Where is it?" I asked.

"It's in the cabinet across the room."

I walked across the room with Layla, holding one of her arms behind her back and my knife against her water balloon tit. She called the men in the car who were holding Joann. "What do you want me to tell them?" she asked.

"Ask them if Joann's hurt and where they have her."

I soon found that Joann was in the desert, and as yet, unharmed.

"Tell them not to hurt her, just leave her there, and come back to the club."

The men didn't ask questions, they followed Layla's orders and immediately headed back to the club, leaving Joann in the desert.

Now, I had to keep Layla quiet until I could get away. I gave her a good hard pop in the jaw to knock her for a loop and before she could recover, I pulled the cord from the draperies and tied her up. Then, I stomped on the radio with my good ol' cowboy boots.

Before I left, I shoved Layla into the closet and I took a poke at her tit one more time. "I otta pop that ridiculous thing just for the fun of it," I laughed. "You gonna make a peep?" Layla shook her head no.

"Oh, and by the way, it's been nice seeing you again, Candy."

Candy had no threats of revenge this time. I closed the closet door and propped a chair under the knob; she didn't make a sound. I carefully opened the dressing room door, slipped out of the club and got away.

I made a quick stop at the hotel, picked up my things and started driving the highway home. I had everything that I needed for my report, my job was finished.

As far as Joann, (being the top notch investigator that she was,) I figured that she could at least find her way back to civilization.

When Ray found out what Joann had done, he fired her before she even got home. He told me that he was impressed by the way that I had handled things. "You're good under pressure kid, and I think that you've got what it takes." Ray apologized to me for sending Joann, and then he promoted me to detective. He told me up front that being a detective would sometimes be dangerous, but the way my life had been, hearing that it might be dangerous, didn't faze me.

Even though I was now considered a detective, I didn't expect things to change much. I thought that Ray was simply trying to give me an ego boost by calling me Detective Wells, and that the title didn't really mean anything…but I was wrong.

After the promotion, I was assigned to a variety of interesting and challenging cases. They were sometimes dangerous, but I was always well protected.

Like Joe, most of the men that I worked with were former law enforcement. They were great, a bit overprotective, but we always got along quite well. In my opinion, cowboys, bikers and cops, they were all the same to me, tough guys.

Working as a detective, I enjoyed a feeling of safety that I had never known before. The bad guys that I met while on a case would never know my real name, where I lived, who my family was or any other pertinent information about me.

After I had worked for several months as a detective, Ray found that I had a knack for catching sexual offenders. He called me his secret weapon and said that I had a special gift, but I had always thought of it as more of a curse.

All of my life I had suffered with this curse, the curse of being a "weirdo magnet." Even as a child they would bother me. The first time that I remember it happening, I couldn't have been more than five or six years old. I was at a nursing home singing Christmas Carols with a church group. A crazy old man singled me out, grabbed hold of my arm and was trying to kiss me. I went screaming and running down the hall, trying to get away from him, but the old man was in a wheelchair and all I was doing was pulling him along with me. It took two orderly's to pry him loose. Needless to say, that was the end of my Christmas Caroling.

Through the years, suffering with this curse was never easy. If there was a weirdo within range, man or woman, as soon as they saw me, they locked on and made a beeline straight for me. I have left many a store and restaurant because of this curse. At the time, I could have never known that someday I would be a detective and that this "curse" would actually turn out to be an advantage.

Now that I had been educated about sex crimes, I realized that Kurt really had raped me. It was called date rape and men had been getting away with it for years. As a rule, women who have been date raped tend to react pretty much the same way that I had; confused, ashamed and blaming themselves.

Working these cases brought up a lot of bad feelings, and it was then that I realized I had been wrong; being raped by Kurt really had been a big deal. At the time that it happened, I couldn't cope with any more stress, so I buried it and I had felt like a dirty disgrace ever since. Rape is a strange crime; it takes something from you that is difficult to regain, but with work, you can recover.

Being a victim of rape myself, I was determined to do something about it and as fate would have it I had been placed in a unique position, a position where I could do some good. That's how I worked through my issues; giving those dirty bastards exactly what they deserved!

Because of my special "gift" it was never difficult for me to catch the slimy perverts, they came running right to me, every time. They intended me as their next victim, but their plans soon backfired when I caught them and I caught them fast. I eliminated a lot of dangerous people and restored peace of mind to our clients. When the police couldn't help, the victims called us.

Ray saved a lot of money getting quick results for his clients and he was happy. I was lucky, and never failed to solve a case. I loved my new position, and no surprise it was exciting. Getting these scumbags off the street was like an addictive rush. I was driven; when I closed a case I couldn't wait to go out on the next one.

Many times after working a difficult dangerous assignment, the clients wanted to meet me to say thank you, but of course that wasn't possible as my identity could never be revealed. There are people who love me for some of the jobs that I did, but they will never know who I am.

I was on a job; it was a Saturday, two o'clock in the afternoon. I was working surveillance on a child molestation case. Our client, Ben Wright, was divorced and had a four-year-old daughter named, Cindy. He had custody of the child and his wife had been awarded visitation every other weekend.

Mr. Wright discovered that Cindy had been molested by his ex-wives father, Cindy's grandfather. Since finding out about the incident, the mother continued to allow the molester to visit with Cindy alone, during her visitation. We found that the man had molested his own daughter as well, (the client's ex,) when she was young and she then set her daughter up to be molested by him, intentionally.

As shocking as this may seem, I learned that it was actually common. The mother's reason being, that she didn't have the courage to fight her father herself, so she hopes that her daughter will be stronger and expose him. Sick, but true.

When Cindy's father, our client, found out that his ex-wife was allowing these visits, he tried to get her visitation denied, but to no avail. He then called us to ensure the child's safety.

Every other weekend, during the mother's visitation, we kept the family under surveillance and made certain that the grandfather didn't have contact with the child. It was always a tense assignment, waiting, wondering and being prepared to take action should the molester come on the scene.

I was settling in for a long shift when Ray paged me; I called him back immediately. "I'm sending someone to relieve you, something's come up and I need you here A.S.A.P."

"Okay boss, I'll be there as soon as I can." I wondered what could be so important, as Ray had never called me off a job before.

As soon as my relief arrived, I raced to Ray's office and walked right in. He was on the phone and hung up as soon as he saw me. He didn't say a word, but after a long sigh, began to speak. "Penelope, sometimes I just don't have the stomach for this job," he said shaking his head. "If you have any fear or reservations about what kind of assignments you'll take, tell me now," then he paused. "Do you want me to go on?"

We had plenty of other operatives much more qualified and experienced than me, so I knew that Ray needed me specifically. I was concerned, "What is it Ray? Tell me."

Then Ray began to tell me the whole horrific story, "The case is located at an upscale condominium complex. The people that live there, mostly single mothers, have poured their life savings into their homes and now they're stuck with no way out, short of bankruptcy. There's a family of three that have owned and managed the complex for the past four years, name of Rakker. The father and his son, who is in his late-twenties, have been repeatedly raping the young girls who live in the complex. Apparently, it's been going on ever since the Rakker's took over the property. The girls are in such terror that not one of them has ever said a word to anybody about it, not even to each other."

"Three weeks ago, a twelve-year old, named Maggie Ross, contracted an STD and her mother got the whole story out of her. After that, the floodgates opened and it was discovered by the parents that nearly all of the girls in the complex have been repeatedly raped by the Rakker's. The families didn't to go to the police because the girls are too afraid to say anything against their attackers. None of the parents think that their children can handle the stress of a court battle; several of them are already on the verge of suicide. The only evidence so far, is the testimony of the victims, which we can't use."

"There's also the questionable death of a thirteen-year old girl, Melissa Stage. Two years ago, she was found dead in an abandoned car, in an alley across town. It was ruled a suicide by drug overdose, but I'm convinced that the Rakker's murdered the girl. Melissa was an innocent, and had no history of drug use of any kind."

"Sounds like these girls have good reason to be afraid," I concluded.

"They're terrified, and could never face their attackers in court, they're much too fragile. It's all up to you Penelope; we need hard conclusive evidence, evidence so strong that the Rakker's will be forced to plead guilty, and it won't be easy. I've been working on this case for two weeks now, using female detectives as bait. I put Sally out there first and then Sandy gave it a good shot; as you know, both Sally and Sandy are former military. Apparently, they're not the Rakker's type, they like young girls, so no dice."

"Sally and Sandy were my first choices because they both have the muscle and the ability to take care of themselves should it get rough, but their physical ability doesn't do me any good if they can't attract the bad guys. I really don't want to send you in, these are extremely dangerous men, but you're my only hope. Well, what do you say, Penelope, are you up for it?"

"You should have called me first, Ray, you know that I'm your secret weapon." What's the plan?"

"My main concern is for your safety, so I'll send you in with Sandy, and Joe can go as your backup."

Joe was back to work now, his wife had had the baby and they were both doing fine. This would be the first time that I would see him since the strip club job and I was happy to have him onboard, but I wasn't happy at all about Sandy.

"Your cover story," Ray went on, "is that you're visiting a friend for a few days. That should speed up the timeline and compel them to act quickly if they think that you'll be leaving soon."

"Wait a minute, Ray stop right there, I don't think that it's a good idea for me to work with another woman on this case. It could take twice as long, and maybe never come together at all if the bad guys don't trust or like her. It could turn out to be a real problem, and no offense, but Sandy looks like G.I. Joe.

Besides that, when I'm alone, I seem vulnerable and the perverts think that they can take advantage me. It makes things so much easier when I'm by myself. This is important Ray; I've got to get these sickos fast, before they have the chance to rape another girl."

"I understand what you're saying," Ray said, "and it probably would move faster if you were alone, but after that strip club case, I don't want to take any more chances with you. You could have been killed."

"I could have been killed alright, but that was because of that idiot, Joann. Don't worry, Ray, I'm more likely to get hurt with another woman there. It makes me uptight having to deal with her ego, and constantly worrying if I'm stepping on her toes. The other woman always wants the credit for the bust and they try to 'one up me' and start competing with me. I'm constantly concerned that she'll speak out of turn and blow it. Just let me go by myself, I'll be fine."

Ray reluctantly agreed, then went on to tell me, "The Rakker's like short shirts, drop earrings and high heels."

"Great, high heels again, oh my aching feet. Why couldn't any of these creeps ever have a thing for sneakers?"

"You're easier to catch in high heels," Joe answered.

"You know you're right, high heels do make a woman more vulnerable; I never thought of that before. They must have been invented by a sick mind. High heels and short skirts, sure make it easy for a rapist." I shook my head and asked, "When do we start?"

"I'll call Joe in from the newspaper case; you can leave as soon as he gets here."

"I'll run home and change," I said.

"Wait a minute," Ray stopped me, "bring some dirty laundry with you. The laundry room is located right next to the Rakker's parking spaces and they also can see it from their unit."

"Okay I will," I shouted as I rushed out the door. "I need to do laundry anyway," I whispered to myself.

This was just the kind of case that I wanted to work. Watching these perverse sexual predators think that they were luring me into a vulnerable position, and then, BAM! You're busted sucker!

Yes, I was happy to get a vile criminal caged, of course, but it was the look on their faces when they realized what was happening to them, it gave me a thrill that there are just no words to describe. When it clicked in their mind, I saw it in their eyes, the exact moment when they realized, that not only had they failed at their sick perverse plan, but also that they had been trapped. That was the moment that I felt the rush of victory.

This particular case was a little tricky because there were two perpetrators and I wanted them both. I wasn't about to let one of these scumbags slip through the noose.

When I arrived home, I changed into a short little skirt with a sexy blouse and my highest heeled shoes, then I sat at my vanity and glossed my lips with bright red lipstick. I selected my flashiest drop earrings and after I put them on, I stopped for a moment and checked myself in the mirror; I was ready.

I grabbed my laundry and when I got back to the office, Joe was already there waiting for me. Ray gave us the particulars and we headed out. Joe and I were on the hunt ready to take down our prey; the murderous serial rapists, the Rakker's.

The Rakker's, father and son, got home from work by six p.m. I decided to get set up in the laundry room and be waiting for them, within view of their parking space when they arrived. I figured that that would be the best time to get their attention, right when they pulled up in the car.

As Joe and I rode along, we exchanged niceties and I began to prepare for battle. I slipped the wire down my side; it was about two feet long. Our equipment wasn't the greatest; Joe merely listened to what was happening through the car radio.

"Do you have enough quarters?" Joe asked, "You might end up in that laundry room all night."

"Yeah, I'm ready for 'em," I answered as I checked my makeup in the visor mirror.

Joe stopped a block away and we made sure that the wire was working properly.

"Well, I've got a lot of static, as usual," he said, "but I can hear you."

"Do you miss working on the police force, Joe? I'll bet they had great equipment."

"Penelope, I'm sorry to say that the police force wasn't much better. We rarely could hear half of what was going on. You stay in my line of sight, otherwise I might not know if you get into trouble."

"Of course Joe, I know these guys are dangerous."

Joe got out of the car and gave me a tight hug, "Be safe Penelope, and don't take any chances, I'm responsible for you."

I walked down the street in my high heels carrying the laundry basket and found my way to the laundry room. There were the Rakker's parking spaces, 301 and 302, right by the door, just like Ray had said. I loaded a washer and then walked the premises to familiarize myself with the area. It was an impressive complex with tennis courts, swimming pool, steam room, the works.

I checked my watch and it was getting close to six o'clock. I ran the descriptions of the Rakker's over in my mind as I headed back to the laundry room. "The father's name is Harry and the son is Nicky."

When I looked up, here came a sleek black sports car with the Rakker's inside. This was it; I had to get their attention. I pretended to check the washers and slowly walked back and forth in front of the big windows of the laundry room as they passed by, then I made my way outside. Just as they pulled into their parking space, I slowly sat down on the curb. With that short skirt on and the high heels, I flashed a lot of thigh and it got their attention.

Father and son, both got out and when they closed the car doors; they didn't take their eyes off of me.

"Hey, good lookin'," I greeted them in a friendly cute tone.

They both looked at each other trying to figure out which one of them I was referring to.

"Don't ask me which one of you I'm talking to," I said. "With two gorgeous men like you getting out of that car… why, I'm a bit overwhelmed."

BAM! … They were on me, they had taken the bait! I glanced over at Joe to make sure that he could hear what was happening. He gave me the signal, smiling and shaking his head in disbelief.

I had to shake my head for a minute too and realize just who these guys really were, they had totally caught me off guard. The Rakker's were two of the most incredible looking men that I had ever seen; they had handsome faces with beautiful smiles and broad-shouldered, flawless bodies.

"We've never seen you around here before. Are you a new girl?" the father asked as they both walked toward me.

"I guess you could say that I'm a new girl, but I don't live here, I'm just visiting a friend. She lives on the other side of the complex."

"What's her name, we might know her?"

"I'd rather not say in case you do know her, she's turned out to be a total bitch. I come all the way out here from Kentucky to visit her and then she ends up treating me like crap. What a bore she is, she doesn't want to do anything and I'm not having any fun at all. As a matter of fact, this is the most fun I've had since I've been here, doing laundry and talking to you."

"So you're not having any fun, huh? Well, maybe we can change all that."

"Well maybe you can, what'd ya have in mind?"

Just then, I heard a woman's voice, "Harry hurry, we've got to leave in twenty-minutes."

"That's my wife, don't go anywhere, I'll be right back," the father, Harry said, before he hurried off to his condo.

The son, Nicky, stayed behind with me, "My dad and I have to go to an important meeting tonight. What are you doing tomorrow?"

"I figured that I'd lay by the pool all day."

"We're not working tomorrow, we'll meet you out there."

"Okay, sounds great." YES! I had made the connection!

"I've got to get ready now, see you tomorrow," Nicky said with a smile.

"Bye, handsome," I replied and waved good-bye.

Before I could walk back into the laundry room, Harry came running back outside to make sure that we had a plan for the next day, and I assured him that I'd meet them by the pool.

When the Rakker's left the grounds and were out of sight, I pulled my laundry from the machine and Joe picked me up.

"You are so good Penelope, I couldn't believe how quick you snagged them, you made it look easy. I've been sitting in this parking lot for two weeks now with Sandy and Sally. They have all the training, but nothing can compete with good ol' instinct, the way you sat down on that curb… genius! Have you decided how you're going to play it?"

"I'm too old to fall into the realm that they're comfortable operating in, young girls, naïve, easily intimidated and manipulated. I think I'll be a sleazy friend that's even more vile than they are. They'll feel much more free to talk and willing to give me information that way. I'd like to start tomorrow at about noon, if that's okay with you Joe; I have a date by the pool. I'm hoping to have them wrapped up in a neat little package by tomorrow night."

"I know you're good, Penelope, but don't you think you're pushing it a bit? Don't get in a hurry and overlook something. Remember everything's riding on you, you have to make the whole case, all by yourself."

"Don't worry Joe, I won't blow it."

Joe dropped me back at the office and I started the drive home. I thought about my plan; it was perfect. A woman lying by the pool, vulnerable and alone, covered with slick shiny oil, in nothing, but a tiny bikini. "That should make them all hot and bothered and easy for me to manipulate."

There was only one problem with this plan; Penelope Wells didn't own a sleazy bikini. I realized that I would be embarrassed wearing the kind of a bikini that I had in mind, but after all, I was an actress playing a part; a part in which lives weighed in the balance and I had to take it all the way. So, I went to the mall and bought the tiniest bikini that I could find.

The next morning, I met Joe at the office and we began to drive to the location. Wearing the skimpy bikini, I didn't have any way to hide the wire and it had to be extended its full length. Joe and I decided that I would take an extra towel and carry it over my arm with the wire concealed inside. He dropped me off and I walked to the pool. When I got poolside, I spread my beach towel on a lounge chair and positioned the towel with the hidden wire near my head. We were fortunate, Joe was able to inconspicuously park very close to the pool, in the shade, right where he had a perfect view.

Now it was time to wait. I was sure that I had made a good connection with the Rakker's, but I hoped that those few minutes that we had spent together, the day before, had been enough to get them to the pool.

I was out there ten, maybe fifteen minutes, when here came Harry trotting up the walk. I sat up so that he would be sure to see me. "Hi, I'll be right out," he shouted as he waved hello.

"I'll be here waiting." I giggled and gave my shoulders a little twist. Harry chuckled and quickened his step. "I've got him now," I whispered in delight. "I hope that Nicky shows up too." It was vitally important that I got them both, but if Nicky didn't show it would prolong the investigation, and give the two time to rape again.

Ten minutes later, here came both of the happy frolicking rapists, ready for action. I wondered just what their perverse sick plans were for me. After all, I wasn't twelve years old and this was quite a stretch for them.

I greeted them as they came through the gate, "Hi guys, I'm glad you could make it."

"We wouldn't pass up a chance to spend time with a beautiful girl like you," Harry said.

"Yes, I'm sure you wouldn't pass up an opportunity to hurt a woman, you sickos," I thought grimly to myself.

The two of them sat down on the lounge chairs next to me, one on each side. I could see how it would be easy for them to get an innocent inexperienced, young girl in their clutches as they were both so attractive and charming.

I got deep into my character, "Thanks for calling me beautiful, that's a sweet thing to say. I'm feeling better already, you guys are really cheering me up. How do you like my new bikini? I got it last night, especially for you." I stood up and modeled the obscene little suit for them. I slowly turned around, did a little dance and then I bent over to talk to them, "Well what'd you think? Do you like it?"

No one knows just how difficult it was for me to stand there in that horrible bikini and be ogled by such perverse sick men, but I kept my eyes on the prize, putting them in the cage where they belonged.

"Baby, I don't like it, I love it!" Nicky answered enthusiastically with excitement in his eyes.

I already had them both worked up, and they were ready for the next step in my plan. I sat back down in my chair and opened the magazine that I had brought with me. The cover was a gardening magazine, but on the inside, it was pornographic; full of graphic photos containing sexual acts with young girls.

I pretended like I was trying not to let them see my trick magazine, but of course they were interested in what I was reading. "What's that magazine you've got there?" Harry asked me.

"Oh nothing, just a little ol' gardening magazine. Can't you see the cover?" I giggled and playfully lowered the magazine for a second or two, just long enough for them to get a quick glance at the bare skin on the pages.

"That doesn't look like gardening to me," Harry answered. His eyes were bulging and he laughed a sick perverse laugh.

"Why you boys are good looking and smart too, but I'd bet there's still a few things that I could teach you."

"Oh really? Like what, for instance?" Nicky asked.

Then the father, Harry, took gentle hold of the magazine, "Come on now honey, let me have a look at your magazine." I let him pull it from my hands and he quickly looked it over.

"Nicky, come over here," Harry bellowed, "I want you to get a look at what our new friend is into." Nicky got up from his chair and walked over to Harry, he knelt down and they both thumbed through the magazine together.

Now it was time for the next step, "Come on, let's get in the spa," I announced, and then I stood up and started my "hooker-walk" toward the spa. Both men leaped up, drooling and panting, and followed close behind me. I slowly lowered myself into the bubbling water and before my bottom even hit the seat they were both in the spa pressing close beside me.

Harry started talking about massage; he apparently had taken some courses. I knew that he wanted to get his hands on me, so I took the easy way out. "You know what really turns me on? A foot massage."

That was all I needed to say and Harry instantly had my feet in his hands massaging them. It made my flesh crawl, but once again, I kept my eyes on the prize.

It has been my experience that perverts like to brag about their exploits. It's not something that they're free to do very often, but when sexually aroused and coaxed at just the right time, it's really not a difficult task to get them to "share their experiences."

The sexual tension was building; I could tell that Harry and Nicky were nearing the point that they would get loose and sloppy and I would be able to get them talking.

Just as I was preparing to make my next move and begin coaxing them, a man came walking past the pool. When he saw me in the spa with the Rakker's, he stopped at the gate and started to open it. "Miss, you better get away from those guys!"

I could see it coming, another client interfering with a case, it happened all the time. What was wrong with these people? They hire us, and then when I'm out there working, they're trying to stop me. What did they expect, a man in a trench coat with a big magnifying glass? It always happened, even on employee theft investigations. The owner would hire us and then be there on site, at the time of the investigation. Then they would call Ray and angrily tell him that the operatives hadn't shown up. When Ray gave them the verbal report, they were always shocked that we really had been there, stating that they couldn't pick us out in the crowd. On a case like a bar shop, it really didn't matter much; if they wanted to waste their money playing games, it was their business. But in this situation it did matter. I had to get the Rakker's stopped, and fast.

I felt bad for what I had to do as the man was just trying to help me, but I decided to use him to create a camaraderie between myself and the Rakker's. "What's your problem anyway, Buddy?" I rudely shouted at the man. "Why don't you shut up and mind your own business. What are you, jealous? You want a piece of this for yourself?" then I stood up and slapped my fanny. "If there's anybody that I should stay away from it's definitely you, you sick jealous freak."

The man looked like I had just punched him in the stomach. He didn't say another word and walked away. But of course, the Rakker's loved it and after that, I was their buddy. I had hoped it would make things easier for me, and it had.

68

The conversation quickly got more and more vulgar as we talked about the obscene magazine that I had.

"Are you into girls?" they both asked.

"Listen, I'm into anything that feels good. Sure I like girls, but I wouldn't complain about a nice hard dick either."

I hadn't read anything about Harry's wife in the complaint, but I wanted to know if she was involved. "What about your wife? Is she into girls? Maybe you could invite her out here and we could get to know each other. That would really be fun."

"No way," Harry answered, "that uptight bitch, I'm lucky if I get it missionary style once a month. Oh no, not her, she's perfect; she never does anything wrong and she's always rubbing my nose in it. Nothing's ever good enough for her. I'd divorce her except for my property, it would just be too damn expensive."

"Okay man, I didn't mean to bring up a sore subject, let's never mention the bitch again." I was satisfied that the wife wasn't involved.

"What turns you guys on?" I asked.

"We like girls too, just like you," Nick answered.

"Well I guess that puts us on the same team. You like them young? I think the young ones are the best, they have such soft smooth skin and tight little bodies."

"Yeah," Harry said, "double digit, ten years old and up; at ten they already know what's going on. I wouldn't want to be considered a child molester."

"You're not kidding," I added. "These parents are just deluding themselves thinking that their little girls are so innocent, when all the time they're parading around just asking for it. They dress them like sluts, and the girls act like sluts."

At that moment, a darling little girl came walking into the pool area with her mother. The little girl was carrying a fluffy kitten in her arms. She quickly got into the pool and left the kitten standing on the edge. She was splashing water at the kitten and strangely enough, the kitten was splashing her back. Her mother waved to the Rakker's, said hello, and then sat on one of the lounge chairs and began reading a magazine. When the little girl was sure that her mother wasn't looking she gave the Rakkers the okay sign with her hand.

"Who's that?" I asked. "One of your playmates? Take her, for example. Did you see the way she came walking in here? All that little bitch needs is a pimp. I've noticed that there's a lot of young stuff around here. You guys ever get any?"

The question had been asked. What would they say? I held my breath and felt the paranoia trying to grab hold of me. "They know who I am! I made my move too quickly!"

I hoped that they weren't worried about getting caught and that they felt invincible, untouchable, above the law as so many criminals do when they've been getting away with their crime for a long period of time. I prayed that they didn't suspect me.

It seemed like forever, but they finally answered, "As a matter of fact, we have big plans for her tonight. She's a new one, she and her mother just moved in and the mother goes to work tonight. The little bitch will be alone and she's expecting us."

What did they just tell me? I couldn't believe what I had heard! I looked at the sweet little girl innocently playing in the pool. What had the Rakkers told her? Certainly not that they had planned to hurt her and destroy her life that night.

I felt the pressure, I had to get them today, there was no time to waste and I moved ahead. "If she's the new one, does that mean that you have other playmates? Why don't you do me a favor and call one of them to come out and play with me?"

"Damn you're fun, girl," Nicky stated with glee. "Dad and I have had every one of these girls around here, but they're all in school right now."

"Of course, they're all in school, that sounds like a good excuse. You're so full of shit, I don't believe a word of it. You've had every one of the girls here? You wish."

"He's not lying and I can prove it," Harry said defensively.

"You can prove it? You got videos or something? I sure hope so, I could really use a good nasty video right about now, just a little something to get me going. As a matter of fact, I've made some videos myself. I've been working in the adult industry for five years now. Believe me, I know how to handle a man, I can give you pleasure beyond your wildest dreams, and teach you things that you've never even heard of."

"Could you get me in a movie?" Nicky asked.

"Well you're good looking enough, that's for sure, but I haven't seen the rest of your equipment yet, or if you know how to use it. I suppose that I could give you an audition."

Nicky started to get up, "I've got the keys to the clubhouse, let's move this party inside."

"Okay baby, let's go and get on with this audition," I said enthusiastically.

"Hey wait a minute you two, is the old man invited?" Harry asked.

"If you want to know the truth Harry, I prefer a more mature man. Come on, let's see if I can get you into the business too, then you can leave that old bitch you're married to."

I couldn't take my wire in with me, wrapped in the towel, it would be too easy for me to get caught with it. But I didn't hesitate, I had to take the risk and go with the Rakker's; they had evil plans that very night for the little girl by the pool. It was up to me to stop them before they ruined another young life.

When the three of us started walking toward the clubhouse, I heard Joe shouting, "Blow it out! Blow it out!" I couldn't ignore him, he was out of the car and running the fence line for the gate. Joe was doing his job protecting me, and he was right.

"Just a minute," I said to the Rakker's, "let me go see what this guy wants. I think he's someone that I met last night at a bar; I'll get rid of him."

"What do you want, sir?" I shouted as I walked my "hooker walk" to Joe; the Rakker's were watching and I couldn't get out of character.

I knew exactly what Joe was going to say and I didn't have the time to get into it with him, so I got straight to the point. "Joe, you see that little girl playing in the pool? She's their next victim and it's going down tonight." Joe's oldest daughter was about the same age as the little girl and I knew that it hit him hard. "Trust me Joe, I know what I'm doing. They're not going to hurt me; I'm their buddy and they're too busy trying to impress me."

"If you go into the clubhouse I can't hear or see you, I won't know if you're in trouble. We'll intervene and do something to protect the girl tonight. I'm responsible for your safety and there's no way that I can allow this."

Joe was my superior and if he said no, there was nothing that I could do about it. "Come on Joe, we have no way of knowing what that kid's mother will say or do. If we start manipulating people the Rakker's might get wise and we could screw up the whole investigation. I know I can nail them today, just give me the chance! The Rakker's are going to get suspicious if we stand here talking much longer. Please, just let me go! I know I can do it."

"Okay, I'll let you have ten minutes, then I'm coming in."

"Joe there's no way that I can put a time limit on this, it'll take as long as it takes. If I hurry I could blow it and there's too much at stake. What's wrong with a good old-fashioned scream? You sit here by the pool, where you can hear me, and if I get into the slightest trouble, I'll scream."

"Any question of your safety and you scream." Joe reluctantly agreed to let me go, and I left immediately; I didn't want to give him the time to change his mind.

I got back into character and skipped a few times as I approached the Rakker's. "Wow, I'm glad to get away from that creep," I said to them. "I shouldn't have told him where I was staying, but how could I know that he was going to track me down? The nerve of some people! Now where were we? Oh yes, your first lesson, I'll reveal an incredible sex secret while I bring you to ecstasy and then… the audition." I slipped a hand through Nicky's arm and the other through Harry's and the three of us walked off to the clubhouse.

Nicky pulled out the keys and opened the door. "This clubhouse is kind of our own private sex emporium, Dad and I are the only ones with the key and everything is safely locked inside."

"Wow, that's great," I acted impressed. What did these monsters have hidden in this room? I braced myself, "Whatever happens, don't lose your cool."

It didn't look like much at first, but then Nicky said, "Come on, let's go into, "The Den of Secret Desires.'"

"The Den of Secret Desires," just the sound of that is making me excited!" I exclaimed.

It never ceased to amaze me how these creeps would tell me things so easily. Was this really happening? Were they actually taking me into their confidence this quickly? Or did they know who I was and the whole thing was a trap? I was deeply concerned; did they have a plan to kill me?

Nicky led the way and we walked into "The Den of Secret Desires." These guys had every kind of sex toy imaginable, along with books, magazines, movies and torture devices. Nothing was taboo to them; sick, painful, it made no difference. I pictured the little girls that had been brought into this room and tortured and it started to affect me; I tried to block it from my mind and move ahead.

I kept talking and teasing while I moved around the room, trying to locate evidence that tied the Rakker's to the rapes and the murder of Melisa Stage.

Meanwhile, by the pool, Joe was trying to hold himself back from calling the whole thing off. He always carried a big bag of peanuts in the car to eat when he was on stakeout and couldn't leave to get food. He was sitting at the pool eating one peanut after the other, crack, crack, the pile of peanut shells was getting higher and higher as the time slowly dragged on.

I was locked in a room with two of the most perverse sick and cruel predators that I had ever encountered. At one point, when we were viewing a film, I became so appalled by what I was seeing that I didn't think I could go on. The film made the horror of the abuse so real, that I became sick and was starting to lose it. I excused myself and headed for the restroom, thinking that I might have to quit. I didn't see how I could find the strength to continue. But then I walked by a window and glanced outside; I had a clear view of the swimming pool and I saw their next victim, the little girl, splashing and playing in the water. The cost of quitting was much too high, it wasn't an option.

I barely made it to the restroom before I threw up. I had to pull myself together, but I didn't know if I could. I sat on the floor sobbing and feeling desperate, completely overwhelmed by empathy for the victims. What the innocent little girls, had endured was more than I could bear and I was crushed by their pain and horror. I forced myself to stand up and I rinsed my face and mouth, then I took a hard look at myself in the mirror. This wasn't the first time that I had to face a formidable enemy. I had learned from childhood how to draw from my inner strength, and as I stood there, I felt the might of the warrior within me, and I went back to face the enemy.

More time passed; Joe was poolside, still cracking the peanut shells in his strong hands. The pile of shells was growing still higher. He was torn, how much longer should he give me? What if they had me gagged and I couldn't scream?

Joe was responsible for my life and he wasn't going to let it go on any longer, he had started to get up when he felt something strike against his boot. He looked down and saw the kitten, it had noticed the peanuts that had fallen to the ground and was batting them about.

The child's mother got up from her chair and approached Joe, "I'm sorry, I hope that little Fluffy isn't bothering you."

"Oh no, she's fine, no problem at all."

"Do you mind if I sit at the table, in the shade with you for a bit? The sun is getting a little hot."

"Sure, have a seat."

"I'm Madelyn," she introduced herself and then reached to shake Joe's hand. Joe shook her hand and gave a forced smile. His mind was on me, he was trying to listen for the scream. Did I need him? Was he making a mistake allowing me so much time alone with these dangerous men?

"My daughter, Molly, and I just moved in two days ago," Madelyn explained. "I thought we'd take a little break from unpacking and come out here and enjoy the pool for a while. This is sure a wonderful place, I just love it here."

"Yeah, it's nice alright," Joe answered.

"I never thought that I would ever be able to afford to live in such a lovely place like this, but the owners, the Rakker's, made me an incredible deal. My husband died recently after an extended illness and our credit was in shambles. The Rakker's carried the papers for me so I could qualify. Then yesterday, they came by with a housewarming gift, this adorable little kitten for Molly. She had asked me for a kitten when we were here last time and they must have heard her; they're such thoughtful caring men. Little Fluffy is an expensive cat too; I was totally floored by their generosity. They even offered to look in on Molly for me, while I'm at work tonight."

Joe couldn't even find the words to comment, he kept briskly cracking the peanuts and throwing the shells into the pile. Then Molly came over, "Hi mister, may I have one of your peanuts?"

"Sure kid, go ahead."

This little girl had just lost her father, now she was in an extremely dangerous situation and neither her, or her mother had a clue. Joe realized that he had to wait; he had to give me more time. I had told him that I could get the Rakker's that day and it was the only way that he could be certain that they wouldn't hurt this little girl or any others. He had to trust me.

I can only imagine the look on Joe's face, the tension as he cracked the peanuts.

"Are you feeling alright sir?" Madelyn asked.

"I'm fine," he answered. Then Joe thought that he heard something .... He paused and listened ... no... it was just a bird cawing.

"You look so tense, are you sure you're alright?"

"I've just got a lot on my mind today, I'm sorry if I seem a little preoccupied."

Joe wanted to get me out of there, he was struggling to stay by the pool, but he had to give me the time that I needed. Crack, crack, he broke more peanuts one after the other, he wasn't even eating them anymore.

"Thank you mister," Molly said, as she picked the shelled peanuts from the table.

"Now Molly, you ask the gentleman if it's alright to eat his peanuts, you don't just start grabbing. She's so hungry for male attention, I hope you don't mind. I guess the three of us have kind of invaded you over here."

Suddenly, a scream shrieked through the air! And another scream, and another, agonizing, painful, terrified screams! Joe leaped into action; he ran to the clubhouse and kicked open the door, his gun drawn. He cautiously entered the room. What condition would he find me in? What horrific things had the Rakker's done? Would he be able to save me, or was he too late?

When Joe saw what was actually happening his jaw dropped to the floor and he lowered his gun to his side.

The Rakker's were on their knees, naked, bound and blindfolded, sobbing and pleading for their lives. And there I was, dressed in full studded, dominatrix regalia, complete with whip and a huge strap-on.

When I noticed Joe standing there, I stopped what I was doing, "I've got enough evidence to put them away for life!" I exclaimed.

Joe had a shocked look on his face, he was speechless.

"I'm sorry Joe, I know I crossed the line, but these boys needed to be taught a lesson and I was obliged to give it to 'em! Clean it up a little for me, would ya? I've got to get out of here, man."

I dropped my weapons of torture and headed for the door, then I turned back and smiled, "I would have called you sooner, but it's always been a fantasy of mine."

KILLER BOYFRIEND

I loved my job, I was helping to make a difference and I couldn't have been happier or more fulfilled, but unfortunately my private life hadn't changed much. Larry had found out where I lived and I had to be on guard at all times. He was a constant threat always looming in the shadows.

During the time that Larry and I were together, he met a hillbilly. The hillbilly told Larry about a man that he had killed. He described how he rigged up a shotgun in his bedroom window and when the window was opened by the would-be-burglar, it fired and killed him, dead on the spot.

The story excited Larry, he thought that it was a great idea and he giggled with glee as he talked about it, over and over again.

This incident stuck in my mind, I was concerned that Larry might try it on me, in my own home. It was hard to predict what he might be planning next in that evil twisted mind of his. When I went outside, would he be waiting for me in the bushes? Or would he do something to my truck? I always had to check. When I returned home I was apprehensive; had Larry been inside my house? Had he poisoned my food or put acid in my bath oil?

I set little traps, triggers that let me know if he had been there. That way, I knew if I could open my front door without being shot, eat the food in my kitchen, and use my bath oils and cosmetics.

Larry always managed to evade the police and until he actually committed a crime, I couldn't have him arrested. Fact was, when it came right down to it, it was up to me to protect myself, but unfortunately, I couldn't just go out and kill him. I had already made one mistake and destroyed a part of my life by marrying Larry, I couldn't allow him to force my hand and then find myself in prison for the rest of it.

When Larry made his move, I just had to be ready, and if I did kill him, I had better make certain that it was clearly self-defense. I would just have to wait it out until… "The Showdown."

While I was working, I didn't have to think about Larry, so I wanted to work as much as possible. It was sad, feeling more safe confronting dangerous sexual predators than I did in my own home. After closing the Rakker case, Ray offered me some time off, but I asked him to put me right back to work. He assigned me to a routine employee theft investigation at a bar, about sixty miles from my house. I was accompanied by another operative who I liked very much, a sweet woman named Jean.

When Jean and I arrived, we sat at the bar and ordered a couple of beers. About half way through the investigation, an attractive man entered the bar; he tossed his head to throw back his wind-blown hair and then looked at me with a bright beautiful smile. I tuned away and whispered to Jean, "Here comes trouble."

I, of course, was there working a case so I made note of his description: approximately 5'10," medium build, dirty-blonde curly hair, cleft chin, baby-blue eyes.

The man slowly sauntered across the room, then he sat on the barstool next to me and said hello. I didn't answer him; I wasn't going to take the chance of getting something started. I was playing it safe, after what I had been through, the last thing on my wish list was another man.

But this man was persistent, obviously someone who wasn't accustom to being ignored. He kept trying to get my attention, but I refused to acknowledge him and went on with my business.

Finally, Jean felt sorry for the guy and she started answering him for me. They actually got on quite well, with her pretending to be me. His name was Windsor and he was adorable, laughing and joking with Jean and teasing me.

After about a half hour of this phony conversation, I couldn't stand it anymore and I broke down and talked to Windsor. Even though I found him charming, I still had it in mind to get rid of him and I abruptly told him that the only men that I dated were bikers and cops.

After that statement, I expected he would leave me alone, but his answer caught me by surprise, "I'm a biker and a cop," he said.

I chuckled a bit in disbelief, but then he pulled out his wallet and showed me some pictures of himself. "This is me at fifteen years old, on my first Harley." I glanced at the slight teenage boy on the chopper, then he flipped to another photo. "And this is me in my uniform, I'm a Correctional Officer at the toughest prison in the state. You see, I'm not lying, I am a biker and a cop." Windsor had sparked my interest and I realized that he was more than just a pretty face.

Soon the investigation came to an end, but Jean and I stayed longer to get to know Windsor better. We were having a terrific time with him, but it had to be cut short, as Jean was having a barbeque that night and it was time for us to leave.

I was relieved when we said good-bye, but then Jean took it upon herself to invite Windsor to the barbecue! I couldn't believe it, I kicked her under the bar, but it didn't do any good, she didn't un-invite him. Ray was coming to the barbeque and the two of us had important business to discuss, I was obligated to attend, so I could only hope that Windsor wouldn't show up.

Later that night, I was in the backyard talking with Ray, when here came Windsor, with Jean holding his hand and smiling. She introduced him to everyone at the party and then seated him right next to me. "It's time you got on with your life," she whispered in my direction.

Windsor was friendly and cheerful, he was so fun and entertaining that all of the people at the party loved him. He was a big hit. Jean pulled me aside and whispered, "If you don't go for it, you're crazy! Every woman here wishes that she were you." Well maybe so, but every woman there didn't have my track record with men.

The night went on without a hitch, about midnight the barbecue began to break up and I decided to leave. Windsor walked me to my car and asked me to go out to dinner with him the next night. I accepted; I really did like him, even though I didn't want to.

The next night, while I was getting ready to go out with Windsor, half of me was hoping that he wouldn't show up and the other half was praying he would. Terrified to get involved with another man and have my life turned upside down again, I planned to keep him at a distance and just be friends. After all, we could all use another friend.

Windsor showed up and right on time, happy and smiling. I suggested that we go to a little pizza shack a short distance away. Windsor liked pizza and we had a nice time, he was a pleasure to be with, just like before. By then, I didn't know what I was expecting or hoping for.

After dinner, we drove back to my house and Windsor parked the car and walked me to the door. We had a short conversation and I tried to quickly get rid of him, but then suddenly, I changed my mind and decided to invite him in for dessert.

We sat on the sofa, ate chocolate cake with ice cream and talked late into the night. Windsor had a way about him that made me feel at ease; he was intelligent and intuitive and somehow we ended up talking about intense subjects that neither one of us had ever been able to discuss with anyone else before.

I found that Windsor and I had something unusual in common; he too, had been dropped on a violent scene at a High School in the middle of a race war. I was actually able to talk to him about the things that had happened to me in school and he understood. He had been through it too, and learned the rules the same as I … fight or die. There weren't many people whom I could tell that I had tasted human flesh, but I felt a kinship with Windsor; he knew who I was and he didn't think ill of me; quite the contrary, he respected me.

As the night went on, it was as though Windsor knew me better than I knew myself and I even dared to tell him about Larry. Windsor didn't think that there was something wrong with me because I had been foolish enough to marry a crazy like Larry; he actually understood that too. I couldn't believe it when he told me that he had just come out of a marriage from an abusive woman himself.

"In my opinion, being with an abuser is worse for a man than it is for a woman," he told me. "No one has any sympathy for you. People have a hard time understanding how a woman can abuse a man and even physically harm him. My ex-wife used to attack me when I was asleep or hit me from behind when I was sitting on the sofa. I couldn't defend myself from her or I'd be the one who ended up in jail. It's a real problem and I think that few people know just how many men are suffering; we're too embarrassed to talk about it. I was fortunate to escape. I really loved her and it was difficult, but I just couldn't let it go on any longer. After I left, she had another man move in with her three days later, the poor sucker."

Windsor had been through it all and we validated and supported one another. I could talk to him about the nightmares of my past, things that I had had bottled up for most of my life. It was an incredibly freeing experience. It seemed as though Windsor had been dropped from the heavens; he was the breath of fresh air that I needed.

Before we knew it, the sun was rising and when I realized what time it was, I jumped up, "I've got to go to the office this morning, I better start getting ready."

"When can I see you again?" Windsor asked.

"Why don't you call me later, I've got to get rolling here."

I quickly walked him to the door and we said good-bye. Windsor took me in his arms and kissed me passionately, then he held me firmly by the shoulders and studied my face. It was as though he was trying to read my mind.

He had a wild look in his eye and it turned me on.

Late the next night, I was awakened by someone frantically knocking at my kitchen door. I quickly got out of bed and looked out the window, I was surprised to see that it was Windsor. I opened the door to let him in, his hair was a mess, his shirt and pants were tattered and I could see blood oozing through a tear in his shirt.

"You're hurt, get inside!" I pulled him into the house and took a quick look around outside, I didn't see anyone, then I closed the door and locked it shut.

Windsor was out of breath, he lost his balance and fell down on the kitchen table. "I'm sorry Penelope," he said as he struggled to stand back up.

I firmly grabbed his arm. "Take it easy," I told him, and helped him to sit in a chair. Windsor slumped over, exhausted and I could only guess what had happened to him. How badly was he hurt? I wondered if I should be calling an ambulance or rushing him to the hospital.

Neither of us spoke as I carefully removed his shirt, trying not to hurt him. I knelt down at his side, to examine the bleeding wound and when I did, I knew… he had been stabbed! There was dirt, mixed with blood in his hair and all over his body, then I found three slash wounds, from a knife, across his chest. Obviously someone had had Windsor down on the ground beating and stabbing him. My mind flashed back to the many times that sharp knives had been wielded at me, how familiar it all seemed. It gripped me by the heart and gave me a sick feeling, deep inside. I was alarmed, what would the repercussions be? I was apprehensive and looked up into Windsor's face.

Windsor could see my concern, he smiled sweetly and gently took my hand, "Don't worry, it's not bleeding much anymore. I'm okay now, now that I'm here with you." Even in this situation, Windsor was still as charming as ever. I was glad to see that he was holding it together, and then I asked him what had happened.

Windsor began to explain, "I shot and killed a man and I'm out on bail. It was self-defense, I swear!" he declared adamantly. "The friends and brother of the dead man tried to kill me tonight, seeking their revenge. I managed to fight them off and came running here to you. Please forgive me, but I didn't know where else to go; you're the only person I knew that would understand." Then Windsor broke down a bit, "Please don't make me leave Penelope, I don't have anywhere else to go, they'll be sure to get me! Nobody knows you; they'll never find me here! They couldn't have possibly followed me, they were all lying on the ground when I drove off." Windsor paused for a moment and grinned, "If you think I look bad, you should see the other guys!"

I had a hard time believing my ears. Did Windsor really just tell me that he had killed someone? What was I involved in now? Was it really self-defense, or was he a murderer? Then there's the third option; he could be a nut! In any event he was in my house and I thought it best not to risk agitating him. I had to make a quick judgment call and I decided to believe him.

Windsor was stabbed and bloody, and if what he had told me was true, he had done nothing to deserve it. I knew all about the self-defense scenario; no matter what the situation, somehow it always makes you look bad. I also knew what it felt like to be innocent and bleeding and I couldn't help but have sympathy for him.

I tried to take Windsor to the hospital to get checked out and to get a tetanus shot, but he refused to go. "I'm not hurt that bad," he argued.

I finally gave in and quit pressuring him, "If you won't let me take you to the hospital, I guess I'll have to patch you up myself; get in the shower." I gave Windsor a couple of towels and turned the shower on, "Throw your clothes out in the hall so I can wash them for you, and then call me when you're ready."

Windsor took a long shower and then wrapped a towel around his waist; when he called me, I took him to my dressing room and sat him down on a comfortable chair. Slowly and carefully I ran my fingers over his smooth moist flesh. He winced when I pressed on his ribs, they were bruised and tender, but not broken. His wrist was swollen and purple and he had cuts and gashes scattered over his entire body. It was a big job tending to the wounds, but I gently treated each one while Windsor tenderly watched me with his dreamy blue eyes, his damp hair curling on his brow.

When I had finished, I gave Windsor a pair of old sweatpants to wear. He tried to put them on himself, but he couldn't bend down far enough and was struggling to get into them. I took the pants from him and slipped his feet through the legs, then I carefully and slowly eased them over his wounds, trying not to hurt him. I pulled the pants past his calves and over the knees, but when I got to the middle of his thighs, I felt my face turning red, "You're gonna have to stand up now," I quickly stated, hoping that he hadn't notice me blush. "Wrap your arms around me and I'll pull you to your feet."

Windsor tossed his head to throw the hair from his eyes, then he smiled brightly and reached up for me. He wrapped his arms around my shoulders and stood to his feet and pulled me close. Windsor held me tightly in his arms, "You're wonderful baby," he said as he kissed my neck, breathing hard. "Let me show you how much I appreciate you," he ran his hands down my silk robe and started to pull it up, "you're so beautiful."

A typical man; half dead and still trying to get laid. "Windsor, knock it off or you'll start bleeding again!" I scolded as I pulled up his pants. "Come on let's get you to the sofa."

Windsor was shaky and weak from blood loss and trauma; I slipped under his arm and let him lean on me while we slowly walked into the living room. I gently lowered him onto the sofa and put a pillow behind him, then I went to the kitchen and got him a cool drink.

"Thank you, I don't know what I would have done without you," Windsor said gratefully.

Once I knew that he was comfortable, it was time to go outside and see what I was facing. If Windsor had been followed, things could quickly develop into a deadly situation and I had to be prepared. I changed into dark colored clothing and put my .38 Special in my pocket. Then I went into the living room and flipped my heavy wooden coffee table over on its side. "Windsor, I'm going outside to investigate, if you hear gunshots, get on the floor between the table and the sofa. If trouble breaks out, I want to know exactly where you are, so I don't end up shooting you by mistake."

When Windsor heard what I had said, he tried to jump to his feet, but his wounds slowed him down. "Wait, wait," he cried, "I don't want you going out there!"

"If they're here, I need to know about it."

"Then let me go with you, just give me a hand up," Windsor reached his hand out for me to help pull him to his feet.

"Forget it man, you'll be more of a problem than a help. What are you gonna do if you do see one of the bad guys? Fall on 'em? I'm better off without you, and like you said, they don't know me."

I turned out all of the lights, inside and outside of the house and then, I went out to check the area. I walked up and down the streets and the neighboring properties … no sign of anyone. With all of the lights out at the house, if the enemy was about, I figured that they would make their move, thinking that we were asleep. I hid in the bushes and waited and watched, still no sign of anyone. Windsor was right, no one had followed him; things were safe … at least for now.

When I got back in the house, Windsor was dozing off; he jumped when he heard me come inside. "Go back to sleep, I'll see you in the morning," I said and I threw him a quilt.

That night, I slept with my .38 Special under my pillow not knowing what to expect, I was prepared for anything. "I'll get rid of him tomorrow; I've got enough to deal with without his problems too. That damn Jean! I knew better than to get involved with another man!"

It was a restless night for me, I didn't get much sleep and when I got up the next morning, Windsor was already dressed. "Good morning," he cheerfully greeted me. "I'm glad you're up, I was just looking for a pen to leave you a note. I didn't say anything about it last night, but today is my preliminary hearing. I have to stop at my folk's house to get ready, so I don't have much time."

"Be safe," I responded and reached to hug him good-bye.

Windsor quickly grabbed me and held me close, "I'll see you soon, but I've got to get going now, thanks again," he said, but he didn't let loose of me. "I've got to go now," he repeated, and then he finally released me and started for the door. He was trying hard to be brave, but he was so vulnerable and unsure, his hands were shaking and I could tell that he was in tremendous pain. I didn't know if he could make it on his own and I couldn't believe it when I heard myself ask, "Would it be alright if I went with you?" What the hell was wrong with me???!!!

"I would love it if you came with me," Windsor answered, "but I don't want you involved, it might be dangerous. None of these people know you, and that's the way I want to keep it." Then he opened the door and quickly left.

I stood in the doorway and watched Windsor walk away, his loose curls bounced as he turned his head back and forth, flashing his eyes up and down the street. He strutted to his blue Corvette in his boots and leather jacket, climbed in and dashed off. "Damn he's cute," I bit my lip, "Ouch!"

I waited on pins and needles that day, anxiously hoping to hear from Windsor. Was he dangerous, crazy, or the best thing that had ever happened to me? He didn't call me all day; it was one of the longest days of my life, and that night I still didn't know anything.

The next morning, someone was knocking at my door and I ran to answer it. It was Windsor, with a big bouquet of roses and an even bigger smile. He was holding a large envelope under his arm. "I've been cleared!" he exclaimed.

I was happy to hear the news, but still wondered what had really happened. How good was my judgment? Had I believed a liar? Had I helped a murderer?

Windsor and I sat next to each other on the sofa and he handed me the envelope. "My attorney called in a favor and got it for me right away," he explained.

I quickly opened the envelope and enclosed was the entire court transcript. I read the whole thing through and found that what Windsor had told me was true. The killing was ruled self-defense and all charges had been dropped.

The whole incident was explained in the transcript: A woman who lived in Windsor's neighborhood named, Tracy, was being attacked and severely beaten by her boyfriend. She knew that Windsor was an armed officer, so when she managed to escape, she drove straight to his house for help.

The woman's boyfriend was extremely dangerous; only days earlier he had put Tracy's head through a plate glass window. He was out on bail at the time, but was facing charges for attempted murder.

The boyfriend knew that Tracy had gone to Windsor's house. Already enraged, the fact that she was with another man put him into a murderous state, and he became determined to kill Windsor and steal back his girlfriend.

The boyfriend made his plan to carry out the murder/kidnapping and brought a friend along who was an expert in martial arts, named, Kyle Whittaker. During the violent attack, Windsor was able to save Tracy and defend himself, but in the process, ended up shooting and killing Kyle.

As I read it through, it brought back painful memories of Parker, another man dead because of a woman's bad judgment. Why didn't this woman simply drive to the police station instead of putting Windsor in jeopardy? It was a miracle that he wasn't the one lying on a slab at the morgue. It was a hard story for me to read, but I was happy that Windsor had been telling me the truth.

Windsor said that he had been living with his parent's since the incident, and that there had been several attempts on his life while he had been there. He wasn't sure how much more stress his mother could handle, her doctor had informed the family that she was on the verge of having a heart attack.

Windsor explained to me that he would be returning to work very soon and then he asked in his sweet way, "Would it be alright if I stayed here with you until I get back to work?"

I wasn't prepared for him to ask such a thing, the words hit me like a ton of bricks and I quickly rose to my feet. No way! I wasn't willing to put my life on the line for this guy, I barely knew him. Besides that, I had planned to keep him at arms-length and just be friends. This was much more than that.

Windsor didn't get up, he wrapped his arms around me, buried his face and squeezed me tight. "I haven't slept and I can't eat. The only peace I have is when I'm with you. Please let me stay," he pleaded with me, tears streaming down his face. It was clear that he was at the end of his rope.

Windsor was a sweet person and I enjoyed being with him. He had killed not out of viciousness or hatred, it was because he had helped someone in trouble, and now he was the one who needed help. But I knew that my family wouldn't stand for it, still married to Larry and living in sin with another man. And let's not forget about the neighbors, what would they think? We all know that nothing is more important than what the neighbors think.

How much was my reputation worth? Windsor's life? His mother's life? How would I feel if these wicked men succeeded and Windsor was murdered in his parent's home? What would I think of myself if I heard that his mother had suffered a heart attack and I had done nothing to help prevent it?

Then there was my own situation; it was difficult for me being alone. Because of Larry, I couldn't have a roommate; it wasn't safe or fair to anyone. But Windsor was different and his circumstances were similar to mine. He knew how to handle a gun and was good in an emergency. He had already proven that he could be a loyal friend and had taken it all the way to the death. I began to think that maybe this wasn't such a bad idea after all.

Chainsaw Charlie had helped me when I was in danger, and Windsor was practically thrown at my doorstep. It was within my power to help and I decided to protect him. "Well Windsor," I said, "I'll make you a deal, I watch your back and you watch mine."

Windsor smiled and wrapped his arms around me, he tenderly rubbed his hands up and down my back. "I've always had a thing for beautiful backs," he said, "it'll be a pleasure to watch yours."

Windsor had been laid off from work until the incident could be sorted out. He wasted no time and called his Union Representative to let him know that the charges against him had been dropped. "I followed shooting procedure that they taught me at the academy, to the letter," I heard Windsor say. "Oh, that's great, just a couple of weeks. I can't wait to get back to work; I'll send you the papers right away. Have a great day!"

Windsor was smiling and happy, "Just a few more weeks and I can put this whole mess behind me! We're going out tonight and celebrate!"

Windsor and I had a nice time that night, and the next morning, I went to work. I was busy doing paperwork when Ray called me into his office. After meeting Windsor at the barbecue, Ray had done some inquiring and wanted to give me the information. "I hope that you won't be offended Penelope, but none of us know this guy, Windsor. I did some poking around and found that he was recently involved in a fatal shooting. We have to be careful; we can't have any trouble around here. Everything you do can reflect on the company.

"I know all about it Ray, Windsor told me everything. In fact he was at my house again last night." I had brought the court transcript to work with me and I showed it to him. When Ray read the details of what had happened he understood that it was a righteous shooting, but was concerned that perhaps Windsor was in love with Tracy, the girl that he had killed for. He thought that Windsor might be using me until the heat was off and then he planned to return to her.

"Ray, why don't you call Cliff?" I suggested. "He might know something about this."

Cliff was on our payroll; he worked at the prison, and got information for us regarding prisoners and prison activity when we needed it for a case. Ray immediately got Cliff on the phone.

As it turned out, Cliff was Windsor's immediate superior; he not only worked with Windsor, but was a personal friend as well. Cliff raved about what a great guy Windsor was. He said that Windsor cared about other people and he believed that that was how this woman had gotten him involved with her problems. "Windsor just felt sorry for her, there was never anything romantic between them," Cliff said, "at least not on Windsor's part, I'm sure of it."

Cliff was looking forward to Windsor returning to work. He went on to explain to Ray, that Windsor was completely safe and not to be concerned about me being involved with him. He stated that, "Any woman would be lucky to have Windsor."

This completely eased my mind, Windsor came with references. Despite the fact that he had recently killed someone, he was still a nice guy and I thought that I could trust him.

It was a short day at work, and when I returned home I asked Windsor if he would like to go to the ranch and meet my horses. He was excited to go and we walked hand in hand out to his Corvette only to find, that it had four flat tires. All had been punctured in the side wall with an ice pick and there was no saving them.

It looked like the cowardly work of Larry to me. I realized that he must have been watching my house and saw Windsor come inside. Sneaky and underhanded, too afraid to face another man, Larry would stoop to vandalism as his yellow-bellied way of telling another man to stay away.

I called the Auto Club, only to find out that Larry had cancelled my membership. Duh, what was I thinking? Windsor and I stood by the car assessing the damage, and when people saw our dilemma they stopped and a small crowd gathered.

I noticed a brawny man coming from the condos across the street. He stepped forward and offered to put the tow on his service. He told

Windsor to stay with the car and wait for the tow truck, and then suggested that I come with him, in case the Auto Club needed additional information.

It sounded reasonable to me and I followed him back across the street, down several winding sidewalks, deep into the condominium complex. When we arrived at his home, the man fumbled with the key and stumbled inside. It was then that I suspected that he might be drunk.

He went to the phone and called the Auto Club while he mixed himself a drink. He was told that his membership had lapsed, but he insisted that they renew it and make the tow anyway. The agent on the other end of the line agreed to check with the manager for approval, (so the man told me,) and they were to call us back shortly.

While we were waiting for the return call, the man showed me a picture of himself with an old western, movie star; they were both wearing green berets. He told me that he was a Green Beret and that he had been on many top secret missions. He had museum boxes full of medals and ribbons hanging on the walls of the condo. I saw a framed newspaper article, with a picture of a General presenting the man with a medal. I was impressed; I was in the presence of a real live hero.

As the man was showing me his treasures he began to cry, not just a few whimpers this guy was really crying tears. "My boss died today, he was my best friend for twenty years, that's why I'm drinking. I don't know what I'm going to do. Oh … my buddy… my buddy…how will I make it without you? I don't have a job anymore. I worked for him and now I have no income. What am I going to do?"

"You'll find another job," I tried to console him. I really did feel sorry for the guy; here he was trying to help Windsor and me in the midst of his own misery.

He came close and put his arms around me; I felt uncomfortable, but I didn't want to be cruel, so I patted him on the back. "You'll be okay," I said calmly.

It was a hot summer day, and I had on a pair of little red, silk shorts. The next thing I knew, he had his hand up the back of them. I grabbed his wrist and tried to move away, but he wouldn't let me. "Oh my God, a Green Beret, how will I ever get out of this one?"

I had no backup, Joe wasn't waiting to come bursting through the door to rescue me, I was unarmed and on my own. This man had seen combat, he was a trained killer and could take me out with one move. I tried to be nice, not panic, and talk my way out. There were things in the room that obviously belonged to a woman. "Why don't we call your wife?" I suggested. "She should know about your friend."

"I don't have a wife anymore, she divorced me," then he cried even harder. Well that didn't work, I tried to wiggle away again, but he had a strong hold on me and he wasn't going to let go.

He kept telling me how beautiful I was, and how much he needed me. He asked about Windsor, "What are you doing with that little twit? Why don't you dump him and move in here with me?" All the while he was trying to kiss me and his hands were all over me.

He was pulling me upstairs to his bedroom, when I managed to break away. I made a dash for the door, but he caught me before I could get the deadbolt unlocked and threw me to the floor. The man stood over me blocking the doorway, and when I got up and tried to fight my way out, he knocked me down and brutally kicked me.

After my third attempt to escape, I was sitting on the floor looking up at his overpowering figure and I realized that it was useless, I couldn't force my way past him. But physical power wasn't all that I had in my arsenal; I would use what I did have, my head. I sized up the situation; my only advantage was that this man was drunk and I expected that his reflexes and thinking would be impaired. I quietly sat on the floor and didn't try to get up again.

"Had enough?" he asked as he reached down and took hold of me. He dragged me to the sofa, climbed on top of me and started trying to undress me.

My body remembered the pain of being raped before and I felt rage welling up inside. I wouldn't get raped again! I decided at that minute to do whatever it took to escape and if I couldn't, he was going to rape a dead body.

Strangely enough, at that exact moment, a scene flashed through my mind of an old movie that I had once watched, a woman of the old west in the same predicament that I was in. I decided to try the trick that she had, and I smoothly told him, "Slow down now cowboy, no need to get rough, I didn't know you wanted it that bad, just relax and I'll show you a real a good time."

After I said that, the man did relax a bit and I managed to move him off of me and position myself on top, all the while pretending that I wanted him. It was at that time that he loosened his grip on me, only for a split second, but that was all the time I needed. I took my knee and I slammed that creep in the balls with all my might. He screeched in pain, I pushed him and fought to get up, but before I could break free, he grabbed hold of my leg. I was still in his grasp, but at least I was on my feet.

The battle was on, me, against a skilled assassin. This man had been trained to take out the enemy, and I was now the enemy, I wasn't fool enough to believe anything else.

This was my only chance and I couldn't blow it. He was hurting, but I knew that he would recover quickly and there was no telling what he would do to me when he did, especially now that I had struck him.

There was a heavy ceramic lamp on a small side table near the sofa. I quickly lunged for it and bashed it down on top of him. The lamp broke into pieces, but he still didn't let go of me, and now he was even more angry.

The man was struggling to get up and screaming at me, "You little bitch, you don't know who you're messing with, you're going to pay for this! I know how to handle a cunt like you!"

He didn't have to repeat himself, I believed him. I also knew that I had to keep him down; if he got up, it was all over. I reached for the only thing within my grasp, the side table. I grabbed it by the leg, swung it above my head and slammed it down on him. I hit him so hard that the table leg broke off in my hands. "You're the one who doesn't know who you're messing with, you bastard!"

The man was knocked for a loop and he let go of my leg, but he was tough and still trying to get up and come after me. I knew that he might catch me again before I could get out the door and I had to make sure that he couldn't. He kept threatening me and trying to scare me, so I hit him again with the table leg. The more he threatened, the more I hit him. I pounded him again and again and again and I didn't stop until he quit moving.

At first, I thought that I had killed him, but when I looked closer, he was still conscience. He was lying there looking at me and I was looking at him; there was complete silence as we stared at each other. Then I yelled, "I know how to handle a dick like you!" and I gave him another sharp kick to the groin.

After that, I knew that he would be down long enough for me to make it out, and I ran for the door. It was an old fashioned, complicated lock and my hands were shaking, but I managed to get it open. I looked back at him, he was sitting up by this time and I told him in a calm and sober voice, "If you ever see me again, you better run, because if I see you first, I'm blowing your brains out."

Then I ran, and I just kept on running; my adrenaline was pumping, my heart was pounding fast and I couldn't calm down.

I saw Windsor ahead of me, running toward the street, waving a gun over his head and screaming my name at the top of his lungs. I wanted to cry out, rush into his caring arms and tell him what had happened, but I knew that I couldn't. I straightened myself up a bit and I called to him, trying to act like everything was fine.

"My God," he said, as he ran up to me, "I didn't realize what I had done until you were out of sight. Letting you go with a strange man, he could have done anything to you. Are you okay? What happened? You were gone for forty-five minutes!"

"Oh, has it been that long? I didn't realize," I said casually. "We had to wait for the Auto Club to call us back."

"Wait a minute, why are you out of breath? You're shaking, your legs and arms are red. Is that blood?" Windsor had me by the shoulders, he was screaming and wild eyed. "That guy did something to you! Where does he live? You tell me where he lives! He's a dead man!" Scraped and bruised, his stab wound still tender, Windsor was prepared to kill again to protect me.

"Windsor, I'm okay, really, he was a perfect gentleman," I lied. "I got lost, I was running, trying to hurry back to the car and I tripped on the uneven pavement, but I'm fine."

Windsor didn't believe me, he could tell that something was terribly wrong. It was then that I felt the full weight of the situation grip me. What if the Green Beret was coming after me? If he and Windsor saw each other I knew that one of them wouldn't survive. Was I leaving Windsor at a disadvantage by withholding information? Should he know the real situation that we were facing? If he didn't know, would the Green Beret get the jump on him?

Windsor was in a protective state of mind and very much capable of killing. I was rattled, but I couldn't forget the consequences of a rash emotional or selfish decision. I quickly thought it through, and decided that it was more dangerous to tell Windsor than to withhold information. I had to protect him; he couldn't be involved in another killing. They'd lock him up for sure this time, maybe even execute him. If the Green Beret showed up, I decided that I would throw myself between them and hope for the best.

Even though I felt half-crazy myself, I tried to calm Windsor down and eventually he gave in and believed me. One of my best acting jobs.

I carefully took the gun from Windsor's hand and put it in his pocket. I teased him a little bit and slipped my arm through his and we headed for his car. Now, I'm hoping that the Green Beret wouldn't be there waiting for us. I started shaking as we got closer, my chest was tight. I was looking around every corner wondering if he would be there, waiting in ambush. Finally, I saw that the tow truck had already loaded the car and was ready to leave. The Green Beret wasn't there, we had made it!

That night, Windsor and I watched a movie, but my mind was on other things. I thought about what had happened that day. I was happy that I had kept my head; I hadn't been raped and no one was dead. If I hadn't have played my cards right, it would have been a very different situation that I was facing that night. I put my head on Windsor's chest and breathed a sigh of relief, we were both safe at home.

I thought about my attacker, was he really a Green Beret gone bad, or was he an imposter; using phony newspaper clippings, photographs and dime store medals and ribbons? Was the fact that he presented himself as being a Green Beret, supposed to paralyze me with fear and make the rape an easy task? Then, was I also supposed to be too afraid to report it to the police because of his hero's reputation?

Fact was, I was afraid to go to the police, but not for that reason. It was my word against his, and he was the one who had taken the beating. I thought that I would be the one to go to jail for battery if I brought attention to myself, or if I admitted that there had been a problem between us.

I couldn't go to Ray; I didn't want to take the risk of jeopardizing my job. I could soon become a liability and a risk to the company's stellar reputation if word got out that one of their operatives had been involved in any violence or a scandal.

I didn't worry too much about the Green Beret; I figured that having his ass kicked by a girl had been enough, and assumed that he wouldn't be back for more. I simply threw him on top of my pile of troubles, along with Larry, and Windsor's enemies as well.

Our world was a dangerous place, and Windsor and I needed each other to survive in it. I felt lucky to have a man who would protect me, and not one that I needed to be protected from. Windsor gave me a sweet kiss on the top of my head, he gently held me and softly stroked my hair, while we watched the movie together. I felt safe with him, a feeling that I hadn't felt in a long time.

I enjoyed the way that Windsor touched me, he was gentle and caring. But then, I thought about what a disappointment sex had been for me. All those years looking forward to it and waiting until marriage, only to be abused by my own husband. Then Kurt raping me, and now another man trying it today. It was sad to say, but the only gratifying sex that I had ever had was when I was brutalizing the Rakker's! Had I become too bitter and hateful to even have a normal sexual relationship with a man? Truth was, I didn't even want to try, yet here I was with an attractive sexy man. What was I doing? Would I need to tie him up and torture him to enjoy myself? I knew that the subject of sex would come up and probably quite soon. I didn't want to be hurt anymore, but I didn't want to be alone either. After the horror of my marriage to Larry, I knew that I was in dangerous territory. I had to be careful, I couldn't make another mistake. But enough for now, I tried to relax and enjoy the peace of the evening. I would put off worry until another time.

Later that night, when the movie ended, I went to get blankets for Windsor to sleep on the sofa and he followed me into the bedroom. I wasn't surprised, but didn't want any part of having sex with him.

He sensed it right away and said, "Don't worry Penelope, I won't pressure you, you get a good night sleep." He kissed me on the forehead, then he dropped his arms, took a step back and turned to go down the hall. When he reached the doorway to the living room he looked back and smiled at me, gave me a cute little, salute-type wave and said, "See ya in the morning."

I went to bed alone that night, disappointed and relieved at the same time. I was exhausted; what a stressful day it had been.

The next morning, Windsor wasn't pouting like I expected he'd be, he was as sweet as ever. He was happy just to be there and I was happy to have him.

After breakfast, we climbed into my truck and went to the ranch to see my horses. I saddled up Lucky Loop and Carol Lee, and Windsor and I took a nice little ride on the local trails. We spent the afternoon at the ranch and by the time we were ready to leave I felt wonderful, just like I always did after a day with my magical horses.

Windsor had a nice time too; he had been raised in the city and had never been close to a horse before. I enjoyed watching him, he was fascinated by the horses and I think that they were fascinated by him.

When we got home that night, we had a nice dinner and another comfortable evening cuddling and watching movies.

Weeks went by, with Windsor patiently sleeping on the sofa. He never complained or brought up the subject of sex again. Then one night, I was in my bed nearly asleep when I heard him walking into my bedroom. He climbed into bed with me and pulled me close. He was on one elbow resting his head in his hand and looking into my eyes, "What happened to you baby? Why are you so afraid of me?"

"It's not you Windsor, it's just that I can't afford to make another mistake."

"You're so tense, you just need to relax," he said, "let me give you a massage."

He sat up and grabbed some lotion from my vanity, then gently and thoroughly he rubbed my tense shoulders. I was surprised, it was actually working and I was beginning to relax.

Slowly and methodically Windsor massaged every inch of my body with his strong caring hands. No one had ever done anything like this for me before. When he finished the massage, I was waiting to see what was next. He had a fur glove and he slid it up and down my body, it tickled my skin and heightened my senses.

Finally, Windsor took me in his arms and asked if he could make love to me. I didn't say a word, but tried to co-operate, hoping for the best. I wanted Windsor, there was no question about it, but when the moment came, I tightly closed my eyes and turned my head to the side. Sex, it was something that had to be done and I decided to get it over with.

Then I heard him sweetly say, "Open your eyes and look at me Penelope, I want you to know who's making love to you."

I reluctantly opened my eyes, Windsor was looking at me and smiling a soft caring smile as he gently stroked my hair. This man wasn't going to hurt me, he was going to love me. I could see the love in his eyes and feel it in his body, it was as though the energy went from him all the way through me. I felt warm and safe, he loved me and I knew it, and it was wonderful.

I had never had a man make love to me before. Finally, I found out what I had been missing, and I couldn't get enough. I don't know how long we went on, it must have been hours before we both collapsed in exhaustion, laughing and glowing with pleasure. I wasn't a twisted person after all, I didn't have to hurt Windsor to enjoy myself and he didn't hurt me. I was finally freed of my fears.

Windsor was something that I had always longed for, but never had. He filled a void in my lonely battered life and from that point on things changed; I had a man who loved me and I loved him and we were inseparable.

Windsor and I never wanted to go out anywhere or be around other people. We just wanted to be at home, alone together. We had found each other in this crazy dangerous world and we were going to enjoy every minute of it.

Windsor's motto was: "Keep your woman satisfied, and you'll be happy. Never get in a hurry, and make it special every time." He believed in quality, not quantity, but even so, we spent most of our time together in the bedroom. We still had the problems of the cruel outside world, but we had a safe warm haven in each other.

Windsor and I knew that we had to be together for the rest of our lives, and we wanted to be married as soon as possible, so I made a daring move and filed for divorce from Larry. Larry wasn't going to make it easy, and tried everything he could to drag it on.

Windsor and I loved being together, so while he was waiting to be reinstated at his job, he went with me on my investigative assignments, whenever it was allowed. With his training and background he was a great asset; Windsor knew how to write reports, collect evidence and was very observant. He had a good eye for detail and a great sense of direction. Unfortunately, I wasn't getting paid extra because I was bringing my boyfriend to work with me, but it was nice having him around and working helped to keep him in practice.

Windsor had just bought his new Corvette, right before the killing. He had a high car payment and had to carry full coverage insurance. He was behind on his child support and all of his credit cards and other financial obligations, but it wasn't a problem, I was making plenty of money and we were having a good time.

Months flew by, and Windsor didn't get called back to work as he had expected he would. After investigating, we found what the problem was; the warden had been embarrassed by the front page newspaper headlines describing the shooting - "Prison Guard Kills in Love Triangle." The warden refused to reinstate Windsor and there was nothing that the Union or anyone else could do about it. Windsor got screwed, his career was ruined, health benefits, pension, security, all gone.

Up until that time, he had managed to maintain a good attitude. Living with me away from the stress of his enemies had given him the break that he needed. Windsor had been looking forward to getting back to work and reclaiming his life, but hearing that he had lost his livelihood was the straw that broke the camel's back. He had a lot invested in his job and this news was more than he could handle. It was at this time that he made a bad decision and started drinking his troubles away.

Adding to his stress, Windsor suffered from night terrors. One night, shortly after losing his job, he was screaming and crying in his sleep. I woke him up and he described to me what he had seen the night that he shot Kyle. "I didn't want to shoot him, I really didn't," he cried, "but he wouldn't show me his hands. I asked him twice and then he made a move for me and I shot him in the face. It was like slow motion, I watched the bullet go in on the left side of his nose, the hole got bigger and bigger and his head blew off in pieces. They found his nose on the mailbox by the street and his brains and parts of his skull clear in the neighbor's yard. Kyle kept coming at me with no head, blood gushing from the hole in his neck. I backed up and he fell on me. He was holding throwing stars and a knife in his hands, they fell with a clank to the ground and the sound echoed in my head."

"I'm afraid to go to sleep; I feel like I'm dying every time I start to drift off, it's like I'm falling into a bottomless pit. When I finally do fall asleep, I see Kyle, he has no head and he's coming after me again. This time, the blood doesn't run from his neck, it drips from my hands. Then I hear his voice from across the yard, 'You shouldn't have killed me, I was only being a good friend.' It's true Penelope, he was only there to back up his friend, I shouldn't have killed him, I should have killed the boyfriend! Kyle had a candy bar in his back pocket and that's what bothers me the most, it makes him so real, so human. Oh, will this agony ever end?!"

I couldn't help Windsor myself, and I didn't think that he could get over this on his own. The next morning, I did the only thing that I could think of and made him an appointment for him with a therapist, and pressured him to go.

Windsor only saw the therapist one time; he explained to me that things were far too difficult for him to discuss. He decided that drinking was a better option; if he drank at least he could sleep. I guessed that he was medicating himself.

I was disappointed that Windsor hadn't followed through with therapy, but realized that it was understandable. A sensitive person like him could be expected to be traumatized by all that he had been through. I would try to be supportive and patient. Where was he to go from here? He had to figure it all out. I believed that he just needed the time to heal and recover.

Since he didn't sleep much at night, I told Windsor to get plenty of rest during the day, "Lay by the pool and relax." Sooner or later, I expected him to get over it.

Even though Windsor wasn't working, it wasn't as though he brought nothing to the party. Because he was always home, he was excellent security and I had no more worries about what Larry might do, while I was out.

I decided to make good of my killer boyfriend's reputation and told everyone who knew Larry all about him. I was hoping that the news would get back to Larry, and eventually it did. Larry was a wimp and I knew that as long as Windsor was there with me, he wouldn't risk getting caught in my neighborhood, especially since he was the one who had punctured Windsor's tires.

Having Windsor at the house was a comfort; I no longer had to set traps and look behind every bush. He had defused the situation just by being there and had made my life safer and more comfortable. Our arrangement wasn't a bad one and if I had to pay for it, it was alright with me.

And I did pay for it … and pay for it … and pay for it. Years passed, and Windsor never looked for work or made any effort to seek help for his problem. I didn't want to be cruel and uncaring, but I was growing impatient. If he had at least been trying I would have had hope to hold on to, but it became obvious that things were never going to change. I had to face the fact that this was the way that my life with Windsor was going to be, putting up with an unemployed drunk.

This was not the way that I wanted to spend the rest of my life and I wasn't sure how much longer I could stand it. But there was one thing that kept me hanging on, one thing that Windsor never let his drinking or anything else interfere with … he was still "prime beef" and always up for a good time. Windsor was the only good sexual experience that I had ever had, and I wasn't sure if it would be possible to ever replace him. I decided to stick it out and hoped that it was worth it.

PAT AND PENELOPE KICK ASS

My sister, Pat, and I, hadn't seen each other in months. I was working long hours and no matter how we tried, we could never get a day off at the same time. Finally, we were able to schedule a day, the next week that we could spend together. We decided to spend our special day at Pat's and bake cookies, cupcakes and apple pies, just the two of us. Our plans absolutely did not include the drunken Windsor.

The day before Pat and I, were to have our bake-a-thon, Windsor got a call from his father. He explained that Windsor's uncle from out of state had stopped in for a surprise visit. His father believed that it would be safe for Windsor to come to the family gathering the next day, as long as he didn't bring his car. His father planned to pick Windsor up and disguise him with a big floppy hat and sneak him into the house. Then, he would drive him back home when the party was over.

I thought that it was perfect, Windsor would be occupied and wouldn't be pestering me while I was at Pat's and I wouldn't have to worry about him driving home drunk.

Windsor wasn't happy about the whole arrangement, he insisted that I cancel my plans with Pat and go with him. I thought that his request was reasonable, but I wasn't budging. I'm not psychic, but in this case I was able to see the future very clearly and I knew exactly what the day would be like. I would uncomfortably make conversation with Windsor's relatives, while they sized me up and watched him get sloppy drunk. They would then decide that I must be driving him to drink. And finally, when Windsor was about ready to pass out, (but hopefully could still walk,) I would shuffle him out to the car, make excuses and drive him home. No thank you; not interested. I wasn't about to change plans with my sister for a day like that.

The next morning, I was expecting Windsor's father to arrive, when he let me know that he had decided to drive himself. He wanted to show the Corvette to his uncle.

"Windsor, that's not a good idea, you let your father come for you. You know that your enemies are still threatening you and that they're probably watching your parent's house. If they see your car parked there, they're bound to catch you."

"No, I'm driving my Corvette; I promised my uncle that I'd give him a ride."

"Windsor, I'm warning you, you're asking for trouble, but I'm sure that you'll do what you want to, no matter what I say. At least promise me that you won't drive home drunk; you stay the night at your parent's house."

"I would never get so drunk that I couldn't drive, don't be ridiculous."

"You know that you're going to be drinking; it's a party. Please promise me that you'll stay the night there."

"Hey wait a minute, why are you so eager to get rid of me? Are you planning to meet some guy or something?"

"Yeah sure, I'm planning to meet some guy, cut the crap and just tell me that you won't drive home after the party."

"Okay, I won't," he promised.

I didn't think that I could trust him not to drive drunk, but I at least had the hope that his parent's and the rest of his family were responsible enough to stop him.

I got in my truck and went to Pat's, trying not to worry. When I arrived, there was a dirty old pickup parked in her driveway with a rifle in a gun rack in the rear window. I got out of my truck and went inside. "Hi Pat," I greeted her, "what's with the old truck?"

"Oh, it belongs to Lance. He's away on a business trip and he asked me if I would open and close the yard for him today (Lance's family owned and operated a junkyard and quarry). It's so dusty and dirty out there and you know Lance, he doesn't want me to get my Cadillac dirty, so he insisted that I drive the old work truck."

"Why are you opening and closing the yard, what happened to Jim?"

"He hurt his hand, just a few stitches, nothing serious, but Lance insisted on giving him the day off."

"That's good," I replied, "I'm glad he's okay, I like Jim, he's a good man."

"I can't believe that this happened today, of all days," Pat said disgustedly. "The one time that we can finally get together, and Lance has to be out of town when there's an emergency. I have to be at the yard before the men knock off work. Why don't you take a ride out there with me, then we can spend a little more time together."

"Sure, I'd like that," I answered. "I hear that Lance got a new bulldozer, I'd love to get a look at it."

"I have to leave here about three," Pat informed me, "I need to pick up the mail and messages and it takes a little time to do the bookwork and lock up. We better get baking if we're going to be finished in time."

Pat and I put on our frilly pink aprons and started pealing apples for the pies.

A short time later, the phone rang, Pat answered it and called me, "Sissy, it's for you."

"Hello," I said; it was Windsor. "Yes I'm really here. Are you at your parent's house? Okay, great, have a nice time. Good-bye," I hung up the phone.

"Hopefully that will be the end of it, now that he knows that I'm really here with you. Windsor's got some crazy idea that I'm having a wild fling with a mystery man today while he's gone."

"Oh, Windsor's gone today?"

"Yes, he's at his parent's house for a family thing. He'll get drunk and probably drive home. Hooray, hooray."

"Well don't let it bother you, let's just forget about him, we're going to have a nice time today, remember?"

Unfortunately, we couldn't just forget about him, that stupid Windsor called every fifteen minutes.

"I'm sorry about Windsor, Pat, but I have to keep answering the phone or he'll come charging over here."

"Don't worry about it," Pat said, "all us gals have been through it at one time or another."

Windsor kept right on calling, and each phone call was worse than the last. He was getting drunker and drunker as the day went on, slurring his words and telling me how much he loved me and how he couldn't handle it if I cheated on him; it was pathetic. I felt sorry for Pat, Windsor was ruining the whole day.

We finished our baking at ten minutes to three, putting up with Windsor's annoying phone calls the whole time.

Lance called; somehow he had managed to get through on the line. Pat gave him his messages and told him that we were getting ready to leave for the yard. He said that he had some men coming out to pick up the backhoe that night for a job. "I hate to ask you girls to wait out there for them, but I'm in a spot; I've got to get that job started right away. You know how it is when you leave town, everything falls apart. I know it's banged up, but that's a good rifle on the truck, you girls keep it with you so I won't worry, it's pretty secluded out there."

"We'll be fine Lance," Pat said. "Don't worry, besides we like it at the yard."

Just as we were getting ready to walk out the door, Windsor called one more time. I told him that he wouldn't be able to reach me for a while because we were going out to Lance's yard.

"Oh, so now it's time for your date! I don't believe that you're going out to Lance's junkyard, not for a minute! What are you girls planning to do out there? Dig in the quarry? No way, I'm not buying it!"

"Believe what you want," I said and hung up on him.

Pat and I got in Lance's old truck and started on our way to the yard. We pulled in the gate, and slowly drove down the bumpy dusty, dirt road. Pat parked in the passing lane up against the cliff.

"Why'd we park so far from the shack?" I asked her.

"We have to, the men coming off the job need the space, there's too much equipment parked up by the shack right now."

We got out of the truck, and I looked around the property; high at the top of the cliff above us was the biggest bulldozer that I had ever seen. "What in the world is that?" I asked.

"That's the new earthmover. Isn't it a beauty?"

"Wow! It's as big as an apartment building!"

We walked on down the road to the shack. We hadn't been there long, when the workers came in from the job and punched out; it was quitting time. Pat and I were friends with the men who worked for Lance. They were a group of great guys and I hadn't seen them for a while. We happily greeted one another with hugs and kisses and Pat broke out a bottle of Lance's whiskey. We all smoked cigars and chatted for a while before they went on home. Pat and I stayed behind and waited for the men to come and pick up the backhoe.

"Did Lance say how long we'll have to wait for these guys?" I asked.

"I have no idea," she answered, "could be five minutes, could be five hours. How'd you like to check out the earthmover while we're waiting?"

"Great idea, I was thinking the same thing, let's get going!"

Pat and I rushed up the steep incline and approached the gigantic machine, then we walked around it looking it over. It was impressive.

"Lance says that it weighs over forty tons," Pat explained. "It runs on this track thing here, like a tank."

"Yeah look at it, it is like a tank … let's get in."

We climbed up into the cage and sat in the driver's seat together.

"You wanna hear how the engine sounds?" Pat asked.

"Really think you can start it?"

"Now let me see if I can remember how … umm … I saw Lance do it. He said that you have to prime it and throw some switches, and umm … I think you do this, and then you…." VROOM! The big engine started up. The motor roared and the earth trembled beneath the monstrous machine.

"Pat, you did it! This is so cool! I know we shouldn't, but let's try to drive the bloomin' thing!"

We pushed and pulled at the different levers and devices, trying to figure out how it worked, and slowly Pat began to maneuver the mammoth bulldozer. We were on the move, laughing and yelling, pushing the gravel and dirt around the yard and having a great time. It was turning out to be a fun day after all!

"Pat, you've been driving long enough, it's my turn now," I complained.

"No it isn't, it hasn't been that long yet, it's still my turn. Keep an eye out for the men coming to pick up the backhoe, we don't want to miss them."

Being on top of the cliff and up so high in the earthmover, I could see way down the road. I glanced toward the intersection, before the turn-off to the yard, and saw a blue Corvette swerving recklessly around the corner. "Pat, isn't that Windsor down there on the road?"

"It sure looks like him," she answered. When the Corvette got closer, Pat screamed, "It is Windsor and that Camaro is chasing him!"

"The guys that are trying to kill him drive a Camaro! They must have followed him from his parent's house! He's headed here! What should we do?!"

"Where's the rifle?!" Pat shouted.

"Oh no, we left it in the truck!"

Windsor came screeching around the turn and through the gate of the yard. He made it as far as the turnaround, but the Corvette was too low to the ground to handle the rough road and it bottomed out. Windsor was spinning the wheels, digging himself deeper and deeper in the dry powdery earth. When he realized that he couldn't get free, he jumped out of the car and started clumsily running down the road toward the shack.

"Pat, we've got to do something, they're going to kill him! Let's try to drive this thing down the cliff, we can block the road, then I'll get the rifle and run them off. I think we can make it!"

"Let's go!" Pat said and she maneuvered the giant earthmover to the edge of the cliff. "Hold on!" she shouted. "Here we go!"

We both took a deep breath and … over the cliff we went. We tilted downward and the earthmover was beginning to tip over! We both screamed and braced ourselves for the perilous fall. "It's okay Pat, we're in the cage we'll be alright. Try to head for that ledge near the truck, it'll break our fall. But just keep on going!"

We charged ahead in the earthmover, thrashing back and forth wildly as it slid down the cliff.

Meanwhile, the Camaro started the turn into the yard, it wasn't as lucky as the Corvette had been and it was stopped as soon as it hit the gully at the front gate, where the big trucks dig in to pull out onto the road. There were three men in the car, they all got out with baseball bats in their hands, prepared to carry out their revenge and kill Windsor.

"I've got to get the rifle before they see it!" I screamed.

Sliding down the cliff, that earthmover was going lick-e-ty-split. We had nearly reached the ledge, when one of the men spotted the rifle and started to run for it.

"We've got to make it Pat! Go! Go! Go!"

The man reached the truck and started to open the door. These men had murder on their minds and I didn't know what were they capable of. Would they shoot us if they got their hands on the rifle before us?

KABAM! The earthmover crash-landed on the ledge. "Don't worry Sissy, hold on!" Pat shouted as she made a desperate move. She sharply turned the massive machine and we plunged from the ledge, straight down and hit the ground with a tremendous, BOOM!

The earth shook beneath the forty ton load, dust billowed as if there had been an explosion; we had landed squarely on top of the truck. Pat raced the gigantic engine, VROOM! VROOM!! The beast was raging in uncontrollable fury as it smashed and crashed over the top of the demolished truck. The truck buckled and crunched beneath the tremendous weight as we emerged roaring, from the dense cloud of dust.

The bad guys didn't manage to get the rifle; as a matter of fact they all dropped their bats and ran for their car, screaming in terror.

The truck was crushed and we were headed for the Camaro; they knew that it was the next target of the unstoppable force.

The bad guys hurried, trying to save their car and make their escape, but Pat and I were gaining fast, the enormous angry monster would soon be upon them. The evil men were in a panic, frantically trying to get their car out of the gully and Pat and I just kept right on going, straight down the road, right for them.

"Stop! Stop!" they screamed.

"You wanted trouble, now you got it!" I yelled back at them.

We hit the front end of the Camaro and started to crush it down.

"Sissy, one of the guys is still in there, his shirt's caught!" Pat exclaimed.

"He'll get out, don't worry about it. We can't stop now that they're on the run, and don't forget what they came here for! Murder!"

Just as we started to smash in the roof of the car, the frantic man managed to break free and run away. "I told ya Pat, vermin have a way of wiggling free."

All three of the men were running down the road hysterical, crying and screaming in a panic. "Come see us again sometime!" Pat yelled loudly as we laughed in both amusement and relief. "Guess things didn't turn out the way that those boys had planned."

The bad guys ran fast and were soon out of sight.

Still sitting atop the crushed Camaro, Pat and I stayed in the earthmover for a minute to catch our breath. "Whoa, that was a wild ride!" Pat exclaimed.

"You're not kidding," I agreed, then looked up at the cliff towering above us. "I can't believe that we actually made it down that thing, look how steep it is!" Then, I glanced back at the crushed truck, "What do you think Lance will say about his truck?"

"Oh he doesn't care about that old thing, but we better hurry and do something about this car."

"Why don't we push it into the pit at the back of the quarry," I suggested.

"That's a perfect idea, that pit's been mined out for years and it's so far out of the way, nobody ever goes back there anymore. Forget about Windsor, we'll look for him later, we better get this taken care of right away."

Pat shifted the earthmover into reverse and we began to backup off of the Camaro. It squealed and screeched as metal grated against metal. "Hurry Pat, I can't stand that sound! It's like fingernails against a chalkboard!"

"I know, ahhhhh!"

When we were clear, we drove the earthmover back up on the ridge where we had found it. It was too big to maneuver around the yard. We quickly got into one of the smaller dozers with a blade attachment and headed back for the Camaro. I threw the bats inside of it and we began to push the car down the long bumpy road toward the quarry pit.

Pushing the car down the battered crude road didn't turn out to be an easy task. It raised so much powdery dust, that Pat and I were having difficulty breathing and our eyes watered so badly that we couldn't see very well. Coughing and wiping the dust from our faces, the car got caught in a big pothole.

After a difficult struggle, we were free from the pothole, but then the car was soon hung up again, wedged under an enormous tree root. We positioned the blade underneath the car to pry it loose, but when it broke free it flipped over and landed, stuck between two boulders … what a predicament!

"Why can't anything ever be easy?! That blasted Windsor, look at all the trouble he caused!" Pat shouted in frustration.

It was a difficult struggle, but we continued to persevere. When we got close to the pit we carefully maneuvered the car between two huge boulders and pushed it over the edge. The car flipped and tumbled as it fell and then crashed with a bang at the bottom of the deep quarry pit.

"Well, that's one," I said, patting my sister on the back, "now let's go get the truck, we don't need anybody asking questions about what happened here."

Pat agreed, and the two of us drove the dozer back down the road to get the truck. The truck was bigger than the car and more difficult to maneuver, but we managed to avoid the previous obstacles and made it to the pit without incident. We pushed the truck over the edge and it tumbled down and landed with a crash, right next to the Camaro.

Pat and I climbed down from the bulldozer, and stood at the edge of the pit, looking down at the bent twisted vehicles lying at the bottom. "That was a big job," I said, "I think we deserve a break."

I pulled two cigars from my pocket. Pat and I lit the fat cigars and sat on the edge of the quarry pit with our legs dangling over the side. "Sure is a long way down, I don't remember this pit being so deep," Pat said as she took a puff.

"Yeah, it's deep alright," I agreed blowing smoke from my mouth.

Pat threw her head back with the cigar clenched between her teeth, "These are pretty good cigars, Mack give 'em to ya?"

"Yeah," I answered, "they're good alright."

"A little too good, I wonder if Lance is paying these guys too much."

"Oh, come on Pat, Lance is probably the one who bought the cigars for Mack."

"Yeah, he's is a great guy."

Pat and I talked and joked as we relaxed and enjoyed the expensive cigars, flicking our ashes over the edge of the deep precipice. When we were about done with our smokes, we both stood up, "Ya know Sissy, that Camaro's got a gas leak, could prove to be dangerous."

"I know," I said, and with that … the two of us flicked the cigars from our fingers; they soared through the air and plunged down into the deep pit.

Pat and I threw our arms on each other's shoulders, as we turned and walked away. We heard the explosion, the sky lit up and we felt the rush of heat at our backs.

"Wonder if the men are here for the backhoe yet?" I asked.

"Yeah," Pat answered, "it's about time they showed up."

We climbed on the bulldozer and headed back for the shack. Just as we arrived, the construction workers were pulling up for the backhoe. "Is there a fire around here?" they asked.

"A controlled burn," Pat told them and then said sternly, "don't worry about it."

The men loaded the backhoe and after they pulled out the gate, we locked down the yard.

"We might as well start looking for Windsor now," Pat said. "Let's take the Jeep and drive out into the woods, that's probably where he headed. There's no telling how far he could have run by now. He probably thinks that they're still after him."

We climbed in the Jeep and started down the road, "Windsor, Windsor," we called as we crept along.

"Does Lance own all of this land?" I asked.

"His dad does, but he never comes out here, nobody does."

"Sure a lot of dead trees. You think that Lance would mind if I cut some firewood?"

"Hey, that's a good idea, I could use some firewood myself. Lance should be getting home soon, so we better come back out first thing in the morning."

"I was just going to write reports tomorrow, nothing that I can't put off," I said. "We should get started about five, don't want to burn daylight."

"Five it is," Pat agreed and we continued to look for Windsor.

"Windsor, Windsor, it's okay to come out," we called to him.

"We're not ever going to find him," Pat said.

"Yeah, you're right," I agreed. "I'm sure he'll show up sooner or later, let's turn back."

When we returned to the yard, we got the Corvette out of the rut. It was the only vehicle that we could take. We pulled out of the yard, locked the gate and raced down the country road in the sleek fast car.

"I don't think that those city boys will give Windsor any more trouble," Pat said chuckling.

"Yeah, they were running scared alright, probably didn't stop until they run all the way home."

"All sixty miles of it."

Later, we arrived at Pat's and divvied up the goodies that we had baked earlier that day. Then enjoyed a piece of delicious apple pie.

"I don't envy you sister," Pat said, "you have enough problems to cope with without Windsor too. You've got to get rid of him, he's a freeloader and nothing, but trouble. Look what happened today, the whole thing was his fault, if he had listened to you instead of disrespecting you the way he did, it would have never happened.

"I know, I'll do it first chance I get. I'll break up with him and kick him out." Pat was right; I was tired of fighting the uphill battle with Windsor.

Having trouble come your way, and asking for it are two different things, and that's exactly what Windsor had done, blatantly asked for trouble. He had placed Pat and me in a position where we were forced to defend him or stand by and allow him be killed. He had endangered all of our lives, and who knew what stupid thing he might do next? I didn't want to put up with his nonsense any longer; I had had enough.

When Pat and I finished our pie, I drove the Corvette home. Pat was to pick me up in the morning in my truck.

When I arrived home, I opened the front door and walked inside and I couldn't believe what I saw … Windsor sleeping on the sofa. He jumped up when he heard me come in. "So, you were at the junkyard today huh?" he said with a snooty attitude. "For your information, I went out there to check and, guess what? Surprise, surprise, you weren't there! Just as I suspected, you've been lying to me. Where were you really? Who is this guy you're seeing? I'll kill him!"

Pat and I had been through so much that day because of Windsor and his nonsense, and I couldn't believe that it wasn't over yet; now I had to deal with mister smarty pants. I was too angry to talk, and I walked past him toward the bedroom. I was tired and didn't want to go through the drama of breaking up with him that night. I decided that I would wait for a better time.

"Oh, so you can't even answer me huh?" he said indignantly as he followed behind me. "Having trouble coming up with a good story? While you were out having fun, I had a horrible day; by the way, somebody stole my car from Lance's yard! What do you have to say about that?!"

I paused and turned, and I gave Windsor a look that expressed the deep anger that I was feeling toward him at that moment, "Nothing," I answered, "I have nothing to say to you. I'm tired and I'm going to bed and I suggest that you do the same thing before you dig your grave any deeper." The tone of my voice scared even me and I hoped that Windsor had enough sense not to take it any further; I was afraid of what I might do.

Fortunately, Windsor did have enough brains left in that drunken head of his. He backed off and didn't say another word. I took my shower and went to bed, I was going to sleep. I planned to get up early and cut firewood the next day.

The next morning, I got up early prepared for a day of hard work. Pat was waiting for me out front in my truck, at five a.m. sharp. We went to my tool shed and pulled out two chainsaws, a sledgehammer, wedge and a long-handled axe. We threw them in the truck and headed back to Lance's yard.

"Have you heard tell of Windsor yet?" Pat asked.

"Sure did, he was home on the sofa when I walked in the door last night. He thinks his car was stolen."

"Oh no, that's so funny. Can you believe that after everything that happened yesterday he doesn't have a clue?"

"I know, it's unbelievable isn't it? And you know what else? He says that he knows that I was lying to him, because he went to the yard and I wasn't there."

"That would stand to reason," Pat commented, "he didn't see my Caddy or your truck, he could think that we weren't there. But Sissy, how in the world did he think to look for us, he was running scared with three men after him trying to kill him?"

"Amazing isn't it, even while fleeing for his life he still had to check up on me."

Pat and I arrived at the yard and greeted Jim, the foreman. We asked about his injured hand and he assured us that he was fine. Pat told him not to work too hard, and let him know that we would be in the woods cutting firewood. "Don't wait for us," she instructed, "we'll probably be out there until dark."

We hooked a trailer to the junkyard Jeep and headed for the far back gate of the quarry. The yard was surrounded by a tall chain-link fence, topped with razor wire. Pat pushed open the heavy gate and I drove the Jeep and trailer through. She closed the gate and climbed back in the open battered Jeep and we continued down the primitive road looking for dead trees.

We weren't too far out when I spotted a dead tree on the side of the road and decided to cut it down. "This tree's dangerous Pat, it's close to the road and ready to fall, I'll start here. Why don't you hike out a ways and see what you can find. I'll catch up to you with the trailer when I'm done here; shouldn't take long."

"Sounds like a good idea," Pat agreed, "this scrawny little tree's not enough work to tie up the both of us." She grabbed a chainsaw and started heading north over the ridge and down the ravine toward the river.

I put on my safety glasses and gloves and started the chainsaw. I easily cut through the tree; it fell and I started cutting it into sections. The powerful saw was ripping loudly through the wood, RREERRR, RREERRR, I couldn't hear anything else.

Suddenly, I felt Pat tap me on the shoulder and I shut off the saw so I could hear what she had to say. "Why'd you come back? I was going to pick you up." I lifted my safety glasses and turned around, but it wasn't Pat that I was looking at, it was Larry and in his hand… my long-handled axe.

I felt a charge of shock go through my whole body, but I tried to keep my cool. "What are you doing out here Larry?" I asked.

"It was just my good fortune," he answered. "I came out to Lance's junkyard to pick up a part for my car and just happened to see your truck. The foreman told me that you were out here in the woods. I followed the sound of the chainsaw and well… here I am!"

He was strangely chipper, but I didn't trust him; he was completely unpredictable. And why was he holding my axe? Whatever the reason, it couldn't be good. I was alone with Larry in a secluded place and Pat hadn't planned to come back. I had to be careful how I handled it. "What do you want?" I asked in a pleasant, but firm tone.

"It's not what I want, it's what you want."

"What do you mean by that, I don't want anything?" What in the world was this crazy screwball talking about? I wished that I hadn't turned off my saw.

"I know that you didn't renew the restraining order against me," he cheerfully explained. "That can only mean one thing, that you want me. I know honey, don't be shy, I know you want me back!" He was smiling from ear to ear and his eyes were twinkling with delight.

I had been told that a woman isn't supposed to give this kind of a madman any hope, but I didn't think that not renewing a restraining order against him would be seen as a sign that I wanted him back. It was shocking, especially since it had been years since our separation and the divorce had been final for at least six months. "Oh, why didn't I renew?" I agonized.

Larry went on, "I've been waiting for the right opportunity to talk to you about us getting back together, and fate decided that today was the lucky day. I can't wait for you to see the house; you're going to love what I've done with it. I had the whole thing painted inside and out; I bought new furniture and draperies and had every room carpeted in your favorite color, purple! Dark deep purple! It's beautiful, you'll love it; I wanted everything to be perfect for you when you came home."

"Sounds lovely," I said reluctantly.

"Yes, and you can take all of the credit for it too, after all, you're the one who worked in interior design, not me. All I did is go by what I thought you would do, and I know how you love purple. It's the color of royalty you know, and that's what you are to me, my 'Royal Highness.'"

"You don't know how excited I was when I found out that you hadn't renewed that restraining order. I waited and counted the days and when the last day passed and I found out that it had expired I was thrilled!"

I interrupted, "Larry, Pat's out here with me, wouldn't you like to see her? Pat!!" I screamed at the top of my lungs. I hoped that she wasn't too far out yet and could still hear me.

"Don't try to get funny with me, the foreman didn't say anything about Pat being out here with you. I know that we're alone Penelope, it's just the two of us and there's nothing that you can do about it. You don't have a restraining order anymore and it's perfectly legal and natural for me to want to see my wife."

"You don't have to be afraid of me honey; why, I'm completely harmless." Larry said it in a quiet soothing tone, but then he abruptly changed and sharply shouted, "But this axe certainly isn't harmless!!" Larry's eyes shifted from side to side as though he had gone completely insane and he ran his finger along the blade of the axe head, "It's very sharp, a person should be careful with something this dangerous." He swung the axe above his head as though he was going to strike me with it.

"That's one thing about you honey," he let the axe handle slide down through his hands, "you always maintain your tools so well." He held the axe close to his face and caressed it, "Look at this axe head, not a speck of rust on it. How often do you have to sharpen it to keep such a…NICE … SHARP…EDGE?!!"

I had triggered him that easily. All bets were off, Larry was flipping out and he had an axe in his hands. I realized that the day that I had been dreading for so long had arrived, today was…"The Showdown."

Larry started to swing the axe back and forth and in circles. He swung it toward me, pretending that he was going to strike me with it, but then pulled back.

"Larry, really, Pat is out here, I guess that Jim just didn't think to mention it. I know that she would like to see you. Pat!! Pat!!" I frantically called to her again.

"Oh why did I shut off my saw?" I agonized. I had to figure out a way to get it started again without alerting Larry. "Larry I really would like to see the house. Why don't I finish up here and then we can both leave together when I'm done."

I reached for the pull cord, but before I could tug it, Larry pushed the axe down firmly on my glove. "No, stop right there, don't think that it's going to be that easy to get rid of me."

"I'm not trying to get rid of you, I just want to finish my work."

Larry screamed at me, "You don't want to finish your work, you want to get away from me! Now don't bother to argue with me Penelope, you know damn well that I'm smarter than you, but you'll never learn, you still try to trick me. You're so stupid and transparent to me. I know exactly what you're trying to do and it won't work! First you try to scare me by telling me that Pat's out here; I know that you think I'm afraid of her, but you're wrong. Just because she carries a hunting knife on her hip doesn't make her tough and she doesn't scare me, not one bit. I'm a real man and Pat's nothing but a frail little girl, just like you are!"

Larry paused, took a deep breath and then rolled his eyes as if he were disgusted. "And then Penelope, you made your next stupid move and tried to start the chainsaw, but as usual, I'm one step ahead of you. I know that you're lying to me, you don't want to go home with me at all, you just want to make a fool out of me again!" He smiled strangely and then screamed, "But don't worry, I have a back-up plan!!"

Larry's hands were shaking and he began to speak in a quiet monotone as if he was trying to control himself, "Honey, why don't you want to come home with me?" When I didn't answer him, he screamed in a shrill piercing voice, "It's because of that boyfriend of yours, Windsor, isn't it?! You didn't think that I knew about him did you? Yes, I've known about it the whole time, how you've been cheating on me. You used to be a nice girl, but now you're nothing but a dirty filthy slut!"

"I haven't been able to see you at all because of that guy. Before he came there, I could at least hide across from your house and watch you walk in and out. Now I can't even do that! It's been hard not being able to see you, not to even lay my eyes on you. I would be satisfied for the rest of my life just watching you walk in and out of the bathroom. I'm not asking for much, please just come home, I'll do anything!"

Larry went on and on, he was whimpering and begging one minute, and screaming and threatening the next. I tried to calm him, "Larry why don't you put the axe down and we can talk about it."

"You think I'm stupid don't you?" he snapped back. "But I know a lot of things, it might surprise you to find out how much I know. For instance, I know that you're coming home with me today, whether you want to or not. You see, if you resist, I will be forced to follow through with my plan and don't kid yourself, I'm plenty of man for the job."

Again with the plan, I shuddered to think what it might be.

He went on, "You saw what I did to all of your good-for-nothing animals. Didn't you? Oh, that's right, you didn't see everything that I did. I'm good with an axe by the way, I got a lot of practice after you left me ... left me all alone with all of those dead animals! That axe that you kept in the barn worked quite well on little Snowball. Just try to cuddle with her now!! Oh I'm sorry, I guess you can't, good luck trying to cuddle with pieces of bloody meat!!" Larry patted his stomach, "Ahh... ha...ha, ha, ha! You know how well I barbecue. I gave Snowball exactly what she deserved; every time you hugged and kissed that little rat dog she gave me a dirty look to let me know that you loved her and that you didn't love me. She thought that she was better than me, but now she knows that I'm a real man. I taught her what happens when someone crosses me!"

The horror of the scene filled my being; my body heaved and I was nearly overwhelmed with repulsion, but I didn't let on. I couldn't let this madman know that he had gotten to me or he would move in for the kill.

Larry certainly hadn't improved, his insanity had escalated and he was more cruel and dangerous than ever before. Once again, the devil was looking at me through his eyes, the black B-B eyes of the rattlesnake.

Larry raised the axe above his head, I held the chain saw in front of me and backed toward the trees. "Don't do this Larry, calm down and get a grip on yourself," I pleaded uselessly.

Larry took a swing at me; the blow crashed into my saw and glanced off. "Pat!!" I screamed at the top of my lungs. Pat was the only hope that I had of anyone hearing my cries for help, the men working the quarry were too far away and the heavy machinery much too loud.

Fight or flight? Running away was out of the question, when I turned my back on him, Larry would throw the axe at me and was more than capable of hitting the mark. A picture crossed through my mind … me falling with an axe in the back of my head!!

Even if I avoided that peril, I could never make it to the gate and be able to open it before my vile attacker would catch me. I had to stand and fight, but I needed a chance to start my chainsaw to battle him. I planned to work my way to the dense trees, use them as cover and hopefully avoid the axe long enough to start my saw.

Larry was screaming and wildly swinging the axe at me. I continued to dodge and block the blows as I backed toward the protection of the trees. But my saw was taking a beating and I hoped that when the time came it would still work.

I kept backing up, moving toward the river, in the direction that I had seen my sister go. Walking backward through the rough terrain, it was difficult for me to keep my footing and fight the battle for my life. The crazed maniac, his eyes blazing, screamed wildly, and in a flurry of relentless brutal blows, he nearly sliced my throat. I jumped backward and avoided that agonizing death, but stepped on a dead branch; it broke under my foot and I stumbled. I managed to catch myself, but at that second, Larry lunged and swung the axe directly at my head. I saw the deadly sharp blade coming straight for my face, I quickly moved away, but hit my head on a tree. The axe sliced into my forehead, cutting me in the same place where Larry had hit me in the barn with the rifle, years earlier.

At that moment, it was as though time stood still, Larry stopped and stood watching the blood running from the wound and down my face,

"Good, good!" he giggled with delight.

I was stunned, everything was blurred and spinning around, I leaned on the tree next to me, hoping to regain my balance. I tightly clenched the saw in my fist, trying not to drop my weapon or I would be defenseless.

I couldn't pull out of it; no matter how hard I tried to stand, my legs began to fold, and I slowly slid down the tree trunk. Everything went dark and I knew that I was going out, but I didn't give up and kept fighting to stay conscious. "Pull yourself together Penelope, you've been knocked out before, quit being a weakling and keep fighting!" I opened my eyes, things were foggy for a few seconds and when they came into focus, I was peering through my blood at Larry's hideous smile, just inches from my face. He was pressing the axe handle and his body against me, holding me tightly to the tree trunk. Larry firmly grabbed my face with his left hand and then reached into his back pocket and pulled out a screwdriver. He held it in his fist, pointing it within an inch of my left eye.

Larry's hands were shaking, he was breathing heavily, his lips were quivering and he spit and stammered as he spoke. "I…..t..t..told… you… that I had a p..p.plan," he said.

I tried to break free, but my body wouldn't respond … I was paralyzed! There was nothing that I could do, I couldn't move, I couldn't even manage a scream. I had to listen helplessly to the ravings of this madman and face the terror staring me directly in the face.

"I, d..didn't want to..to do this," Larry stammered, "but..but you leave me no ch..choice. You see Penelope I will have you, one way or another and because you won't cooperate this is the only way. But you should consider yourself lucky, I'm not crazy like other men are. You've heard them say, 'If I can't have you no one can,' and then the fools kill the woman that they love and adore. Not me, oh no, I'm much smarter than that, don't worry honey, I'm not going to kill you, as a matter of fact, I'm going to take very good care of you. No one can ever say that I'm not fair, I gave you a chance to come home with me of your own free will, but you refused. Now, I will have to force you to do the right thing. It's up to me darling, to keep the marriage together. In time, you'll understand and you'll learn to appreciate me and even thank me; this is for your own good. You see, my love, I'm going to poke out your eyes with this screwdriver and then cripple you. It's the only way to show you that I'm the one who truly loves you, no matter what; me and no one else."

I couldn't believe that this horrible thing was actually happening, and on top of it all, I couldn't move a muscle or utter a sound. "Penelope, pull yourself together!" I kept repeating over and over in my mind, "Fight! Fight! You have to fight!"

"Not to worry honey, you can depend on me," Larry kindly uttered, "I'll take very good care of you. I'll push you in your wheelchair and take you on little outings. I'll bathe you in a tub full of bubbles and wash your hair, and make sure that you eat only the foods that are good for you ... except for a little chocolate once in a while, I know much how you love chocolate."

Larry smiled when he spoke of this, but then his face went dark, "But there is one thing that I will regret, I'm going to have to scar your beautiful face, it's the only way. I must scar it so badly that the only way that Windsor will ever look at you again will be in horror! Complete and utter horror! That pretty boy doesn't care about you and you're going to find out! I'm going to prove it to you! You'll see, I'm the only one who will stand by you when you're ugly pathetic and helpless! Larry began to grind his teeth, "The thought of that dirty filthy man running his fingers on your soft smooth skin is more than I can bear!" he screamed wildly. "I'll see that it never happens again! I want you and I will have you!! Oh Penelope, why do you make me do these things?!!"

Larry pulled back his fist with the screwdriver pointed, ready to pierce my eye. Just when I thought that all was lost, my coordination returned, I bowed my head and with everything I had, I rammed him with my shoulder and pushed him away.

Larry wasn't prepared for the blow and he began to fall, but as he did, he held tightly to the axe, the head of it caught my chainsaw and yanked me down with him. The two of us tumbled down a long steep slope and into the brisk muddy river at the bottom of the canyon.

When we hit the rushing shallow water, I quickly got to my feet and looked around trying to figure my next move. I saw that the river had cut a deep narrow canyon with steep slopes on both sides, and behind me, a solid, rock faced waterfall. Downstream, only feet away was Larry, still clutching the axe, blocking the only way of escape.

I still had the chainsaw in my hands, the only chance I had was to get it started and attack. I reached for the pull cord and gave it a yank, the saw sputtered, but it didn't start. "Please don't be broken!" I cried. I tried again, and again; it didn't start, but I had to keep trying.

Larry got to his feet and began to move toward me; he was walking slowly, swinging the axe back and forth, taunting me. I backed away from him, the only way I could go; toward what I knew was a dead end, the waterfall. The river was getting deeper, but I kept trying to start the saw, sputter… sputter… sputter. The saw hadn't started and I had gone as far as I could, my back was against the rock and the plunging waterfall was drenching me with sheets of water. Larry was laughing a fiendish hideous laugh, "This is it sweetheart! There's nowhere to run, get ready for your new life!" He swung the axe toward me and the fight was on again. I jumped to the side; Larry missed me and hit a large piece of driftwood. The axe was wedged in deep, and before he could pull it out, I hit him in the back with the chainsaw. When I tried to take another whack at him, he abandoned the axe and slammed into me. The saw flew from my hands and landed out of reach on the riverbank, the axe was still wedged in the driftwood.

Larry grabbed me and pulled me under the swift running water. Now it was a hand-to-hand battle and Larry was insane and had superhuman strength. He grabbed me by the hair and held my head under the water. I struggled to get air, but his hands were firmly fisted in my hair.

Instead of continuing to try and raise my head up to the surface, I jerked and twisted to the side and got Larry's finger in my mouth. I bit down hard and felt it crunch; the river water ran red from my mouth. Larry screamed in pain and released me; he fell to his knees holding his hand and whimpering.

I saw my chance, the axe was just feet away. I went for it, but before I was out of his reach, Larry jumped up and grabbed my legs, then he yanked me down and pulled me under the water again. I punched and kicked, fighting to get free. During the perilous struggle the strong river current pushed us to the more shallow water. Larry got on top of me and pulled my face just above the waterline. I was spitting water, gasping for air and screaming bloody murder. I was in a desperate fight, a fight that if I lost, held a fate for me worse than death!

Larry had the screwdriver in his hand, "Take a good look sweetheart, burn it into your memory, because my face is the last thing that you will ever see!"

Above my own screams, I suddenly heard a loud war cry crack through the sky. I raised my eyes and there was Pat standing at the top of the waterfall. She started her chainsaw and held it above her head. The sound of the loud saw blasted through the forest and Pat jumped over the fall. She flew through the air and before her feet even hit the water, Larry was trying to climb over the top of me and get away.

Things had suddenly changed, I was no longer trying to get away from Larry, I was trying to keep him there; I wasn't about to let him escape! Larry punched me, he kicked me in the face and tried everything to break free, but I was locked onto him like a vise-grip and wouldn't let go!

Pat positioned herself down river; she stood in the rushing water with her chainsaw raging, blocking Larry's escape. Larry was focused on Pat now; she had things under control, so I released him and he stood up.

Now that the odds were against Larry, his demeanor changed drastically, "You stay away from me now Pat," he whimpered in a timid whiny voice.

I took the opportunity to run for my chainsaw. I quickly pulled the cord and RREERRR, RREERRR the saw finally started!

I stood on one side of Larry and Pat the other, our saws raging, RREERRR, RREERRR. The two of us walked toward him, closing the gap, he was stiff, frozen with fear. There was nowhere for him to run, he, as I had been, was now trapped in the canyon.

"You're a joke Larry," Pat laughed.

Larry just stood there with a dazed look on his face, then he started blubbering, his lip quivered and his hands shook. "You girls stay away from me," he said crying. "The foreman knows that I'm out here and he's coming here and he'll catch you!"

Larry began slowly backing out of the water toward the canyon wall, but he stepped in a hole and slipped and fell down. "Oh no Larry, are you alright? I hope you didn't hurt your BACK!" Pat taunted him. "I better take a look at you and make sure that you're okay, you know how bad your BACK is."

Pat walked on one side of Larry and I walked on the other. We stood over him with the chainsaws loudly roaring, RREERRR, RREERRR.

"My back is fine, Pat, please, please don't come near me!" Larry cried.

"That's not what I heard, you better let me check anyway… ROLL OVER!" Pat demanded.

Larry didn't move, he stiffly laid there sobbing. Pat didn't wait, Larry hadn't moved and she buzzed the saw toward his side. "I can't believe that this is happening to me!" Larry screamed as he lunged toward me to get away from her. "Help me Penelope!" he begged. "I'm your husband! Please don't let her hurt me, I just wanted you to come back home! I miss you, I love you! Help me, please help me!"

I looked down, what a pathetic sight, the merciless cruel snake, now crying and pleading for himself. I stood over Larry, the fierce chainsaw in my hands. I was so enraged that I was out of my head. All of the cruel things that he had done were angrily shouting to me as they raced through my mind.

I slowly raised the saw above my head, RREERRRRRR! The noise was deafening. "You made a big mistake coming out here today Larry, today is the day that you're going to pay!!!" I struck hard and fast with the raging saw, attempting to deliver a fatal blow. Larry, like most snakes wiggled out of the way and I merely nicked him, but the saw caught his shirt and was pulling it into the blade.

Larry jerked it away and rolled toward Pat, "Help me Pat! Please!" he cried.

"Don't herd him over here, I don't want this sidewinder near me." Pat took a poke at him and drove Larry back over to me. "There you go sister, finish him off this time!"

"I don't want him by me either." I buzzed at him again, RREERRR, and grazed his leg this time. For once, Larry was the one who was bleeding instead of me.

Larry pulled away, screaming in terror, crying and begging for mercy. "Mercy, you want mercy?" I screamed back at him. "After you just tried to blind and cripple me! You'll find no mercy here, you scum!"

Up until that point, Pat had just been playing rough with Larry and letting me get in a few cracks at him. But, when she heard what Larry had tried to do to me, she was outraged, and things became serious. "What?" she said, "You threatened to blind and cripple my sister?" Pat came down hard with the chainsaw and hit Larry, he went screaming back towards me and I buzzed him back to Pat.

It had turned into a gruesome, bloody game, and Pat and I played it well. Back and forth, back and forth, we cut at Larry and watched the snake-like venomous creature wiggle and squirm.

Finally, Pat had enough, "I'm tired of playing this game," she announced.

"Yes, yes," Larry cried, "I'm tired of it too, let me go, you girls are crazy!"

"You know Pat, Larry could be right, maybe I am crazy. Wouldn't that mean that I'm not responsible for my actions?"

Thinking that we were about to kill him, Larry screamed, "No, no, you would never get away with it!"

Pat stopped him, "Shut up weasel! You're the one who's not getting away with anything. I haven't forgotten that day at the ranch, when I picked up my sister covered in blood the day after her surgery. We would be doing the world a favor, ridding it of vermin like you." Then she turned to me, "Let's butcher him! It's exactly what he deserves, to be cut up alive, piece by piece!"

Larry went hysterical and started trying to crawl away. I stepped in front of him and lunged my saw in his face. "Get necked," I demanded.

"Please, don't hurt me, please, please, no, no, no! You've always been such kind and caring girls, you don't want this on your conscience! You couldn't live with yourselves!"

"You're wrong about that," Pat screamed, "after what you done to my sister, I couldn't live with myself if I don't kill ya."

"No, no!" Larry whimpered. "I won't, I won't ever do another thing to Penelope, I'll leave her alone, I promise!"

"It's too late for that," Pat answered. "My sister told you to get necked, now get moving! We need to see the cuts of meat for a proper butchering."

I gave Larry a swift hard kick and he stripped down to his underwear. "Not good enough… I said necked!"

"No! No!" he kept screaming as he stripped all the way down.

I stood looking at the naked Larry before me, "There's the cut of meat that I want to start with, I believe you called it tube steak, didn't you Larry? You remember how you used to hurt me and then tell me that I was a weirdo? The doctor had to stitch me up because of what you did to me with that thing. You said that it was just too big. Well I'm going to remedy that problem right now; it won't be too big when I get through with it!"

"Tube steak it is!" Pat chimed in.

"Oh my God! No! Not that! Please, I'm sorry! I didn't know what I was doing when I did those things. I didn't mean it when I said that I was going to blind and cripple you either. I was just joking, it was just a bad joke! I'm sorry, I'm sorry!"

When Pat made a move for him, Larry couldn't take it; he wet himself and then fainted. After all the evil that he had committed, when something bad was happening to him, Larry couldn't handle it.

"Well," I chuckled, "it seems that Larry can dish it out, but he can't take it."

"Yeah you're right about that one, Sissy. But seriously, we have to figure out what we're going to do with this guy; we can't just let him go."

"I know," I agreed. "The first thing we better do is pack him up and go further into the woods, we're too close to the yard and we don't want anyone walking up on us. Wait here, I'll be right back."

Pat stayed with Larry, and I ran to get the Jeep. In the few minutes that I was running I thought about my situation; it wasn't just this episode with Larry, it was the dreading what he might do next. The years of torture; the dark cloud that I had endured constantly looming over my head. Every minute of every day, living with the tension and uncertainty of not knowing when he would strike.

What abusers do to women is unthinkable; even if the man never physically attacks, just the threat of it is enough to devastate a life. It's hard to imagine how horrible it is, a miserable fear-filled existence.

Once again, I found myself faced with the question … What was the right and honorable thing to do? I quickly realized that I had no other choice. I had to save myself while I had the chance. I had to put an end to it and stop Larry once and for all; it was my only promise of survival. I couldn't trust it to the courts to decide.

When I reached the Jeep, I disconnected it from the trailer and started driving back to Pat. My head was pounding and blood was still dripping down my face. I was shaky and badly injured, but I didn't care, this would be the last time that Larry would ever hurt me.

I thought about sweet little Snowball and what he had done to her and my other precious animals. My anger toward Larry kept building, and by the time I reached my sister, I was enraged. I jumped from the Jeep and wiped the blood from my face with my shirtsleeve, "I've taken all that I'm going to! Pat, help me strap him to the hood! We're going to finish him off!"

We tied Larry and strapped him naked on the hood of the Jeep. Then we gathered up his clothes, and threw the chainsaws and the axe in the back; and then started to drive far into the woods on our deadly mission.

I hadn't driven very far, when I began to feel dizzy and nauseous, so I stopped the Jeep. "Pat you're going to have to drive." I wasn't surprised at the way I felt, I knew that I had a concussion, and I had also lost a lot of blood.

Pat ran around the Jeep and climbed into the driver's seat. "Here take this, you're head's still bleeding." She handed me a bandana and I held it to the wound. "And put the seatbelt on, I don't want you falling out." Pat looked at my face, "You don't look too good, do I need to get you to the hospital?"

"No way, we have business to take care of!" I sternly answered.

"Well, okay then, let's get going," she hit the gas pedal and we went crashing through the brush.

Larry came to, screaming and crying, "I'm getting all scratched up!"

Pat snapped back at him, "That's the least of your troubles, now shut up weasel, you're bothering me!"

"Sissy, you know that we're not just playing games here, we really do have to kill him, there's no other way. He's more than earned it and he proved it today, he's not ever going stop. It's just a matter of time before he tries this again, and the next time you may not be so lucky. What if you had been out here alone? What if I hadn't heard you screaming? It comes down to the basics; it's either him or you, that simple. What else can you do? Go to the police? You know what they'll do, throw him in jail so he can bail out the next morning and come after you again."

"I know Pat, you don't have to convince me; the only question is, how do we do it? I don't want to get caught."

"Oh come on now Sissy, don't worry about that, you know as well as I do that real life isn't like the detective shows on television. The cops don't want to make more work for themselves, they would never come all the way out here looking for a missing person. And even if we do get caught, with everything that Larry's done, it's clearly self-defense, and if that doesn't fly the worst we'll get is manslaughter. I can do the time if I have to. It would be worth every minute of it just to know that that lunatic won't be able to harm you ever again. At least it will bring an end to things. Face it, you have a better chance of surviving in prison than with this crazy out gunning for you!"

"If I go down, I go down alone Pat, I'll kill him myself; I don't want you involved. We'll have to figure out a way to keep you out of it."

"I think that it's a little late for that," Pat answered, "I told you, I'll do the time if I have to. It's already cost you too much; you've been tortured ever since the day that you married that creep. You didn't ask for this and it isn't your fault that he went insane. You made an innocent mistake and married the wrong man and the suffering ends today! I don't want to hear another word about keeping me out of it either, I want to kill him! Did you hear me? I... want... to... kill... him! He deserves it a hundred times over! Now, how do you propose we do it, and get rid of the body and the evidence?"

From that point on, harsh reality laid heavily upon us; Pat and I were devising a plan, a plan to kill a man. Yes, he was a poor excuse for one, but by law a man just the same. This was a man who I had once cared for and married, and now my sister and I were discussing how to kill him and dispose of his body. Strangely enough, there was an eerie calm about the two of us. It was almost as though we were planning a trip to the mall to shop for shoes.

I offered my suggestion first, "I think that butchering really is a good idea, but cut him up real good. Chop him into little bite-sized pieces, then we can drive the Jeep through the woods and scatter them for miles. The chainsaws can easily cut through bone and if we cut the pieces small enough, no one will ever suspect that it's human remains. The coyotes will probably eat every bite of him."

"Yes I like that idea," Pat said, "but it's so bloody."

"Are you serious?" I asked. "Just look at us, we're completely splattered with blood already."

"That's my point exactly," Pat said, "all we've done is nick him a few times and look at the mess we have. Can you imagine what it would be like, chopping him up? I don't know if I can stomach it. There has to be a better way. I know, how 'bout we hang him? We could stage a suicide, a lot less messy."

"Hum, not a bad idea," I said thoughtfully, "but, I don't think that the evidence will add up to a suicide. If we leave him hanging, it'll make it too hard for the animals to get at him. His body could turn up in pretty good condition, and he's been cut with the chainsaws and I just noticed ...

I bit off his finger."

"You did?" Pat said with surprise, and then she glanced at Larry's hand to see his finger loosely dangling by a piece of skin. "Yeah, I guess you did alright. Well good for you!"

Pat paused momentarily and then went right on planning, "You know, if we don't want it to be messy, why don't we break his neck and throw him off a cliff. We could make it look like an accident."

"Oh I like that idea," I said, "very believable, everyone knows how Larry likes to hike by himself, it's perfect, a flawless plan. Then all we have to do, is get rid of his car, but that should be easy enough, we'll just push it into the quarry pit with yesterday's problems."

Pat chuckled thinking about the vehicles that we had smashed and burned the day before. "Yes, I guess that's the obvious solution, sounds good."

"Okay, it's settled then," I concluded, "we break his neck and throw him off a cliff. If he's ever found we don't know a thing."

"Oh, I wouldn't worry about that," Pat said confidently, "we'll make sure that that weasel never turns up, we'll find the perfect place."

Pat and I rode in the Jeep for hours, going deeper and deeper into the mountainous woods. We weren't sure where we were going, but we knew what we had to do when we got there.

I kept holding on, my vision was fading in and out and the dizziness wouldn't let up, but I had to keep it together until the job was finished, when my ex-husband was dead.

The sun started to go down, Pat and I had to make a decision and we picked the place to do the dreaded deed. A tall cliff, with huge boulders at the bottom, and lots of full trees for cover. We stood at the top looking down. "No one could ever see anything down there," Pat said. "We found it, the perfect spot!"

Pat cut Larry loose from the Jeep and he fell with a thud to the ground. He lay there quietly whimpering, his reign of terror, coming to an end.

Pat tugged at his bonds to be sure that they were secure and the two of us dragged Larry near the edge of the towering cliff. We weren't strong enough to break his neck with our bare hands, so we wedged him between two big rocks with his head hanging over a sturdy log. I got on top of him and pushed down hard to hold him securely while Pat climbed up on a boulder, just above, and prepared to jump down and snap his neck.

"Pat, can't we just throw him over the cliff? Do we really have to break his neck first?" I shouted to her as she climbed.

"It's the only way to be sure that he doesn't survive," she shouted back to me. "You don't want him reappearing some day! Do ya?"

Pat was definitely right; I surely didn't want that, this bloody horrid creature wielding an axe at me again, like a scene from a bad horror movie. The thought of it made me shudder. I shook my head to get the image from my mind, and I looked up at my sister standing high on top of the big boulder. The shadowy blue sky and the clouds behind her moved in beautiful designs. It all seemed surreal. Nature was still peaceful and calm, as though this gruesome thing wasn't about to happen.

Larry had forced me into this horrid situation, but it still didn't make it easy and I struggled with what I had to do. Holding Larry while he helplessly waited to be killed was getting to me. Maybe if I had killed him in the heat of the battle, it wouldn't have bothered me, but after the hours of driving I had calmed down. I tried to reason with myself, "Penelope, Larry meant it when he said that he was going to poke out your eyes, cripple you and scar your face. That's what could happen if you don't follow through with this. Larry will keep trying until he succeeds. Is that how you want to live your life? It's his own fault that this is happening to him, not yours! You didn't ask for this, you don't have a choice, but he did! Oh why didn't he just let me be?!"

I kept holding Larry down, listening to his whimpering and waiting for what seemed an eternity. "It's him or me, it's him or me," I repeated over and over again. I was beginning to fall apart, "It will be over soon, just hold it together. Why hadn't Pat jumped? What was the holdup? Why was she taking so long?" I couldn't stand it much longer! "Pat hurry and do it! Hurry up, just jump and get it over with!"

"We're not murderers," Pat said in defeat, "I can't believe it, I want to kill him, you know I do, but I just can't bring myself to do it. Penelope, I'm so sorry, I'm so sorry for letting you down."

"It's okay Pat, don't worry about it. This is my responsibility; I didn't want you involved in the first place."

When Larry realized what was happening, he immediately stopped crying and quickly spoke up. "I have learned my lesson; I really have! I didn't realize what I was doing before, but now I do. I just wanted you to come back to me Penelope! I've never had anything bad happen to me before and I didn't know how to handle it when you left me. In fact, no one has ever even hit me, not once in my whole life and I didn't know what it felt like to be hurt. Now I know better. I know that I was horrible and I'll never raise a finger against you, ever again. I'll leave you alone Penelope, I swear I will. I'll never bother you, you can count on me! Please, please! Just let me go!"

Maybe it was true, and Larry had learned his lesson. It wouldn't be the first time that a good ass-whuppin' had changed somebody. I could only hope that he had been beat down enough and would leave me alone. I didn't know what else to do, and I agreed to turn him loose. "Alright, alright Larry, I'll let you go."

Pat was still standing on the boulder. "It's okay Pat, come on down from there, the sun's setting and it'll be dark soon, we better get going."

Pat jumped down from the boulder and when she hit the ground, the earth gave way beneath her feet and she began to fall through into a deep hole. She screamed for help, "Sissy grab me!"

I left Larry lying between the big rocks and rushed to help my sister. Pat was frantically grasping at fragile tree roots and clawing at the ground trying to catch herself as she fell. I rushed to her aide as fast as I could, but when I reached for her hand, we merely brushed fingertips and she plunged into a deep dark abyss. I heard her terrified screams as she plunged deeper and deeper into the darkness. Then I heard nothing, nothing, but cold empty silence.

"Pat, can you hear me?" I hollered down through the opening. I listened, hoping and praying for a response, but nothing.

What a horrible situation I was in; the murderous snake-like Larry tied up and squirming only feet away from me and my little sister, Pat, laying in a deep dark cavern, probably hurt, dead or dying.

I had to get her out! There was a rope on the Jeep! I jumped to my feet to run and get it, when I heard Pat shouting up to me from the darkness. "I'm okay, I landed in an underground spring, the water's warm and I've made it to the bank."

"Thank goodness," I answered in relief, "don't move I'll get the rope and throw it down to you."

"Wait a minute Sissy, you've got to come down here and see this place. It's a huge magical cave; the walls are glistening. You know what? I'm probably the first person to ever step foot down here, this could be the discovery of a lifetime! Hurry get down here, I want to explore! There could be creatures and organisms that have never been recorded living down here."

"I'm sure there are, all kinds of gross creepy things. Pat, you're coming out of there as soon as I get back with the rope! It's nearly dark, we can come back and explore another time. Now stay put!"

Larry was screaming, "Cut me loose! Cut me loose Penelope!" But I couldn't worry about him; I had to get Pat out of the cavern before something else happened.

"Hold on Larry, I'll turn you loose as soon as I get Pat out of the hole."

I ran to the Jeep to get the rope and I also grabbed a couple of flashlights. When I got back to the hole, the first thing I did was throw one of the flashlights down to Pat and instead of listening to me, the brat immediately began to explore.

I quickly tied one end of the rope to a nearby tree, and lowered it into the cavern. I was thankful to find that the rope was long enough. "Okay Pat, come on up," I shouted down.

"No, wait a minute," she answered. "There's lots of tunnels down here, this is only one small part of a huge system of caves .... Oh my gosh, I hear a baby!"

"Pat, there's no baby down there, your mind is playing tricks on you. It's probably just the wind. You're freaking me out, now just come out!"

"No really, I hear a baby, just give me a second to see if I can find it. Come on down Sissy, you've got to see this place, it's so cool!"

"Oh Pat, why do you always have to be so adventurous? Forget about that baby thing, who knows what it really is? There could be anything living down there in the dark!"

"Wait a minute, I see it. It's really cute Sissy .... Hello little fella." Then I heard a loud hissing shrieking sound and a sharp bang. Pat screamed, "It's a demon! It's a demon!"

"Pat, get out of there!"

I was shining a flashlight down the hole and before I could even decide what to do, Pat had reached the spring and was already climbing up the rope. Seconds later, a big black creature appeared from the darkness and clawed up the rope behind her ... the demon was after Pat! "It's got me, it's got me!" she screamed. I can't climb any further!"

Immediately, I grabbed the axe and started climbing down into the cavern to save my reckless sister.

The creature was ugly with long sharp fangs and claws; it hissed and pulled at Pat trying to force her off the rope. "Get it off me! Get it off me!" she screamed as she struggled to fight it off.

"Hold on tight kid," I yelled as I awkwardly climbed downward holding the heavy axe.

When the monster saw me coming, it showed its teeth and hissed and growled at me. It made a shrill ear-piercing noise that echoed endlessly through the cavern tunnels. This was a noise like nothing that I had ever heard before. It sent shock waves through my body and seemed to sear my flesh. It was a sound too terrifying to even describe.

The demon was furious, fighting for its meal … my little sister!

When I reached Pat, I climbed down the rope to the front of her to get close enough to strike. There was just enough light from the surface for me to make out the monster's silhouette. I took a good hard swing and ... wham! I hit it dead on, but the demon was tough and I didn't knock it off.

When the monster felt the blow, it screeched loudly, and long leathery tentacles shot out from its body. The tentacles whipped in the air and then wrapped around Pat, tightly clenching her legs. "I can't move my legs!" she screamed in terror. "It's pulling me down!"

The situation was more desperate now than it was before. Not only had the tentacles bound Pat, but one of them had wrapped around my ankle as well, and the monster was pulling both of us down into its lair.

We were now further from the surface and fighting in near darkness, the rope swinging and jerking about in the fierce struggle. I couldn't take a hard solid swing; I had to be careful not to hit my sister with the axe. All I could do was hack at the beast with short sharp blows. With each strike the cave demon screeched and made hideous ear-piercing noises, but it wouldn't let go and continued to pull us further down the rope.

Just when we thought that things couldn't get any worse, Pat and I heard screeching screams echoing from inside the cave … an army of cave demons were on the way! "Come on Sissy, hurry and kill it, it's calling for help!"

No matter how hard we struggled, the monster was still overpowering us and we were quickly losing ground. When the ugly demon thought that its victory was eminent, it looked me in the face with its glowing fierce eyes and threw back its head in elation, it began to snarl and laugh a hideous shrill laughter.

I saw my chance, the demon's head was well away from Pat. I pulled back the axe, I had to make it count, I took my swing and …WHAP!! I hit the monster solid and chopped off its head. Fluid gushed from the body and the severed head floated momentarily before it began to fall. Its fierce glowing eyes were wide open and fixed directly on me as it screeched and fell down through the darkness.

Pat and I experienced a moment of hope, perhaps we could make it out before the other demons arrived. We quickly tried to climb up the rope, but still couldn't move; the monster's tentacles remained firmly attached. I wedged the axe between Pat and the tentacles and frantically cut away at them, but they were tough and leathery and as hard as I tried, I wasn't making much progress.

Our hearts clenched, we could hear pounding, tapping sounds and horrid screeches as the army of cave demons got closer and closer. The monsters began to emerge from the dark tunnels and into the steamy cavern, huge black creatures, each one more hideous than the last.

"We've got to get out now kid!" I warned as I pulled and cut away at the tentacles, but still, they held fast.

It looked hopeless for Pat and me, when suddenly, I felt something pulsing and pounding like a heartbeat at the base of the twisted tentacles … the body was still alive! Immediately, I chopped the axe deep into the flesh, it popped and whistled and out gushed slimy smelly ooze and then … the tentacles released and fell off of us.

Pat and I were free and we started scrambling up the rope. "Hurry Sissy, his buddies are heading this way!"

I moved like lighting and quickly reached the surface. I threw the axe on the ground, climbed out and then I laid down on my belly and reached back in the hole to pull out my sister. Pat was just starting to surface, when she screamed, "Watch out Sissy, it's Larry!"

I quickly glanced behind me and saw Larry standing over me wielding the axe, intending to hit me in the middle of my spine. I rolled to the side and Larry drove the axe head into the ground, barely missing me. Pat was only half way out of the hole, but she grabbed the axe handle and gave it a hard yank. Larry's momentum worked against him and he flipped, head over heels and tumbled away.

I firmly grabbed hold of Pat, I had to get her out of the hole before the hoard of demons leapt upon her.

Pat was nearly out, she had one knee on the ground when suddenly, a clamoring black mass came bursting from the cavern. We ran for our lives, screaming and waving our arms trying to escape the swirling twisting menace. What was this new terror that had stricken us?

Pat and I kept running and when the attack ended, I watched as thousands of bats fluttered away into the night sky. "Pat, it's okay, it's okay, they're only bats."

We both stopped running and tried to catch our breath. "Sissy," Pat exclaimed between pants, "we have to hurry back … we've got to cut the rope before the demons reach the surface!"

"Hopefully the bats slowed them down and we can make it in time!"

Pat and I looked at each other, neither one of us had the axe; it had been left behind in the confusion. "I don't know what we're going to do without that axe," Pat exclaimed. "How are we going to cut through the rope, I don't have my knife, that demon knocked it out of the sheath before I could even pull it out."

"My knife's plenty sharp, it'll have to do."

"That knife's the legal limit for a concealed weapon, it's too short to saw through that thick heavy rope, it'll take forever!" Pat exclaimed in dismay. "We have to find the axe and hope that Larry doesn't get it first, or he'll be after you again."

This was the most terrifying thing that Pat and I had ever been through. How we wanted to jump in the Jeep and run for our lives, but we knew that if we didn't prevent the creatures from escaping the cavern, they would be creeping the forest, and neither man nor beast would ever be safe again. Losing the axe was a major setback, but at least Pat was still holding a flashlight. I picked up a good solid, tree branch for protection and we headed back toward the cave.

Pat shined the flashlight ahead of us as we ran, the light bounced up and down and from side to side with each stride that she took. When we were getting close, we slowed down the pace and Pat shined the light toward the cavern hole to see what was going on, and when she did … we were stopped dead in our tracks. We had arrived too late, the huge dark demons were on the surface, scuffling about on the ground with their long clawed arms and legs. When the light from the flashlight hit them, they squealed and covered their eyes.

Pat and I, both realized that we had found a formidable weapon in the flashlight, but what were we to do with it? There were so many of them and they were gigantic. But then, I noticed something and put my hand over the flashlight, "Turn it off Pat," I whispered. Pat clicked off the light and we knelt quietly behind a boulder. We could hear the creatures shuffling about, screeching, snorting and grunting. There was a full moon that night, and once our eyes had adjusted, we could make out what was happening …the demons were after Larry.

Larry had the axe in his hands, and was attempting to put up a fight. The largest of the demons stood menacingly in front of him and let out a loud threatening shriek, he stretched himself up tall, his tentacles whipped wildly in the air. "Look at the size of that thing!" Pat whispered, "I guess the demon that had a hold of me, really was a baby."

"Yeah, you're right about that one kid," I agreed, looking at the massive creature.

The monster reached forward with a long leathery tentacle; it wrapped it around the axe and easily pulled it from Larry's grasp. The demon tossed the axe to the ground while another of its tentacles whipped around Larry's neck and tightened. The demon wallowed in its superior strength, it whipped Larry through the air, back and forth while it laughed and made horrid screeches. The other creatures celebrated and even in the moonlight, Pat and I could see the saliva oozing from their mouths. The big monster tossed Larry around for a little longer and then threw him down into the cavern. All the demons leapt down the hole after him in a crazed fury.

When they were all gone, Pat and I started to quietly make our way toward the edge of the dark hole. Even at a distance, we could hear the feeding frenzy as the demon creatures yowled and pulled Larry apart, piece by piece; feasting on his raw flesh.

"At least they killed him first," Pat commented as we crept along, "they didn't eat him alive like a bear would have."

We reached the cavern opening. "Okay Pat, they're busy eating this is a good time to go for it, let's pull the rope up and hope they don't notice."

I stepped forward and was reaching down to take hold of the rope, when I stepped on something lying on the ground, it was the axe! I picked it up and swung it above my head. I struck with all my might, but the rope didn't fall. The axe had taken a beating and was too dull to slice through, it had only made a small cut. "Guess we'll have to pull it up after all," I concluded. "Here goes!" I reached down with my bloody dirty hands and grabbed hold of the rope. I tried to pull it up, but it didn't move. "It must be hung up on something," I said and gave it another tug. "What could it possibly be caught on?"

Just then, a shrill shriek cut through the air and Pat and I knew what the problem was, two glowing eyes were moving up the rope toward us!

"He's coming up for dessert!" Pat screamed. "Cut the rope! Cut the rope!"

I grabbed the axe again and started furiously chopping, cutting only a few threads at a time, chop, chop, chop, chop, chop! We weren't going to make it, there just wasn't time! It was impossible for the dull axe to cut through the rope before the creature reached the surface, and my small knife wouldn't have been any faster.

"He's coming up! … He's here! He's here!" Pat screamed while I continued hacking away. Pat grabbed the tree branch that I had been carrying. "Don't worry, I'll knock him back down!" The creature reached up and dug its claws into the ground on the surface, and then up came its hideous head. CRACK! Pat clobbered him with the branch.

The demon pulled back, but then … up came the dreaded tentacles! I kept chopping at the rope hoping that I could cut through while there was still a chance, but if I couldn't, we would be the next course of the devil's gruesome feast.

The tentacles were swinging wildly through the air, one flew toward me, I ducked and it glanced the top of my head. Another tentacle snapped out and whipped around, grabbing the tree branch that Pat was holding. The monster pulled it toward him while another tentacle was reaching for Pat's neck. It was the same move that had been used on Larry! "Get back Pat! Let go of the branch and get back!"

Pat let loose of the tree branch and scrambled back, just out of the reach of the tentacle. The demon had missed and it was angry, it began flailing its tentacles and whipping the tree branch around, but I didn't stop, I kept furiously chopping at the rope.

The demon made another attempt to climb out of the hole. It put up its claws, once again and struck at the ground trying to get a grip when … eureka! I had cut through the rope! The rope slid down the hole, but the monster was still hanging on with its claws. I swung the axe above my head to give the claws a whack, and the axe head flew off of the handle. At that same moment, one of the leathery tentacles wrapped around my waist. I jumped back, twisted around and was trying to pry it off.

Meantime, Pat started to stomp on the demon's claws with her heavy boot, the demon's tentacles wildly flailing around her. I looked up for a second and saw the tentacle holding the branch swinging toward Pat's head, "Watch out Pat! The branch!" Pat laid flat on the ground and the branch flew over her. Lying on her back, Pat still didn't waste any time, she pushed against the claws digging her heels into the dirt, breaking it loose.

The tentacles were still reaching, grabbing and trying to latch onto something, but the only thing that they had hold of was me. The monster pulled me toward him, I dug in my heels, but I was still sliding across the loose, pine-needle covered ground. I twisted and pulled at the tentacle and managed to pry it loose from my waist, but as I held it in my hands, the tip of it twisted back around and looped onto my belt buckle.

Pat was kicking hard at the monster's claws and it couldn't hold on any longer. The demon started to slide downward into the cavern and when it did, it jerked me forward by my belt buckle and slammed me down on my face. The monster was taking me with him!

When Pat saw me sliding on the ground toward the hole, she jumped in front of me and tried to hold me back, but now we were both being pulled to the cavern and certain death.

I had to move fast, I reached into my pocket, pulled out my knife and just when we were at the edge of the dark hole … I sliced through the tip of the tentacle. I was free!

Pat and I stopped sliding and quickly scrambled to get out of the way. The demons tentacles twisted about, pawing at the surface trying to grab hold, but then they folded together and went down the hole as the monster fell.

Pat and I tightly hugged each other and listened to the demon screeching and screaming in frustration as it plunged down deeper and deeper into the darkness. There would be no tasty dessert for him tonight!

We fell to our knees in relief; we were safe; we had fought the devil and won. There was no way for the demonic creatures to get back up to the surface from the dark deep chasm.

We slowly stood and walked back to the Jeep for water, but we both knew that we weren't finished yet, we couldn't leave the cavern open; we had to cover the hole.

When we reached the Jeep, we opened our canteen and guzzled down the refreshing water. "I have an idea on how to cover the opening," I said.

"Yeah, what's that?" Pat asked between gulps.

"That boulder that you climbed, you know, when we were going to break Larry's neck."

"What about it?"

"There's a big stone sitting near the edge of it, it looks like it might be unstable."

"Oh, great idea, we'll hook up the winch and pull it down. It might even be close enough to fall right on the cavern opening. It'll definitely cover it, that hole isn't that big!"

The well-equipped Jeep had a winch on the front with a very long cable. When we were finished drinking we climbed in the Jeep and drove as close to the site as we could. There were two small trees, growing side by side and Pat pulled the Jeep up against them. The trees were perfect, they hit each end of the bumper. "Good thinking Pat, these trees won't let that Jeep move forward an inch."

Working in the moonlight, Pat and I climbed atop the big boulder, pulling the heavy cable with us as we went. When we got to the top we examined the big stone, it was definitely large enough to cover the hole and better yet, I was right, it was off balance.

"We can move it back and forth to get it rocking," Pat said, "and then pull hard and tumble it to the ground."

We wrapped the cable around the big stone and secured it tightly, then went back down to find a branch to use as a lever. We were lucky, we found a suitable branch right away and I climbed back up to see if I could get the stone rocking. Pat and I both knew that it was a long shot, but we were still hopeful.

Pat climbed into the jeep and everything lined up at the perfect angle. "Looks good," she shouted up to me.

I put the lever under the side of the stone, "Okay Pat, tighten her up!"

The winch started to take up the slack and when the cable began to tighten, I pried with the lever. The cable lifted from the ground and the pressure was on, the winch whined and the cable creaked as we tried to rock the stone. The giant stone was so unstable that it quickly fell from atop the boulder and came to rest directly on top of the hole, sealing the cave entrance.

I climbed down from the boulder and Pat and I looked it over. "I can't believe that it was so easy!" Pat exclaimed. "Nothing else has been; hanging around with you is certainly no picnic."

Once we knew that the cave entrance was secure, we climbed in the Jeep and got out of there! We rode in silence, we didn't even know if we were going in the right direction, but any direction away from the pit of hell was okay with us.

After we crossed over the highest mountain peak, we could see the floodlights from the yard, "Thank goodness for Jim," we both said at once. There was still a long way to go, but after we had seen the lights at the yard the pressure was off and we started to feel better. Riding through the tall trees in the moon and starlight, I felt free for the first time in years. My head stopped pounding and I could breathe easy. The terror in my life had ended, Larry was gone for good. The further we went, the better I felt.

"Well Pat, I guess that you found your unknown organisms," I laughed.

"Yeah, but too bad we can't tell anyone about it."

"Who would believe it anyway? I don't even believe it myself. What really happened back there Pat?"

"Nothing, nothing happened. All you have to remember is that Larry's dead and buried and you're safe now."

"You're right Pat, nothing else matters. I guess that it was a case of temporary insanity."

Well, that's my story and I'm sticking to it; a demon killed Larry.

Pat and I pulled into the yard in the bloody dirty Jeep. "We made it and it's still dark," Pat said, "we better get moving and take care of things before sunrise, when the men start showing up for work."

"Yeah, we might as well head straight for the quarry pit; I hate to say it, but we're going to have it get rid of this Jeep, it's way too bloody for us to try and clean."

"You're right, I know, and Lance is going to be mad about it too. He loves this Jeep, he's got it rigged up to do all kinds of work around here and he drives it all the time. I'm gonna have to do something real nice for him to make up for this one."

"Why don't you just marry the poor guy Pat? I feel sorry for him, he's got it bad for ya."

"Oh, I know, I've thought about it, that's for sure. Lance is good breeding stock, he's got those broad shoulders and a good solid chest on him, no genetic weaknesses in the bloodline and he's never had a cavity. Yeah, Lance is a hard-working man, it's just that I'm not ready to settle down yet, but I will be someday."

Pat and I drove the Jeep directly to the quarry pit and stopped just at the edge. "Grab that rock over there," Pat instructed as we both climbed out of the Jeep.

I picked up the heavy rock, put it on the gas pedal and Pat shifted the Jeep into drive. We jumped back and watched as it flew over the edge and crashed down into the pit.

"One down, one to go," Pat said as we started to walk to the shack. "It's been a hard day, and I think that we deserve some fun. I've got something special planned.

"What is it?" I asked.

"You'll find out soon enough," she said with a grin, "I want it to be a surprise.

When Pat and I reached the shack, she opened the door and we went inside. "Find Larry's keys on the pegboard and I'll get the surprise." Pat went into Lance's office for a minute or two and then came back out. "Well, what do you think? Shall we blow things up!" she said, waving a stick of dynamite above her head.

I was surprised all right, surprised and a bit concerned. "Pat I've never used dynamite, Dad would never let me. Do you know how?"

"I've seen the guys at the yard blow up a few boulders around here, there's nothing to it! Come on, let's go!"

I pulled Larry's keys from the pegboard and Pat and I climbed into his car. I drove it to the quarry pit and stopped a few feet away from the edge.

"What's next Pat?"

"We do just like the Jeep, but I throw in the dynamite before we send it over the edge."

"Sounds simple enough. How far back do we need to go to get away?"

"With just one little stick of dynamite, not that far, behind those boulders should be fine."

"Well okay Sister, let's blow it up!"

Pat prepared the blasting cap and fuse while I put a heavy rock on the accelerator; the motor raced loudly. Then we put earplugs in our ears and Pat lit the dynamite. The fuse started to "sizzle."

"Throw it in Pat!"

"No wait a few seconds, I don't want it to blow after it hit's the bottom, I want it to go off and make a big firework in the sky!"

"Okay, you're the one who knows about dynamite."

So we waited, and when it was time, Pat threw the stick of dynamite into the car. "Okay Sissy, shift it into drive!"

I shifted the car and Pat and I had started to run for cover when … BAM!!! The dynamite blew! The concussion hit us in the back and we went flying. We were slammed down on our faces, both of us knocked out, lying on the dusty ground.

I don't know how long I laid there before I woke up and opened my eyes. First, I moved my fingers, "My fingers work, my feet work, I can move my arms," I happily discovered. I sat up and then saw Pat lying a few feet away and she wasn't stirring. I crawled over to her and tried to roust her awake, but Pat didn't move and I began to cry.

Suddenly, Pat opened her eyes, "That dynamite has a real kick, don't it?"

"I thought that you knew what you were doing you dumb bunny!"

"I did, that's exactly what I had in mind."

"Yeah, sure it was," I laughed, "now get up and let's check out the damage."

We both got up, ever so slowly, and stiffly walked to the quarry pit to see what had happened. "Wow, we blew half the wall down!" Pat exclaimed. "Consider our tracks covered! Now all we have to do is get cleaned up and get the heck out of here."

Pat and I started the walk back to the shack. I was a banged up, bruised, bloody mess and so was Pat. We were both walking slowly, holding each other up, and painfully limping along. I was worried that we wouldn't make it out of the yard before the men showed up for work, and started to ask us questions, questions that could send us to prison.

When we got back to the shack, the sun still wasn't up and we quickly stripped down and put our clothes in a garbage bag. Then Pat and I looked each other over and pulled out the wood ticks that had latched onto us. We got in the shower and scrubbed ourselves clean, hoping to make it in time. When we had finished, we disinfected the shower and got dressed. I put on coveralls and Pat, a mechanic's uniform. We jumped in my truck and got away, passing the men on the road just as they came in to work.

"I can't believe it, we actually made it, and in the nick of time," Pat happily stated.

We rode down the road for a little while longer; we were both relieved, but then I noticed Pat staring at me, "What's the problem?" I asked.

"You look pretty rough Sissy, especially where Larry kicked you in the face, there's a big scrape scabbing up all the way down your cheek and that cut on your forehead. You better stay at my place until we figure out a good cover story."

"That sounds like a good idea, I've got to get some sleep and I definitely don't feel like going through another interrogation from "Inspector Windsor." I'm liable to drive him into the woods next."

When Pat and I arrived at her house, the first thing we did was start a fire and burn our boots and the bag of bloody clothes. "Well that's the end of that," Pat said, "now let's get some sleep."

We put on silky pajamas, Pat pulled down the blackout shades in the bedroom and we climbed into her soft cozy bed. "Thank goodness today's Saturday, I can sleep all day," Pris said sleepily.

"And I don't have to be at a bar shop until midnight," I yawned.

Pat and I had been up for over twenty-four hours fighting, running, and blowing things up and it wasn't long before we were both sound asleep.

The next thing I knew, the blasted phone was ringing. "This always happens to me, it must be some sort of a curse!" I angrily shouted.

"Yeah," Pat agreed, "no rest for the wicked."

Pat picked the phone up and began to talk, it was Lance. "No Lance everything's fine," Pat told him … "No, I'm not in any trouble …. No, I'm fine, I don't need to go anywhere … Well okay, but only if I can bring Penelope with me … Alright, alright Lance, we'll be at the airport in an hour."

"We'll be at the airport in an hour!" I exclaimed. "Have you gone crazy?!"

"Jim told Lance about the dynamite and he knows that something's up. He's stuck in Louisiana for another week and he wants to fly us out. Before you start freaking out, think about it, it's a good idea for us to get out of town for a while."

After a minute or two, I realized that Pat was right, "It's not a bad idea after all," I agreed. "Things are slow at work right now anyway and Ray's just sending me out on bar shops to keep me busy. I have a vacation coming, give me the phone." I then called Ray and got the week off.

"What about Windsor?" Pat asked.

"I don't care what he thinks," I said as I dialed the phone to call him. "The sex isn't even that great anymore, sometimes he acts like he's doing me a favor and actually has the nerve to tell me to hurry up."

When Windsor answered, I told him that I would be working out of town for a week on a top secret case and that he wouldn't be able to get in touch with me. "I've got to go now Windsor," I said before he could respond. "I can't tell you anything else," then I hung up the phone.

"Now, let's get packing Pat, we have a plane to catch!"

Pat and I called the shuttle, packed our bags and before we knew it, we were on our way to Louisiana.

The trip went by very quickly, it seem as though we had no sooner boarded the plane and closed our eyes than we were landing. Lance had a limo waiting to pick us up and drive us to the hotel.

As we entered the hotel room, I saw a lovely bouquet of flowers on the table. "That Lance sure has class," I commented.

There was a note, "Sorry I couldn't be there to meet you at the airport. Hope you girls had a nice flight, see you tonight for dinner."

"What a break, he's not here and we have some time to relax," Pat happily stated.

We climbed into bed, propped pillows up against the headboard and ordered room service. Both of us were miserable. We were happy just to eat, watch movies and sleep the afternoon away.

When Lance showed up that evening, we didn't feel like going out, and after taking a look at us, Lance understood why. "You girls get some rest and I'll see you tomorrow," he said as he turned out the light and quietly closed the door behind him.

"Thank goodness he's not one of those nosey pushy guys, like that blasted Windsor," I moaned. And with that, Pat and I rolled over and went back to sleep.

For about three days, it rained nonstop and Pat and I stayed in the room recovering. "I feel sorry for Lance," I said, "he invited us here and we haven't spent any time with him."

"Don't worry about it Sissy, I'm sure that Lance doesn't particularly want to be seen with two girls limping around with fat lips and black eyes. We'll make it up to him tonight. Our faces are looking better now, a little make-up and we'll be passable. When he calls today, I'll let him know that we're better and we'd like to go out with him tonight."

Lance didn't call early that day like he usually did, we didn't hear from him until late afternoon. When Pat told him that we wanted to go out to dinner, he told us that he was tied up on the job and I wouldn't be able to make it back in time."

"That's okay," Pat told him, "don't worry about it, Penelope and I will go to the restaurant here at the hotel." She said good-bye and hung up the phone.

Five minutes later, Lance called back, "I made reservations for you at a great restaurant. You girls dress up pretty and have a nice time; the car will be waiting for you."

Pat and I did the best we could patching up our bruised battered faces. "I think we look pretty good," I said surprised. "You can hardly tell."

I hadn't had the time to stop by my place and pick up any of my belongings before we left for Louisiana, so everything that we had with us belonged to Pat. I slipped into one of her short shimmering dresses and I loved it. It was one of those loose fitting styles that plunged down in the back. With it, I wore spike heeled shoes, adorned with sparkling rhinestones and straps that buckled at the ankle. They looked smashing, but Pat's feet were smaller than mine and the shoes were terribly uncomfortable.

"You sure you're gonna be okay in those shoes?" Pat asked concerned.

"We won't be doing much walking, I'll just tough it out," I said as I admired the sparkling shoes in the mirror.

When Pat and I were ready, we rode the elevator down to the lobby and the valet pulled up in the car. "I can't believe it!" Pat exclaimed, "Lance drove the Lamborghini all the way here! Are we going to have fun tonight?!"

The valets opened the doors of the sleek expensive car and Pat and I climbed inside. Pat raced the powerful engine. "What a rush!" she said with a smile, and then pulled out into the street. "I'll tell ya one thing, we're not going straight to the restaurant, we're going to take this baby for nice long drive."

Pat and I drove the showy car down the streets of the strange town. We were just having a nice time enjoying the sights, but everyone was staring at us.

We hadn't been driving long when, as could be expected, some guys pulled up along-side of us at a stop light, in a souped up GTO. The driver revved the loud engine and the car rose up and down. They were challenging us, and Pat couldn't resist taunting them a bit and she raced the engine of the Lamborghini.

Suddenly, the light turned green and our opponent took off at full speed, but Pat just sat at the light without moving an inch and laughed. It was funny playing a joke on the motorheads.

"I'm not getting into trouble with this car," Pat firmly stated. "Lance doesn't even know about the Jeep and the truck yet, and the last thing I need is to damage his Lamborghini next!" We both chuckled and continued to drive around the town enjoying ourselves.

Pat and I were both having a little trouble with our eyes, they were still sensitive and burning. "Pull over into this strip mall," I suggested, "I'll get us some eye drops, they might help."

Pat pulled in front of the drug store and I jumped out and went inside. I searched the aisles and after reading the labels, found suitable drops. I was standing in line at the counter, when I glanced outside and saw the Lamborghini surrounded by people. They were all talking loudly and I could hear Pat shouting.

I immediately left the drops on the counter and ran outside to see what was going on. "Get in the car Sissy, we're going to race these suckers!"

I climbed in the car and then spotted the GTO that had challenged us earlier that night. It pulled out of the parking lot and Pat followed.

"What in the world are you doing? I thought that we weren't going to take any chances with this car."

"You weren't out here to hear what these idiots were saying to me!"

"It doesn't matter what they said to you Pat, quit following them and turn off right here, forget about it!" I tried in vain to talk her out of the risky race.

"It's okay, don't worry Sissy, we're going to race at a quarter mile strip outside the town limits. They say that they race out there all the time, it'll be fine."

When we arrived at the site, we found that it was merely a short strip of road by an old rundown motel.

"Come on Pat, just keep on going and get out of here." But it was too late, all of the onlookers had blocked us in, jumping out of their cars to watch The Big Race. The local boys against the girls in the expensive Lamborghini.

The driver of the GTO got out and walked up to Pat. I thought that it was to collect money and bet on the race, but I was wrong.

"We all know that this car is too much for you to handle, little lady. Why don't you scoot on over and let a man take over. Here, let me give you a lesson, this is the brake and this is the clutch," he said sarcastically. "Do you want me to teach you how to shift the gears? Did you forget how? Or did you ever know how to get it out of first gear?"

Pat looked over at me, "See what I mean?"

"Listen buddy," Pat said to the smart ass, "you're not man enough to fill my panties, now put up or shut up."

Once he realized that his intimidation hadn't worked, the irate smart ass cursed and called Pat filthy names. "I'll show you spoiled snobby, rich bitches a thing or two," he said as he walked back to his car.

Pat pulled the Lamborghini alongside the GTO to get ready for the race and when she did, the smart ass gave her the finger and started shouting more obscenities at her. Pat loudly raced the engine, trying to drown him out.

I tried to hold my temper, but listening to this idiot disrespect my sister was too much for me to take. I pulled my knife from the sparkling little evening bag and started to get out of the car. Pat grabbed my arm, "Well big shot, did you forget about what you were saying earlier? Let me quote you, 'It doesn't matter what they say, just turn off the road and forget about it?'"

"Okay, okay, you made your point, I admit it, the dickhead got to me too," I sat back down in the seat. "Take him down hard Pat, show no mercy!"

The crowd was scrambling about, exchanging money and trying to get a good view of the race, while Pat and I sat quietly in the car waiting.

A girl walked up to the window and told us that she was starting the race. Pat nodded that she understood. The girl then walked forward to where both cars could clearly see her and raised her arms above her head, when she dropped them … the race was on!

Pat hit the gas, the force of the powerful car thrusting forward threw me back into the seat. The GTO kept up with us until Pat shifted gears, and then it was all over, we reached the dead end of the quarter mile stretch leaving our opponent far behind.

Pat slammed on the brakes, the tires screeched and she spun the car around. We sat for a moment revving the engine. The nasty crowd was booing us and making obscene gestures. "Things are getting nasty Pat, get us out of here!"

The only way of escape was directly through the crowd, and that's exactly what Pat did. She angrily raced the car through the center of the pissed off locals. They all screamed and scattered to get out of the way. I stuck my arm out the car window and flipped them off, "See ya suckers!" I shouted as Pat and I drove out of sight. But, just as we turned the corner, I saw the flashing lights of a police car, waiting to pull us over. "Those rat bastards, they had the police here waiting for us!"

"No one has ever gotten a ticket in this car, and I'm not going to be the first!" Pat stepped on the gas, the car took off like a jet and the police were soon out of sight. But our troubles were far from over, only minutes later, I could hear the loud wailing of sirens coming toward us from all directions. We were in big trouble now and there was no turning back! We had to get away!

"We've got to get out of town, but we can't take the Interstate, they'll have it covered." I spotted a country road, "Turn here Pat, we'll try to lose them in the country!"

Pat slammed on the brakes and turned the steering wheel, the tires screeched and the car nearly slid off the road, but she managed to make the turn. We raced wildly down the bumpy country road, but the sirens were still getting closer and it sounded like they were closing in on us.

"We can still lose them Pat, turn here!"

Pat turned, and we drove frantically down the unfamiliar roads, trying to get away. Mile after mile we went weaving and turning and going who knows where, desperate to escape the unfriendly town.

Suddenly, with no warning, the gravel road ended. Pat tried to stop, but we were going too fast; we skidded, crashed through the guardrail and flew down into a gully. "Are you okay?" Pat asked.

"I'm fine, we're both fine, it wasn't that bad."

Pat shifted the car into reverse and tried to get out, but the tires just kept spinning around. "Stop," I shouted, "it's been raining for days, the mud's deep and you're just throwing it all over the place and digging us in deeper!"

Pat shut off the motor and we both looked around at the countryside. It was an eerie atmosphere, the trees were all covered with heavy lacey moss and the air smelled funny. Pat and I found ourselves surrounded by a strange mysterious wilderness, and we soon realized that we were stranded in the swamp.

"Oh great, now we're stuck in the middle of nowhere," Pat said exasperated. "What next?"

"Hold on, listen for a second," I said. We both stopped to listen and we couldn't hear the sirens any more.

"It looks like we finally lost them," Pat said. "But what do we do now?"

"I don't know what we're going to do, my plan didn't go past escaping the cops. Let's just sit here for a minute and calm down, we'll figure out something."

Pat and I took a deep breath and put our heads back on the headrests. "That sure was a wild ride, wasn't it?" Pat grinned.

"We showed them alright! But now it's time to pay for it."

"Yeah, we're never going to get the car out of this mess," Pat said defeated."

"Oh no!" I exclaimed, "I should have known that something like this would happen! I'm going to have to walk for miles in these tight little, fancy shoes!"

"You're right, you're going to have to, I don't know what else we can do," Pat agreed. "We're going to have to hike out of here."

"Okay, okay, let's get going."

When Pat and I got out of the car, we both sunk down past our ankles in the soft mud. It suctioned to our feet and made each step difficult … slosh, slosh, squish, squish. "Good thing that we have on these high-heeled shoes, the little ankle straps hold them on real good," I said sarcastically.

"Ha, ha," Pat replied and gave me a sour look.

It was a struggle, but eventually we made it to the road without falling. We stopped and looked back at the car. "It's down far enough in the gully that no one can see it from the road. It'll be safe enough, we don't have to cover it with branches or anything," I said, and then we started walking.

"Ouch, ouch, ouch," I complained with each step.

"Why don't you just take off the dang shoes and go barefoot?" Pat asked.

"Are you kidding? On this rocky gravel road? There's broken glass and old rusty cans, I'll be cut up and bleeding next."

"Okay, okay."

Pat and I walked at a snail's pace in the fancy high-heeled shoes. I was hoping and praying that someone, not a cop, would come by and help us, but no such luck. On and on we went, ouch, ouch, ouch.

"Wait a minute, I hear something," I said.

Pat and I stopped to listen and sure enough, we heard a vehicle coming, but we had just turned a bend in the road and couldn't see it. "Maybe it's the cops!" Pat exclaimed. We both jumped behind a tree to hide.

Vroom, the vehicle raced by, it was a truck! Pat and I stumbled back out on the road, jumping and shouting and waving our arms, "Stop! Stop!" But, the truck just kept on going.

Pat put her head on my shoulder, "Great, we blew it and that might have been our only chance." We both stood there numb, it was like being on a deserted island watching a plane fly overhead, unable to see your signal fire.

But wait a minute; the truck had turned around and it was coming back! "Oh thank goodness, I couldn't have walked another mile in these shoes!" I happily stated. But now, I just hoped that our would-be rescuers weren't rapist or murderers.

The old beat-up truck got close and stopped alongside of us. There were three, handsome young men inside, and hanging on a rack in the back of the truck was … an alligator!

The gator was hanging by its neck in a noose with its mouth wide open displaying huge razor-sharp teeth. Pat and I gasped and stepped back.

"Oh, don't let that critter bother you," one of the young men laughed, "he can't hurt nobody no more. And anyways, it looks like you two little gals need a lift."

Pat looked at me questioning, "Are we desperate enough?"

I glanced at the gator, and then at my sore feet and the long road ahead, "It's dead … let's get in."

Two of the guys got out of the truck, "I'm Bobby and this here is my twin brother Billy, and him driving is cousin, Sammy, he's married."

"I'm Penelope," I introduced myself, "and this is my sister Pat."

"Them is right pretty names," Bobby said and then, he helped Pat and me climb into the big truck.

There was only room for four people to sit across the bench seat. "Looks like one of you little gals is gonna hafta sit in my lap," Billy smiled.

"No that's okay," Pat quickly answered and scooted onto my lap.

"Well that's fine with me," Billy said, "but your sister here don't look so comfortable."

"I'm fine," I grunted.

The driver started to move ahead; "Now where are you a-wantin to go?" he asked. With Pat in my lap, I couldn't see a thing.

"We're down the road a couple miles," Pat told him, "our car's stuck in the mud, just around the bend up there."

The driver pulled the truck over to the spot where the Lamborghini had skidded off the road. "Looks like you got yourself buried down real good. Let's see if we can help you on outta there." They seemed like nice guys, maybe they weren't going to try to rape and kill us.

We all got out of the truck, Pat climbed inside the Lamborghini and I started to walk into the mud to help push. "Oh no, you let us men do the dirty work," Bobby told me, "I ain't a-gonna let you git your pretty dress all muddied up."

He walked back to the truck and took off a big metal box, then he set it down on the ground and wiped it off with his shirt sleeve. He turned to me with a smile, "Now, that should make a right nice seat for ya. I don't imagine that your feet are feeling too good, walking all that ways in those fancy shoes."

Bobby had a beautiful smile and his eyes were a bright wild green. His sunlit blonde hair was tangled and windblown and he smelled like the outdoors. He was rugged and strong, but he also had a soft caring side, he had noticed that my feet were red and blistered and was thoughtful enough to help me. I felt comfortable with him, so when Bobby reached for my waist, I let him pick me up. He gently placed me on top of the metal box, "Now you just sit there and relax." He started to walk away, but then stopped and looked back at me. "Why I declare," he said with a grin, "if you don't look just like one of those fancy dolls in the department store window!" I smiled, and Bobby went to help the others push the car.

The strong young men got in front of the Lamborghini and easily pushed it through the mud and up and out of the gully. Pat backed out onto the road; she stopped the car and then got out.

Billy carefully looked the car over, "Now this here's a right fancy car. You were lucky, don't see much damage," he stated. "That ol' guardrail's been rotten for years, it probably just fell apart when you hit it."

Pat and I were happy to find that the damage to the car was minimal, just a few scratches. "I'm glad that the car's okay, but it sure is dirty," Pat commented.

"A little mud don't hurt nothing," Sammy told her, "and those scratches should be easy enough to rub out."

"Yeah, you're right," Pat agreed, "once we get it cleaned up, it'll be just fine. Thanks a lot for your help, but we better get going."

Bobby quickly interrupted, "Now hold on a minute. We hate to see you gals leave with a bad taste in your mouth. We're headed to a party. Why don't you come? It's just down the road, there at the dock, at Aunt Hattie's Place. It's just an old warehouse, but you're sure to have a good time. We're gonna cook up this here gator, he's plenty fresh, just caught him today, the last gator of the season. You ever had gator?"

"Pat looked at me, "I wonder what it tastes like?"

"We can't sneak back to the hotel until the cops stop looking for us anyway," I concluded. "We might as well go to the party. What else are we going to do?"

"Sure," Pat told them, "we'd like that."

The polite young men got back into their truck and waved for us to follow them. It wasn't long before we could hear music playing and smell the aroma of delicious food cooking. "Might be a pretty good party," I anticipated, "and I'm hungry too. I'm looking forward to eating that ugly alligator, maybe it'll make us strong."

When we got to the dock, Pat and I parked away from the other cars; we didn't want some drunk slamming their car door into the Lamborghini.

Our rescuers parked their truck and then walked over to Pat and me to escort us to the party. Bobby opened my car door, and then he picked me up, "You don't need to be walking when I'm around."

The swamp water was gently lapping on the boat ramp and I was surprised to see that it looked clear and clean. I pointed to the water, "Take me over there Bobby, I'd like to rinse off the mud." Bobby put me

147

down and I stepped into the water, it was nice and cool. Pat and the boys followed me in and after we splashed around a bit, we all went inside the warehouse.

The band was playing a fun high-spirited tune; they were making music with the banjo, fiddle and a variety of homemade instruments. Everyone was laughing, dancing and having a terrific time.

After introducing Pat and me to the others, the boys went back to the truck to get the gator. They untied it from the rack and dragged it behind the warehouse where Billy and Bobby's father, Phil, and his friend, Frank, began to butcher it. Bobby and I stayed behind to watch, and Pat went inside the party with Billy and Sammy.

Phil, and his friend, Frank, were fast and skillful at their task and there was nothing that they didn't know about hunting and fishing. "We get all the food we need right here in our own backyard," they told me. The men talked about gator fishing and their life on the swamp, and I found them fascinating.

"I heard that it's pretty dangerous around these parts," I said. "My Uncle Glen was somewhere here in Louisiana, years ago, scouting out a job site near a lake when a gator came after him, right on land. He wrestled the thing and killed it, and then had a gorgeous pair of boots made from the skin. I always admired those gator skin boots."

"Yeah," Bobby said, "you wouldn't think it to look at 'em, but the dang gator will outrun a man every time."

The men talked more of the terrors of the swamp; they told me spine-tingling tales of giant poisonous snakes and other horrid creatures. "The swamp is always treacherous, but far more dangerous at night!" Then they went on to tell me about the scourge of the swamp, a dangerous man-eating alligator that they called the Zombie Gator, a monster well over a hundred years old. It had taken many a life and acquired a taste for human flesh. The beast actually stalked and hunted the people living in the area.

Many men swore that they had killed the gruesome gator, but it still continued to return to the swamp and terrorize. Some even believed that the Zombie Gator was an evil spirit, and that it was impossible to rid the swamp of its satanic power. The dreaded gator mutilated the smaller gators caught on the fishing lines, ruining the skins and causing the fishermen great financial hardship.

"Wow," I said, "I was going to ask if Pat and I could go gator fishing with you sometime, but after hearing these stories, no thank you, I'll pass!"

"It's too late anyway," Bobby told me, "even if you did want to go, the season has already ended. The cold weather caused the gators to go into early hibernation."

"Between the Zombie Gator destroying the gators caught on the lines and this cold weather coming early, it's going to be a lean year for us all," Frank sadly stated.

Just then, I heard some commotion inside the party and realized that I had left Pat alone with strangers. "Let's go inside," I said as I stood up, "I need to see how my sister's doing."

"Yeah, you kids go on inside and have a good time," Phil told us. "But don't drink too much Bobby, you and your brother have to go out frogging tonight. We've got to make money somehow."

"Don't worry Daddy, I won't," Bobby told his father and then we went inside and joined the others.

I found Pat dancing with Billy and enjoying the lively music. I didn't know it, but just minutes before, Pat had had a run in with one of the local girls. As it was later explained to me, a girl named Sandy was jealous that Billy was with Pat and warned Pat to stay away from him. Billy set her straight, and told her loud and clear, right in front of everyone, "Sandy, you ain't got no claim on me!" The girl left the party humiliated, and when I came walking in with Bobby, we didn't notice that anything was wrong.

As for me, my feet still hurt too much to dance and I sat down next to the delightful Aunt Hattie. Aunt Hattie was a knowledgeable fun-loving woman and I had a good time talking and joking with her and her husband. I tasted the unique foods that Aunt Hattie had prepared, and she said that she might even give me one of her special recipes.

I was having a nice time, listening to the music and chatting with my new friends, but it wasn't much fun for Bobby. "Why don't you go and dance," I suggested. "There's no reason for you to sit here and be bored."

After a little coaxing, Bobby went out on the dance floor and both of the twins danced with Pat. Between dances, the three of them snuck out on the deck and secretly drank whiskey from a flask that Billy had hidden under his shirt.

We had been at the party for several hours when Phil, Billy and

Bobby's father, told them that it was time to go out frogging. The boys sweetly said good-bye to Pat and me, we exchanged phone numbers and information, and then they went out on the dock to their boat.

"We better get going too," Pat said, "before Lance has the National Guard out looking for us."

"Yeah you're right, just give me a minute or two, I finally talked Aunt Hattie into giving me her recipe for this Cajun stew."

"Okay Sissy, I'll go out and get the car so you won't have to walk so far." Pat walked across the field to the car by herself. She didn't know it, but Sandy hadn't left the property; she and two of her friends were waiting in ambush.

When Pat walked around the car to the driver's side, Sandy snuck up behind her and grabbed her by the hair. "Your better leave this town, city girl, and never come back! You stay away from Billy!" she warned.

Pat wasn't playing games; this bitch had her by the hair, and it was three against one. She quickly broke free and had Sandy in a choke hold before any of the three aggressors had time to react. Pat reached into her evening bag and pulled out her knife, she pressed it to Sandy's throat, "Is that all you got, swamp bitch, hair pulling? You made a mistake, I ain't no city girl. And what about you?" she directed to Sandy's friends, "you want a piece of me too?"

With that, Sandy's friends quickly abandoned her and ran into the woods. "I should cut your throat," Pat told the swamp bitch, then she forced Sandy to the ground and stepped on her head, pushing her face into the mud, "but, I'm feeling generous tonight." Pat left Sandy lying on the ground crying, and stomped back to the party.

Meanwhile, inside the warehouse, I was having a wonderful time, completely oblivious to the problem that Pat had been dealing with. I was just coming outside to meet her, waving good-bye to Aunt Hattie and my other newfound friends, when I saw that Pat didn't have the car. "Pat where's the car? I thought that you were going to get it."

Pat grabbed my arm. "Forget the car, we're going out frogging with the boys. No swamp bitch is going to tell me what to do!"

"No, I don't want to go out on the swamp!" I said pulling back. "You don't know how dangerous it is out there!"

Pat looked at me indignantly, "We're … going … frogging," she said with her teeth clenched.

150

At that point, it was obvious to me that that there was something going on that I wasn't aware of. "Okay Pat, we'll go frogging, but we better hurry before the boys leave."

Pat and I hurried down the wobbly wooden dock, our spike heels catching between the planks. "Hold up boys! We're going with you!" we called.

"Wow, what a nice surprise," Billy exclaimed as Pat and I climbed into the boat. The boys started the motor and we headed out on the foggy, monster-infested swamp. It was dark and eerie and after hearing the horror stories about the swamp, tales of poisonous snakes and the man-eating, Zombie Alligator, I was plenty shook up. And now I found myself in a small boat at night, the most dangerous time of all!

"I hope that you have a good reason for dragging me out here Pat," I said fearfully, "although I can't think of a one. These local people have been working the swamp for generations and are trained from childhood. We have no business out here. And besides that, you and the boys are drunk!"

Pat then explained to me that a girl named Sandy and two of her friends had jumped her by the car, and warned her to stay away from Billy.

"Blasted Pat, you hothead! You already beat her down, we should have just got in the car and left! Now we're out here on this foggy creepy swamp! You don't know what goes on out here, there's a monster, a Zombie Alligator over a hundred years old, a man-eater!"

Billy spoke up, "It'll be okay Penelope, all the big gators are sound asleep, you don't need to worry about them anymore this season. And let me tell you about our boat; it might be small, but we built it ourselves and it's virtually unsinkable." Billy and Bobby explained how they had designed their boat with some sort of pontoons or something. They were trying to comfort me. "Even if it's completely filled with water, it still won't go down." I wasn't very interested, I just wanted the heck out of there.

The boys could tell that I was still uncomfortable, "We won't stay out for very long, we'll just get a few big bullfrogs to sell to the restaurant and go back in."

Bobby slowed down and then stopped the boat, "This is the place I was telling you about Billy, we're sure to get some big ones here."

We worked our way slowly down the shoreline, Pat and I shined the light while the boys caught one frog after another. These were the biggest frogs that I had ever seen, "I didn't know that frogs could grow this big!" I commented. For a few minutes, I forgot how scared I was and I actually started to relax and have a good time froggin' but then, I saw a snake, "A snake!" I warned.

Billy reached into the reeds, and drunk or not, he was still as fast as lighting. He grabbed the snake by the "neck" and pulled it out. "It's a big one!" he proudly stated as he held it up for us to see.

The snake wiggled and hissed and Pat and I shrieked, "EEEWWWW!"

"Don't worry gals," Bobby said, "it ain't poisonous." Bobby opened a cooler and Billy put the snake inside. "We'll get good money for this big boy!" After that, the twins were catching both frogs and snakes. "Whatever it takes to make money," they said. "And we don't waste nothing here on the swamp, we eat 'em, guts and all."

"EEEEWWWW!"

The four of us continued down the shoreline and the boys caught slimy creatures. "We have to tough it out Sissy," Pat said, "I'm grossed out too, but we invited ourselves along and we can't cost Billy and Bobby money, they're having a good night."

"I know, I know, we'll tough it out," I conceded, "I just hope that those snakes don't get out of the coolers, there's no latches on any of this stuff!"

I sucked it up and helped out, shining the light on the bank just ahead of us. "Hold it right there!" Bobby exclaimed and I held the light steady. "Look Billy, the lines taught!"

"Well I'll be, it looks like we might have hooked us a gator after all."

The boys pulled the boat close to the fishing line, and sure enough, there was a small alligator hooked. Billy cut the line and started to pull the gator to the boat.

"Hold on a minute there brother," Bobby said, "I think that these girls might enjoy a good gator wrestle." Bobby jumped into the water and started thrashing around with the alligator.

"Oh no," I said to Pat alarmed, "I told him about Uncle Glen wrestling that alligator and now Bobby's just drunk enough to try it himself!"

"Whoa! He's a strong one!" Bobby shouted as he thrashed wildly in the water. "He's putting up a good fight!"

Billy dropped the line and jumped in the swamp with his brother. "Get back in the boat!" Pat and I begged. But, the drunk, show-off boys didn't listen and they continued to wrestle and put on the exhibition.

With all of the thrashing and splashing about, the boat began to drift away from the shore. "Come on you guys, get out of there! Yes, we're impressed, you're the two toughest men in the universe!"

I nervously flashed the light around the surrounding area and saw a wake moving through the water. "There's something coming!" I shouted, "Something big!" When it got closer, I could see sinister eyes gliding above the waterline, it was an alligator, and a big one!

Pat and I shouted, "A giant alligator! Billy, Bobby, get out of the water! It's headed right for you!"

The drunk boys finally listened, but it was too late; there wasn't time for them to climb back into the boat. The monster gator was nearly upon them, it opened its powerful jaws and was about to strike. Pat and I screamed in terror! Were we about to see our friends killed?!

The two boys scrambled to shore, narrowly escaping, and the giant alligator snapped, consuming the smaller gator in one vicious bite.

Billy and Bobby quickly climbed a tree, and when the brutal beast had finished its tidbit, it began to swim around and around the boat. Pat and I watched in horror as the menacing prehistoric creature struck against the side, trying to knock us into the water. "It wants to eat us!" I screamed.

Sitting in a tree on the shore, the boys were helpless to do anything to help us. "Start the motor girls! Get out of there! That thing can jump into the boat!"

Pat and I knew nothing about motorboats; the only boats that we knew how to handle were canoes. I kept shinning the light on the gator hoping to blind it, or drive it away, while Pat tried to start the motor. She pulled the cord, the motor turned over and the propeller was spinning. "Now let's get out of here!" I yelled.

It looked like we were about to escape, but the motor began to strain and then it came to a stop. Pat looked at me, and I at her, the motor was dead, but the boat was still moving! Faster and faster it went, in zig-zags and in circles! The fishing line had gotten tangled in the propeller and the gator was hooked on the line! We were on a wild jerky ride being pulled through the swamp by the man-eating Zombie Gator!

The boys shouted from the tree, "Get the rifle! You have to kill it!"

"Find the rifle! I have to find the rifle! Pat shine the light and I'll find the rifle!"

At that moment, the bloodthirsty gator swam under the boat, it slammed up into it and the boat started to tip over sideways. The buckets, coolers and gear slid down to the low side. Pat and I lunged to the opposite side trying to balance the boat.

The gator whipped around, it's tail flipped and curled into the boat, striking the buckets and coolers, knocking them over. The frogs and snakes were loose, wiggling, hopping and squirming around inside the boat. The gator kept slamming into us and jerking us around on the line. It was a battle just to stay onboard, but somehow Pat made it to the front of the boat and was doing her best to shine the light for me. It wasn't doing much good; I could barely see while I dug wildly through the disheveled gear, groping and grasping at everything that I could get a hold of. The rifle was our only hope! I thought that I saw the long narrow barrel and reached and picked it up, "AHHH!" It was a snake! The thing bit me and I threw it down and kept searching, there was no time for a reaction. Then I saw something else, long and black that looked like the barrel of a rifle, "I hope it's not another snake," I said to myself. As I reached for it, the gigantic Zombie Gator jumped up high out of the water, its head thrashed from side to side, the water drenched me and the boat rocked and bounced from the waves. I grabbed hold of the small plank seat near the front of the boat with one hand and what I hoped was the rifle with the other.

The enormous alligator lunged forward and slammed down hard, landing on the back of the boat, the tremendous weight driving it deep under the water. The gator was hungry for human flesh, it climbed further onboard and everything was flying to the back, toward the huge fierce jaws. The gator's mouth was full of buckets, snakes and frogs. The angry monster snapped, crushing and tearing through everything in its path.

The boat was leaning, nearly straight up and down. Pat was almost dangling, holding onto a hook at the front and I was clinging tightly to the small bench seat, just under her. At that moment, I realized that I actually did have the rifle in my hand. "I've got the rifle!" I screamed to Pat.

I remembered what Phil had told me earlier that night, and I knew that I couldn't just shoot willy-nilly; I had to hit the gator in just the right spot. Phil had shown me that spot on the gator that he was skinning at the party, it was just behind the skull, a break in the armor, about the size of a quarter. Phil told me that if you didn't hit the spot square on, all you'll do is piss the gator off.

I was clinging to the plank seat with the gator climbing toward me, throwing its huge head from side to side and snapping its fierce jaws. The boat was swaying, rocking, and bouncing up and down; how was I ever going to get the shot, and with only one hand?

The raging alligator was getting closer; his clawed feet were slipping on the wet metal bottom of the boat. It slowed him down a bit, but if I didn't stop him, he would kill me within seconds.

Suddenly, I felt Pat reach for me; she slipped her arm down the plunging back of my dress, bent her arm and hooked it at her elbow, pulling the dress up under my armpits. Then with all her might, she heaved me up toward her.

I stood on the edge of the plank seat in the fancy little shoes; the narrow high heels hooked firmly on and held me fast. For the first time all night, I was happy that I had worn them!

Pat held me tightly by the back of the dress and both of my hands were free. "I've got ya Sissy, take the shot!" she said with confidence.

The gator was so close that I could smell its nasty breath. I knew that I had only one chance to kill it, if I missed, Pat and I would be torn to pieces. I raised the rifle to my shoulder and took careful aim. The boat was bobbing and jerking under me and the gator was thrashing about. I waited for just the right second and when the monster threw his head down … I squeezed the trigger … BANG!! There was a silence ……. and then the gator collapsed and slid back into the water.

The front of the boat dropped down and Pat and I sat quietly together on the little seat, hugging each other.

By this time, the twins had climbed out of the tree and run down the bank. They were on the shore across from the boat, their voices wailing in despair, expecting that Pat and I had been brutally killed.

Pat stood up and jokingly shouted to them, "Hey scardy-cats, running out on us when the going got tough."

Both of the twins shouted for joy, they jumped into the water and swam quickly to the boat. They climbed inside and threw their arms around us, hugging us so tightly that Pat and I could hardly breathe. "Come on now boys," Pat grunted, "we didn't survive the Zombie Gator just to have you suffocate us with crushing hugs." They quickly released us and we all laughed in glorious relief.

"What'd he do, break the line and run off?" the boys asked.

"No, my sister shot him, shot him dead," Pat proudly announced.

"No kidding Penelope! You're damn good, that's a hard shot to make!" Bobby praised.

"I just got lucky I guess."

"Enough with the blabbing!" Pat scolded. "Let's get the dang thing in the boat and get the heck out of here!"

It took all four of us to heave the heavy gator into the boat, and when we finally had it onboard a good part of the massive beast was hanging over the back. The gator was much bigger than the boat was!

The engine had burned up so we had to sit on top of the gator and paddle in. We slowly moved along and it seemed to take forever, but soon enough we could hear music playing from the party. "That's great, the party's still going on," the boys happily stated, "we'll have plenty of help with this thing."

There were two old men sitting on the dock, and when they saw us paddling in, sitting on top of the enormous alligator, they both jumped to their feet and ran inside shouting for everyone to come and see. Everyone at the party came rushing out on the dock and when Phil and Frank saw us, they dove into the water and swam out to help. Everyone was in a state of wild elation, bringing in the legendary Zombie Gator!

The excited men pulled the boat to shore and carried Pat and me to dry land. I was so relieved that I wanted to get on my knees and kiss the ground, but decided not to embarrass myself.

The townspeople assumed, of course, that the boys were the ones who had bagged the ferocious beast and were shocked when they found that the girls in the fancy dresses had made the kill. The townsmen picked us up and put us on their shoulders, they carried Pat and me around shouting and hooting and hollering. They said that we had been sent from the heavens. We had killed the wicked beast and broken the curse. "Now there will be plenty for us all!"

The battle was over and I wanted to leave, but the boys insisted that we have our picture taken with the Zombie Gator. Pat and I posed for a snapshot with the ugly thing, then said our good-byes and left.

We climbed in the car and headed down the road; now it was on to our next problem, the police. We took the back roads to avoid them and I don't know how we did it, but we actually found our way back to town and saw a sign directing us to the hotel. It looked like we were going to make it without getting caught.

"We really should clean this car before Lance sees it," Pat said, "but I'm just too worn out."

"Maybe we'll get lucky and he'll already be in bed," I said hopefully.

But no such luck. When we pulled up to the hotel ... there was Lance, standing outside, right at the front entrance looking for us. "Oh no," I said in dismay, as we stopped in the mud encrusted Lamborghini.

When Lance saw us, he put both of his hands on his face in disbelief. "What in the world happened?" he asked. Pat and I didn't say anything and got out of the car. "And look at the two of you! Your hair! Your dresses! You're wet and just as dirty as the car! And what's that horrible smell? I can't leave you alone for a minute! You know what, I changed my mind, I don't even want to know what happened!" Lance turned and went back into the hotel.

"Oh Pat, I feel so bad."

"Don't worry about it Sissy, he'll get over it in a few days, he always does."

With that, Pat and I went to our room and got cleaned up. We put disinfectant on my snake bite; it didn't look too bad. "I guess the boys were right," Pat said, "it wasn't poisonous, or you'd be dead by now."

We climbed into bed and it felt good to slip under the soft clean sheets. "Pat, why do you suppose that things like this always happen to us?" I asked.

"Oh I don't know," she said in reply as we both drifted off to sleep, "just be thankful that the boat really was unsinkable."

As it turned out, Lance seemed to be over the whole thing by the next day. After he finished work, he took us both out to dinner and didn't give us any trouble, as we had expected he would. "This is weird, even for him," Pat discreetly whispered to me. "Something's up, it should have taken him at least a week to recover from this one."

Lance was holding a newspaper and after the waitress brought our drinks, he opened it and showed us the front page. There was the picture of Pat and me with the Zombie Gator and the headline read, BEAUTIES KILL THE BEAST!

"I blame myself for this," Lance said. "It's my own fault, turning you two loose in Louisiana. I should have known that somehow, someway, you would end up tangling with an alligator!"

When Pat and I returned home, there were two pairs of gorgeous gator skin boots waiting for us there, with a lovely note from the townspeople thanking us for breaking the "zombie curse." I had finally gotten my childhood wish for gator skin boots, and I can honestly can say, that I had earned them.

PANIC STRIKES

As far as Windsor was concerned, he was happy to see me, and I was pleased to find that the house wasn't a pig mess, as I had expected it would be. He wasn't drunk, and I decided to avoid the stress of breaking up with him until another time. Things were bearable between us, at least for the moment.

Now that I was home, I was worried and hoping that there wouldn't be repercussions because of what had happened to Larry. It was strange; there were never any questions asked and no one ever came looking for him. It was as though the world had breathed a sigh of relief that he was gone. I know I had.

After taking the week off from work, I was a little behind, and I started early the next morning finishing up some paperwork that I had put off. I had to complete it and then go out on assignment, and I didn't have much time. When I finished, I jumped in my truck and started hurriedly on my way.

When I got to the freeway onramp, I hit the accelerator and was quickly picking up speed. The onramp was long, and on a steep incline cut into the side of a hill, with the freeway above. It was a blind hill and I couldn't see over. Just as I was nearing the top, I heard a loud bang from the freeway … an accident!

Right before my eyes, a boat came flying through the air, right in front of me. A boat, I couldn't believe it! "It must have flown off of a trailer!"

I slammed on the brakes and swerved trying to avoid it. I thought that I might be able to steer clear, but when I looked ahead, I screamed in terror … a big-rig was barreling down the on-ramp in the wrong direction and headed straight for me! There was no way to safely escape, no matter what I did I was going to get hit. Thinking that it was my best chance for survival, I attempted to go up the side of the hill. I was hit hard by the boat and it started my truck flipping, end over end. I was violently tumbled upside down and right side up, my head was slamming into the steering wheel and roof of the truck. My body was thrashed and tossed about while I desperately clutched the steering wheel trying to keep my hands and arms inside the cab. I knew that if my arm flew outside the broken window it would be ripped from my body or crushed. I held onto that steering wheel with all my might as my truck continued to flip over and over again.

When I finally came to a stop I was balancing on top of the guardrail, the truck teetering forward and back between the steep rock cliff and the road. My face was bloody, but even so I could still see the steep treacherous grade plummeting before me through the broken windshield. I trembled as the truck teetered between safety and certain death, what was it going to be? I was afraid to move or even breathe.

Suddenly from out of nowhere ... BOOM! Another vehicle struck me just as I was teetering toward the road, it spun me around circles, but at least I was on the ground and right side up. I don't know how I ended up where I did, but when I got my bearings I found that I was in my truck, under the trailer of a big rig, between the huge front and back wheels. I looked to my right and saw the rear tires of the massive truck moving toward me. There was no time to escape; this was it, I was about to be crushed. It seemed as though everything was moving in slow motion. The gigantic tires were rolling toward me, but when they hit against the side of my truck, they stopped and bounced backward and then forward again, I had been given the gift of an extra moment. I had to get out of there! The trailer might still roll ahead over the top of me. My truck was sideways on an incline and when I opened the door, I fell out, my legs collapsed under me, and I found that I couldn't stand. A strong odor shocked my senses and noticed that I was lying in a pool of gasoline. I looked around and saw gas streaming from the enormous tanks on the trailer of the big rig; I had to get out of there, and fast! The vast accident wasn't over yet, I could hear tires screeching and metal crunching as rampant vehicles crashed into one another nearby. I had no choice; I had to take the risk of being hit and crawl across the road. The gas could ignite at any second and I was drenched in it.

I was hurt and knew that I couldn't make it very far, but I did the best I could to drag by battered body. I was nearly run over by a pickup, but I made it across the hazardous glass-covered road and pulled myself up and over the concrete barricade. There was a small ledge on the cliff side of the barricade, just wide enough for me to lay on and I tried to stay there in an attempt to protect myself from the impending explosion. Unfortunately, I couldn't keep my balance and I fell from the ledge and helplessly began to roll down the cliff. I hit a clump of bushes that stopped my fall and I rolled underneath them. I laid there, I couldn't move anymore, and I didn't feel any pain. All was still, and then I heard the explosions when the big-rig blew, one … two … three … the sky lit bright, I could see the towering flames of the raging fire! Then I heard sirens; the fire department was on the way. I laid back and closed my eyes, soon they would come for me. I wasn't sure what was real or what was a dream as I drifted in and out of consciousness. I could hear the sirens and the police radios, people were talking and moving about, but it seemed far, far away in another world.

Suddenly, I woke up heaving and screaming in pain. It was dark! Was I dead? No, I was still on the side of the cliff, I had laid there unconscious all day! No one had come for me! Where were they? I listened closely, but all I could hear were the cars moving by on the freeway. No one had found me!

I was in agony, there wasn't a spot on me that didn't hurt, but somehow I had to get help. I looked up at the steep barren grade that led to the freeway and realized that I would have to climb it!

I had one good leg and most of the movement in my right hand and arm. Carefully and slowly, I inched my way up the dark fearsome precipice, clutching to every tiny ridge and crevice. I fought the pain, and finally made it to the top. But that wasn't the end of the battle, I couldn't just throw myself over the barricade and into the road, I still had to find someone to help me. I propped myself up on the barricade in hope that someone would stop for me and take me to the hospital.

A car was coming and the headlights were on me, I tried to wave, but couldn't move much. No result, they didn't stop. Over and over again, I tried to get someone's attention, to no avail. "No one is ever going to stop for me, I'm a dirty mess!" I cried in despair. I looked like a homeless crazy drunk and on top of that, there was no shoulder on the side of the road, no place for someone to safely to pull over.

Then, I dreadfully realized that no one would even know that I was missing until the next day. Ray wasn't expecting my verbal report until morning and Windsor didn't know when to expect me home.

The pain was unbearable and I could feel myself fading. Would I get help, or would I die on the side of a lonely dark road? Another car was coming, I had to keep trying, I couldn't give up! Suddenly, I realized that I was going about this all wrong, instead of waving I decided to try another approach. When I saw a car coming, I propped myself up and stuck out my thumb. It was a police car, and when they saw me they turned on the flashing lights. The police pulled over and the officers got out and approached me. Thank goodness, I was saved!

But wait a minute; these guys looked like they were ready for trouble and one of the officers pulled out his handcuffs! Oh no, was he going to arrest me?! "No hitchhiking!" one of the officers shouted at me. "We're fed up with you homeless wandering out on the freeway, drunk. After the accident today, we have orders to take you all in!"

"Just when you think you've got it cleaned up, another one shows up," his partner commented. They were disgusted.

I tried to explain, "I was in the accident today and they left me here."

The officers didn't hear me, "Turn around and put your hands on your head," they shouted from a distance.

"I can't!" I cried.

And before I could get in another word ...."Okay, you want to go the hard way?"

"No! No! I don't want to go the hard way! I was in the accident today, I'm hurt!"

The two men took a closer look at me and when they saw my twisted leg and the blood, their attitude changed completely. "Don't worry miss, we'll get you out of here, right away. Bud, call an ambulance!"

Before I knew it, I was at the hospital. My neck, back and shoulder were wrenched, my leg was broken and my wrist and arm were sprained. I had to have stitches in my face and I had other scrapes and bruises as well. I was a mess!

I called Pat and told her what had happened. I asked her to let Windsor know and they both came rushing to the hospital to see me.

Windsor walked into the room, and he bent down and kissed me, "Are you in a much pain?" he asked.

Pat was freaking out, she threw herself over me and began to cry. She was a strong kid, but seeing me in this condition was too much for her, and she was falling apart.

"I'm okay Pat, I'm fine really, don't worry," I tried to reassure her. "Don't pay attention to what those doctors say, they just like to make a big deal out of everything."

"Really, you're okay?" Pat said, as I dried her tears. "You don't feel that bad? You sure look terrible."

"Gee thanks kid, but I'm fine, in a couple of days I'll be challenging you to a wrestling match."

I didn't want to stay in the hospital, I wanted to go home, but the doctor insisted that I stay for at least two more days for observation. Guess that my insides had taken a beating and he wouldn't release me until he was sure that I didn't start bleeding internally.

The next day, Pat came and sat with me. "Don't worry about your truck," she told me, "there's going to be enough money from the insurance for Lance to set you up in a nice little car. It's not the best looking thing in the world, but it runs good and it'll get you by until you get back to work."

"Thank Lance for me," I said, "that was real nice of him. But I'm sure gonna miss that old truck of mine, it wasn't worth much, but it never let me down. I would have kept it for the rest of my life."

When two days had passed, the doctor agreed to let me go home as long as I wasn't left alone. Windsor came to get me, he carefully drove me home and then carried me up the steps and gently put me into bed. As I lay there, I hoped that the doctors really were exaggerating, but I found that they had been right, the next day I couldn't move, and I wished that I had stayed in the hospital. I never liked to take pills, but I had to, the pain was unbearable.

It was rough going the first two weeks, I was unable to raise my arms or to move off of the bed by myself. Windsor had to bathe and dress me. Every time that I had to go to the bathroom, he helped me up and walked me in, never complaining, even when I woke him in the middle of the night. He did all of the cooking, and waited on me hand and foot. I was completely dependent on him and he didn't let me down.

Windsor drove me to physical therapy and iced my neck and back. He massaged me every day from head to toe and worked out the pain and tension. Windsor was loving and kind; he had redeemed himself and I was happy that I hadn't gotten rid of him.

The doctor told me that it would be at least four months before I would recover enough to return to work. I was upset about it, but still tried to look on the bright side; I was going to get better. I wasn't crippled and most importantly, I was alive!

Even though I was looking on the bright side, it was still a disaster and with all of my expenses this was more of a financial storm than I could weather. Things were going downhill fast, but I wasn't worried, now that I could get around the house by myself, I expected that Windsor would find a job and start working. It would be alright, Windsor was a changed man!

The fact was, I couldn't have been more wrong. I had given Windsor much more credit than he deserved. He had no intention of working, he refused to get a job and there was nothing that I could say or do to change his mind. He acted as though he didn't care what happened to us. All he did was say, "You'll think of something, you always do."

I could have conjured up an excuse for him, if I cared to … this last episode with his enemies at Lance's yard; it was too much for him to handle, and he was afraid to go out. No, not this time, no more excuses. I was sick of making up excuses for Windsor, and sick of making up excuses for myself for putting up with him. I didn't want to believe it, and it was hard to face, but it looked as though Windsor had only been taking care of me because I was his "meal ticket." I came to the conclusion that he was merely trying to get me on my feet as soon as possible so that I could return to work and continue supporting him. I hated to think such a thing, but I truly believed that that had been his true reason, not that he cared for me.

Everything was up to me; I had to find a way to make it with no help from Windsor. I prayed that I would be able to return to work soon enough to avoid the pending financial catastrophe, but what I had hoped for didn't come to pass, and I didn't make it in time. With no income it wasn't long before the money ran out and cruel reality set in. I had to face it, there was absolutely no way that I could afford my horses. I didn't know how long it would be before I could even brush them and care for them properly. The doctor warned me against getting bumped or jolted, and with horses that's the way it is. They're big strong animals and I got bumped and jolted every time I handled them. I was forced to do something that I never thought I would ever do, but I had no choice; I had to give them up.

Fortunately, Byron had always wanted the horses for himself and he offered to buy all three of them. I wasn't able to bring myself to sell, so the two of us made a deal. I gave him the horses outright with the stipulation I could come and see them whenever I wanted to, and after I got back to work he would give them back to me. We shook hands on it and I lovingly patted Byron's horses, good-bye. "I'll get them back someday soon," I promised myself. The horses would be able to stay together, and I had peace in knowing that they would receive the best of care, until I got back on my feet.

We were deep into winter, it was cold outside and too expensive to heat the big house. Windsor and I moved into one room and burned wood in the fireplace for warmth. I couldn't hang on to the house any longer either. I would have to move into something more affordable and cut down my expenses before I was completely out of money, so I began looking for apartments.

I was disappointed to find that all of the housing in the safer better areas was too expensive for me. I didn't have enough cash left to make the high deposit and move-in costs. I had to lower my standards and eventually found an old rundown house, in the bad part of town with two make-shift apartments in the basement. I applied for the upper level, a two bedroom with the garage.

The landlord really wanted me, so he offered to put plywood on the rafters in the attic, to give me extra storage and to fix the old floor furnace and broken chimney. He agreed to reduce the rent until the work was completed, because I had to heat with an electric heater until then. I agreed, and by the time I moved in, the work was already in progress. It was difficult to leave my beautiful castle behind, but as hard as it was, it was still a relief to get out from under the expense of it.

Even though I had cut expenses as much as I possibly could, it didn't take long before my bank account was empty and there was barely any food in the refrigerator. But strangely enough, Windsor always managed to buy his alcohol. I thought that he must have been getting money from his mother, but who knows what he had really been doing.

Windsor was losing the battle and allowing himself to fall into an alcoholic trance. He was bent on self-destruction and was dragging me right down with him. Windsor wasn't concerned about anything but his next drink and I had lost all respect for him. Our relationship had died a slow agonizing death and I wanted him out of my life, but I had more pressing problems to deal with first ... survival.

I was injured and desperate, it was the end of the line and something had to give. I couldn't call on my family for help; they didn't understand weakness and beside that, I was living in sin and my bad fortune would merely be seen as God's judgment.

I had to find a way out by myself, so I made phone call after phone call to everyone that I could think of looking for some kind of work that I could do in my condition, and I got lucky. A friend from the old interior design shop referred me to a clothing designer and I got an opportunity to design some characters for a children's clothing line. I only had a short time to do three months of work. The designer was under the gun, she was unusually overloaded and had a deadline to meet. It was only a one shot deal for me, but the money would be enough to get me through until I could return to my job.

I began drawing, and hoped that my creativity wouldn't fail me. It was great; I could still draw even while lying down, and that's exactly what I did when the pain got too bad and I could no longer sit up. I worked every day and late into the night, while Windsor sat on the sofa drinking and watching television. He wouldn't even make me a sandwich.

Soon, it was down to the wire and the next day was the deadline. I had to deliver my work to the designer's warehouse for approval. If I didn't have the right images or if payment was delayed for further development, I was screwed.

My leg was out of the cast, but I was still in the collar for my neck and shoulder, so I asked Windsor to drive me, and he agreed. The warehouse was located in a dangerous area, of a big city, but he knew exactly where it was, so I didn't bother to get directions.

I worked until three a.m. and managed to complete all of the drawings. I laid down and rested for a couple of hours and was up again at five getting ready to leave. My neck and back were killing me, but I couldn't take any pain medication; I had the appointment with the designer and I needed my wits about me. I prayed that it would all work out somehow.

The pressure was on, and guess what? Windsor wouldn't get out of bed. "You do realize, that if I don't make this deal, we'll be out in the street!" I screamed at him.

"So we get there a little late, it's no big deal," he grumped, and rolled over.

"Quit being ridiculous and lazy and get up!" I couldn't believe that he was doing this! I was so frustrated that I picked up a cookie from the table and threw it at him. It hit the wall and turned to dust.

What a fit Windsor threw over that cookie, you would have thought that I had thrown a knife at him. Now he had a "real excuse" not to go with me. After all, who would want to ride in the same car with a "mad cookie assassin?"

What a wretched mess, what a waste. What was I doing with this lowlife?

It was getting late and I had to leave; I couldn't miss this appointment; everything was riding on it. I pulled myself together, got in the car and started driving in the general direction of the warehouse. I planned to call the designer for directions when I got closer, and her office would be open.

With all the time that I had spent trying to get Windsor up, I was running late already. It was difficult to drive as I couldn't turn my head in the collar; I had to turn my whole upper body to look for traffic, so I took it off.

It was a long drive to the designer's office, the freeway was huge and traffic, heavy. I was trying to find my way in a strange and dangerous city. I was in horrible pain and I felt desperate. I was going eighty miles an hour in the fastest lane, frantically trying to get there on time, when suddenly, I couldn't breathe. Sounds became tinny, my eyesight narrowed to tunnel vision; I was dizzy and felt like I was losing consciousness. I had to get off of the freeway, but my vision was so bad that I couldn't see the other cars. All I knew was that I had to go to the right. I said a short and earnest prayer, "God please help me!" And I turned across all the lanes of fast-moving traffic. Somehow I made it to the exit and no one was hurt, thank God!

When I got off the freeway I stopped the car, I still couldn't hear or see clearly and couldn't catch a breath. I had a sharp pain in my chest, my heart was racing, and I was sweaty and shaking. I was sure that I was dying and that I needed an ambulance, but I couldn't even gesture to a passerby for help. I don't know how long I actually sat there before I could breathe, see, and hear, but it finally did ease up a bit.

My vision cleared enough for me to make out a nearby payphone and I wanted to call an ambulance. I got out of the car and started slowly walking toward the phone. I was shaking from head to toe and ringing wet with sweat. As I got closer to the phone, I thought about how much the medical care would cost; the ambulance ride, the emergency room visit, testing. It would bury me even deeper than I already was. I realized that if I missed this appointment, I might as well be dead. I decided that if I died, I would go down fighting with my boots on and I pulled out the designer's number and called it instead. "I'm lost, how do I get to the warehouse?" I asked. She told me that I was very close and sent someone out to lead me there.

I don't know how I ever pulled it off, but I made the deal and got paid. Lucky for me, people expect artists to be a little temperamental and it may have worked in my favor.

I left the designer's office and got back in the car to head for home when, BAM! I was hit hard, like a ton of bricks; dizziness, shortness of breath, shaking, I was completely immobilized and I sat there frozen, not knowing what to do. Was this it, was I going to die this time? I put my head on the steering wheel and waited. What was going to happen to me? Then, just like before, the symptoms started to ease up a little, just enough for me to get back into the designer's office and call Windsor.

Luckily, Windsor answered the phone and I quickly told him, "I made the deal, I'm sick and can't drive home. Call Lance, he'll bring you here and you can drive me back home." He argued with me a little, but then agreed to come for me, probably because he knew that I had been paid.

A few hours later, Lance dropped Windsor off. He was a little drunk, but even so, it was still safer for him to do the driving than it was for me to. I was happy to see him and even happier to get home.

When we pulled into the driveway Windsor got out and walked around the car to open the door for me. "See baby," he said, "I told you that everything would be okay. I knew that you would pull us through, you always think of something." What could I say to that comment?

I shakily walked into the house, put on my pajamas and climbed into bed. Things had worked out alright, I had enough money to make it through and I didn't die.

The next day, I had an appointment with the doctor; he examined me and deduced that the incident on the freeway was due to muscle spasms from my injuries causing my rib cage to cramp and lock up. This made breathing difficult and brought on the other symptoms that he believed were caused by lack of oxygen. He expected me to be fine.

It was good news, but the fact was, I wasn't fine, I was still having attacks every day and night. Was I dying or going crazy? I wasn't sure which.

I no longer had the calming force of my horses, it was just too painful for me to see them. They were attached to Byron and his family now, and instead of it being a peaceful experience for me to visit them, I always left the ranch in tears and finally couldn't bring myself to return. The way that things were going, I knew that I would never be able to afford to get them back.

I had wondered how I would cope without the peace and calm of my horses, and now I knew that I couldn't.

During the attacks, I held tightly to the hope that when my back and neck were healed and I was able to return to work, I would be okay. I was patient, and that day finally came. I was still having attacks, but my injuries had improved enough that I thought I could make it through work. I called Ray and he had a job for me.

I happily got dressed, climbed in the car and began to drive to my assignment. When I reached the freeway onramp, BAM! Shortness of breath, racing heart, dizzy. My God, I couldn't drive on the freeway!

I got off at the next exit, pulled myself together and then got back on. I kept trying, over and over again, but it was no use. No matter what I did, I had an attack every time. I finally had to give up and turn back. Now I couldn't do my job, and I couldn't depend on Windsor. What would become of me?

I had to get help; something was seriously wrong and I couldn't handle it by myself. I called the doctor again and he was kind enough to see me right away. He did a more complete exam and diagnosed me as having panic disorder. It sounded terrible, but now at least I knew what I was dealing with. The doctor told me that panic disorder can be brought on by a traumatic experience and / or stress. My God, I had been practicing for this disorder my whole life!

Now I knew what I had to do; get rid of the stress, get rid of the panic.

It all sounded so simple, but it wasn't. Panic Disorder was a kind of enemy that I had never faced before, an enemy attacking me from within. It was as though my own body had turned against me; my own body was fighting me and taking me down.

In the past, I had never had much patience or understanding for people with emotional or mental problems. I thought that they were weak and chose not to control themselves. Now it was happening to me and I found that I had been very wrong. I couldn't control these panic attacks any more than I could control the sun rising in the morning. I was helpless before this enemy; it was a terrible dark feeling.

I continued to struggle with the debilitating attacks; I couldn't breathe, my chest was tight, my heart racing and the dizziness brought me to my knees every time. There was no way that I could even fake my way through one. If anyone were around me when an attack hit, they knew that something was terribly wrong and sometimes tried to call an ambulance. What had I become? A pathetic weakling, just a shadow of the warrior of the past.

The longer that I couldn't work, the more stress I had. The more stress I had, the more frequent and severe the attacks. It was a vicious cycle and I had to find a way out.

Fact was, the investigative work I did was stressful. There was no question about it, my life had been in danger on many of my assignments. Maybe this was a stress that I had to eliminate. I would try to find a different kind of a job, one where I didn't have tremendous responsibility and pressure.

Then there was Windsor, this was another stress that I had to eliminate. I told him to get a job and pull his weight or get out, and I meant it.

It wasn't long before I managed to find an opening at a fine jewelry store as a salesperson. The pay was next to nothing, but I could get there by taking the side roads and avoid the freeways altogether. I was happy to have the job and hoped that I could somehow handle it. But then, I had an awful thought, what would happen if I had an attack at work, right in front of everyone? I started to have a panic attack about having a panic attack, I couldn't believe it! I felt my throat and chest tighten and my heart began to race, it was horrifying! I waited it out, and when I calmed down I thought it through. I just had to be prepared, I needed to have a plan.

Everyone understood what back pain was; I would say that I had occasional back spasms because of the car accident. That way, if I had a panic attack, I would go to the backroom until it ended and my co-workers would think that I was merely in pain. It went against my grain to lie, but I had to lie, I couldn't tell anyone what was really happening to me. I was embarrassed and afraid that people would think that I were insane. I didn't understand what was happening to me myself, how could I expect someone else to?

My panic attacks were still severe when I started working at the jewelry store. I had to leave for work an hour early every morning because I panicked all the way there. I turned on my flashers and pulled over several times when it got too much for me to handle, and then every night, I panicked all the way home. But at least I wasn't on the freeway and I had enough warning to safely pull over. Surprisingly enough, I didn't have attacks while I was at work; it was just the problem of getting to and from work.

After I had been on the job for several weeks, I found out that there was an opening for the Head of Security at the shopping center. Windsor was well qualified and the hours would be perfect for him, so I immediately called and told him about it. Windsor went to the interview and actually got hired.

After he started working, Windsor began to feel better. He was sleeping more soundly at night and his drinking was getting under control. He was never drunk when he went to work, the general manager really liked him, and he was doing a good job. Windsor was on track and things were finally looking up; maybe we were going to work out after all; I was optimistic.

We were expecting Windsor's first paycheck when I figured out our monthly bills. Money would still be tight, but we were going to make it! My optimism soon turned to disgust when I found that Windsor planned to keep all of the money for himself! He actually expected me to continue supporting him and he was making more money than I was! At first I thought that he must have been joking, but I soon realized that he was serious. When he saw how angry I was, he gave me some money, but after that, I was finished with him. I didn't toss Windsor out immediately; I didn't want to be cruel, but it was just a matter of time before I would find a way to get rid of him.

It was about two months later that I came home from work and found the house pitch black. It felt creepy; Windsor always got home from work earlier than me, and had the lights on.

I carefully opened the door and quietly listened, I could hear labored breathing, something had happened. I had a 9 mm. hidden by the door, I grabbed it and called out, "Windsor! Windsor!" No answer. I braced myself, I had to be ready for anything, what was the situation that I was walking into? I found the lamp and turned it on, my eyes quickly flashed around the room. There was Windsor, sitting in the middle of the living room floor tightly hugging an UZI, a look of terror on his face. "Pack the car, we're leaving," he whispered to me.

"What in the world is going on?" I asked.

"They found me, one of the guys came in for a job and I had to interview him."

"What guy?"

"One of the guys that's trying to kill me!" Windsor handed me a job application, then got up and went into the bedroom.

I looked at the application name, address and phone number; it was all filled out. "Looks to me like this guy just wants a job."

"All the way out here?!" he quietly screamed.

"Did he threaten you or do anything strange?"

"No, I don't think that he recognized me, but I knew who he was. It doesn't matter, they know where I am now, and we can't stay here anymore." He began throwing his clothes into a paper bag, "Pack the car, we're leaving!"

We hadn't seen hide nor hair of Windsor's enemies ever since Pat and I had run them off. It was clear to me that this whole thing was just a trumped up act because he didn't want to work anymore, but I played along. "Where do you plan to go?" I questioned.

"To my brother's house, in Reno."

"You go on without me, I can take care of myself."

"No something might happen to you, you can't stay here alone!"

I was so fed up with Windsor at that moment, he was lucky that I didn't shoot him myself. "I'll take my chances. It'll be faster if you travel alone," I told him as I pushed him out the door. "Let his brother take care of him now, I've had enough!" I said as I watched Windsor drive away.

Windsor was finally gone and I was happy. I sat down in a comfy chair and took in a deep breath. What a relief, it was over! But even though I had wanted to get rid of him for such a long time, I still felt a loss; I had failed at yet another relationship. "I'm sure I'll get another chance at love and happiness," I comforted myself.

At long last, I was free from the stress and danger that I had suffered because of the men in my life and it was wonderful! And things at work got better too, I was promoted to store manager with a modest increase in pay, and with the promotion, I got to work a lot of extra hours.

Unfortunately, I wasn't free of the panic attacks; I still never had one at work, but at home, every night when I sat in my recliner, I felt creepy and had a serious bout with them. I wished that I could just stay at the jewelry store and never come home, so most nights I ate dinner at work. When I did get home, I usually "freaked out" for a few hours, and then cracked open the bedroom window for fresh air, and climbed into bed.

HOLLYWOOD FANTASY

One evening, Pat and I went to a Chamber of Commerce mixer where we donated to a charity raffle. I couldn't believe it when we won two tickets for a free dinner at the finest restaurant in town. It was perfect timing; we were already dressed up in our nice clothes and very hungry, so we decided to go to dinner as soon as the mixer was over.

The restaurant was located in a highfaluting hotel and it was incredible; shiny marble floors, sparkling chandeliers and a huge pond with elegant white swans swimming in it.

There was a big party going on at the restaurant that night, so Pat and I had to be seated in the bar. We sat down and ordered two, big thick, juicy steaks.

The crowd in the bar consisted mostly of men, who were soberly talking business. The band hadn't started playing yet and it was fairly quiet, so we couldn't help overhear that they were in town filming a major motion picture. Then in walked the movie's big star, (I'll call him by his first name only) Michael, and sat at a table near us. It was exciting, Pat and I had never seen a movie star before, but we left him alone and made a point not to look at him and make him feel uncomfortable.

A little while later, the band started playing a good old rock-n-roll song, Pat's favorite. She jumped to her feet, grabbed an old man and pulled him on the dance floor. He didn't want to dance with her, but there was no saying no to Pat. This old man had skinny little legs and a big fat, round belly with his pants pulled up to his neck. Pat was having a ball, twirling around him and shimmying up and down his legs.

Back then, it was the style to tint your hair an unnatural color and Pat took it all the way, her hair was fire engine red, (literally,) with lipstick to match and a red-hot body. That poor old man, I actually felt sorry for him. Pat and the old man were the only couple on the dance floor, and it was a good thing too, because Pat needed the room to fling her partner around. It was hard not to notice this great entertainment and soon everyone in the place had forgotten all about business and was laughing, cheering and clapping.

During the wild spectacle, one of the guys from the movie crew came up to me and whispered in my ear, "She's going to give that old man a heart attack." I nodded my head in agreement. The man politely introduced himself as Morgan and asked if he could buy me a drink. I accepted and invited him to sit down; he seemed a fine gentleman.

After the song was over, Pat wanted to keep dancing, but the old man couldn't take anymore. She looked around to find another partner, but as it turned out, the old man was the bravest man in the room. Finally, she had to give up and come back to the table. "All these guys are shy," she said.

Morgan laughed, "Not shy miss, terrified, I'm surprised that your dance partner lived to tell about it."

We all had a good laugh, and a few minutes later, a big husky man came swaggering up to the table. He looked at Pat and said, "Haven't we met somewhere before?"

Pat cocked her head and looked at him from the corner of her eye, "Can't you come up with a better line than that?"

"Well," he said, "I saw you staring at me from across the room, undressing me with your eyes. I know you want me, baby."

"Ewww!" Pat squealed, "You're so icky!"

"How 'bout if I have a seat," he grabbed the chair next to Pat.

"No!" she snapped.

"Hey I'm icky," he said and he sat down anyway and ordered us a round of drinks. "Hey waiter, keep 'em coming!" Icky rudely shouted to the waiter across the room.

I never saw a guy enjoy being called Icky before, but this guy loved it, and the four of us had a great time. We talked and joked and laughed so much that my stomach hurt.

We had been at the bar for about an hour, when a young man who had been sitting with Michael, the movie star, got up and came walking to our table. He handed me a little slip of paper and said, "Here's a message from Michael."

I glanced over at Michael and he was getting up from his table to leave. He turned his head, looked at me and gave me a cute little smile.

Pat and I quickly looked at the note, it read, "You can have me, if you want me."

After receiving such a note, I wasn't flattered, as one might have expected, I was disgusted, the whole world knew that Michael was married. "What a cad," I said and showed Morgan and Icky the note. "That man actually thinks that I'm gonna go to his hotel room; he's a married man, shame on him!" I exclaimed in disapproval.

Pat strongly agreed with me, and then we dropped the subject and started having fun again.

The evening flew by, and the four of us stayed until the place closed down and the manager kicked us out. Icky and Morgan, were walking Pat and I, through the hotel to our car when Icky loudly proclaimed that we were the only cool girls in the whole town, and the only ones that they would let hang around with them. Then he asked, "What were two little girls like you doing eating those big steaks? Shouldn't you have been eating salads?"

"That's what cowgirls eat, beef," Pat answered.

"Oh, cowgirls," he said. "You're cowgirls? Have you ever ridden a bucking bronco?"

"Why sure," Pat told him. "First you get your lasso ready."

I looked at Morgan, "Let her borrow your tie." Morgan responded and quickly removed his tie and handed it to Pat.

"Here, let me show you how to tie a lasso, city boy."

Pat tied the knot and lassoed Icky around the neck, then she jumped on his back and yelled, "Okay Icky, let's see how wild of a ride you are!" Icky started running and jumping through the luxurious hotel with Pat riding on his back yelling, "Yee hah!"

"Uh oh, I'm busting out of the corral!" Icky exclaimed. He whipped around and broke through the decorative fence surrounding the swan pond, ran to the middle of it and slipped and fell in the water.

Feathers went flying, the swans scattered, honking and fleeing everywhere in the hotel. Pat got up on her feet laughing, water dripping from her clothes and hair, "You give me a pretty good ride after all, city boy."

"We better get out of here!" I exclaimed, and we all ran out to the parking lot.

We had a lot of fun that night, and no one wanted it to end, so the boys invited us to come on the set for lunch the next day. They were shooting in Cub Valley, an isolated place, but Pat and I knew where it was and promised that we would be there. Morgan told us to wear boots because it was very muddy.

The next morning, when Pat picked me up, it was raining and had been raining hard for weeks. When we got to the old dirt road that led into Cub Valley we found that it was in very bad shape with rain water was rushing across in torrents. "Maybe we should just turn back?" I said discouraged.

"Hell no!" Pat exclaimed, "I want to see them making that movie, and since when are you afraid of a little rain?!"

With Pat prompting, we decided to give it a shot and headed down the hazardous muddy road. It was rough riding, especially in Pat's, Caddy. The rain was pounding so hard on the windshield that it was difficult to see, even with the wipers on as fast as they could go. We kept forging ahead, there were a few times that we got stuck in potholes, but Pat was able to get out by shifting back and forth from drive to reverse and rocking the car.

There wasn't much that grew on the hills surrounding Cub Valley and when we were well up the hill, we heard a rumble and a crash. The saturated ground had broken loose and a mudslide was headed down the hill, right for us! Pat stepped on the gas and the gigantic chunk of mud landed on the road just behind us. Pat stopped the car and we got out to check the situation and found that the road was completely impassible. "We didn't get hit, but there's no turning back; now we have to find those city boys," Pat said. We stood in the rain and looked at each other, and then at the road ahead. It didn't look good, but we got back in the car and pressed on, there was nothing else we could do. When we rounded the next bend in the road, we saw a pipe gate which was swung open to a lane that was paved with decomposed granite; it was weathering the storm fairly well. "It's heading up the hill, this might work out okay; maybe we can get over and into the valley," I said as we slowly drove ahead.

There was a "No Trespassing" sign, but we decided to take it anyway. "Hope the rancher doesn't catch us and start shooting!"

The road went well up the hill, but it didn't go over the top and into the valley as we had hoped it would. When we saw that the road ran back downhill again, we stopped the car. "Pat, I think that this is as close as we're gonna get. If we want to make it into the valley, we're going to have to take a chance and go the rest of the way off road. It's not that far to the top, looks pretty smooth, I think we can make it. What do you say?"

"Yee hah! Let's go for it Sissy! Let's find those city boys!" Pat backed the car up and lined it up toward the top of the hill. We had to get up enough speed to make it over, so Pat hit the gas pedal and the car took off like a shot! We were flying in that Cadillac when we went off the road, banging right over the dips and gully's and we kept right on going, sideways and fishtailing, wheels spinning and slipping, but we couldn't slow down or we'd be stuck.

We were nearly at the top … "Looks like we're going to make it Pat!" I shouted with a smile, when suddenly the wheels grabbed hold. We had hit some solid ground and gotten friction, it jumped us ahead, right over the top of the hill! "Yee hah!" We were flying, then we hit the ground on the other side with a slam-bang, and went sliding sideways down the slippery slope.

With the heavy rain it was hard to see where we were headed, and when we came to a stop, we heard someone yell, "CUT!" Somehow, we had landed right in the middle of the shoot!

Morgan was quickly walking up to the car. "It's okay, they're with me," he shouted to his co-workers, waving his arms. He was laughing and shaking his head, "What are you girls up to now, are you alright?"

"We're fine, how bout you?" I asked him. "You look a bit pale."

"Why don't you back up and park in the lot, on the left," Morgan suggested, and he pointed to a graded leveled area. "We've got to get this mess straightened out."

"Okay, Morgan," we agreed, and Pat started the engine. Pat and I had interfered with the filming and destroyed the set, but when we started to drive away everyone was waving to us, laughing and giving us the thumbs-up. I had expected to get thrown off the property, but instead we were treated like celebrities. The director assigned two young men to carry umbrellas for us, to see that Pat and I didn't get wet.

Later, we found out that the movie company had cut a nice wide road for access to the site and everyone asked us why we didn't just drive in on it. We had to tell our story over and over again that day.

When the shock of our arrival wore off and the set was rebuilt, everyone started back to work. Pat and I walked with Morgan to a field where they were filming a high-speed, motorcycle chase scene. There were two motorcycle riders, we heard the director instruct them to race through the field, jump into the air at the end of a row of trees, and then crash into each other. Each driver was to land in a precise place, facing toward the camera.

It was exciting, the stuntmen started the bikes and began racing wildly through the field. At the end of the trees they jumped the bikes into the air and crashed into each other, landing exactly as the director had told them to. It was amazing to me that anyone could be so precise, crashing in mid-air at high speed. The stuntmen were incredible! They had performed the stunt perfectly, but unfortunately the director didn't like the shot that he got and wanted to use a different lens, so they had to do it all over again.

When the crew left to replace the mangled motorcycles, the director turned to Pat and me, and jokingly asked if we would please do our stunt again for him in the Cadillac.

"No, we're not as nice as your stuntmen, we're more temperamental. If you didn't get the shot right the first time, that's just too bad," I answered laughing.

"You girls are going to go far in this business," he said with a smile.

Pat and I, met everyone on the set that day. They said that we had brought life to a dreary week and invited us to come again. We ended up going back to Cub Valley every day, and during that time, we understood why the crew enjoyed our company so much. We found that the people working on the movie (accept for Icky of course) were very quiet and reserved. Filming was slow-moving and boring most of the time; they needed us to liven up the place, and we surely did. When the movie was completed, Pat and I were invited to the wrap party.

We went to the party and had a great time dancing and drinking champagne. Morgan was leaving the next morning and I didn't expect to ever see him again, but he had different ideas and asked me to come to L.A. for a visit. I of course said no, and just gave him my phone number. "Call me if you're ever back in town."

Morgan didn't waste any time, the very next weekend he made the trip to see me. He checked into a luxurious hotel in a nearby costal city, then surprised me with a phone call. I was excited to hear from Morgan and wanted to go and spend time with him, but because of my panic attacks, I couldn't make the drive to the city on the freeway. I was embarrassed; I didn't want Morgan to know about the attacks, so I told him that I was having car trouble. Morgan quickly solved the problem and sent a car to pick me up.

When I arrived in the big city, the driver took me straight to the marina. Morgan was waiting for me there; he had rented a beautiful yacht with a full crew. We spent the day in luxury, sightseeing and being pampered. The weather was sunny and cool and I couldn't remember when I had ever had such a relaxing wonderful time.

I was sad when the day was drawing to an end and we were heading back to the marina, so I was happy when Morgan suggested that we take a stroll downtown. We held hands and slowly sauntered down the bustling sidewalks looking in the windows of the fashionable shops.

As we approached the corner, I saw a mannequin standing in a store window; it was cloaked in the most gorgeous, red-fox, fur coat that I had ever seen. When we got near, I stopped and admired the lovely fur.

"Let's go inside and have a look," Morgan suggested, and we stepped inside the lavish shop. "Why don't you try it on?" he suggested.

The salesgirl was within earshot; she quickly removed the fur from the mannequin and helped me on with it. When my arms glided through the silk-lined sleeves, it felt as though they belonged there. The coat was a perfect fit, and Morgan thought that it looked incredible with my red hair.

"She'll wear it out," he said as he reached for his wallet and walked to the counter. The girl rang up the sale, $9,000.

I was stunned and I just stood there; I wasn't sure how I should react. I didn't want to seem ungrateful and refuse Morgan's gift, I was concerned that it might insult or embarrass him. Morgan was a highfaluting man and I thought it best to talk to him in private, we could always return the fur later.

When Morgan had finished the transaction and was walking toward me, he had a big smile on his face. I could see that giving me the coat had made him happy. I took his arm and as we moved toward the door, I was nearly breathless; I stroked the luxurious fur covering my body and it felt fabulous.

When we got outside I stopped, "You know Morgan, I can't accept this gift, it's far too expensive."

Morgan looked at me intently, "You really would return it wouldn't you," he responded. "But what do you mean expensive? Why I consider this getting off cheap, you could have wanted the Jaguar over there across the street," he laughed and pointed to a lovely flashy car.

"Oh, you mean I could have had the Jag? Well how 'bout you buy it for me too! But actually, I prefer a Porsche." I laughed and glanced at him, expecting him to smile, but he didn't.

"Penelope I need to tell you something," Morgan said in a serious tone. I tensed up; had I done something wrong? Then he went on, "I hope that you won't think me too bold, but I'm a busy man and I don't have time to play games, I want you to know how I feel, right up front. I've led a rigid structured life, an existence of great responsibility and drudgery. I know that I'm not the most attractive or exciting man in the world. It's not me that women want, they're after stardom or money and whatever else that they can get from me. But Penelope, you're different, you've never asked for anything and it makes me want to give you everything! Since I've met you, I feel alive and I'm actually happy. The time that we've spent together has been the most incredible of my entire life. I've never felt this way about a women before and I'm prepared to do whatever it takes to have you. Please be honest with me, do I have a chance?"

Wow! This guy was wild about me! I stepped back and took a good look at him, he didn't seem drunk or crazy; maybe he was serious. I didn't have any idea what I had done to deserve his admiration, but it was definitely worth checking out. After all, what did I have to lose? "If I say no, do I have to return the coat?" I asked and then started to giggle.

Morgan grinned, "I should have known better than to think that I'd get a straight answer out of you." He gave me a big hug and lifted me off my feet. "I'm hungry," he said, "let's get something to eat. I know a superb seafood restaurant only a block from here."

As we walked arm in arm toward the restaurant, a damp wind started blowing in from the ocean. I pulled my fur coat tighter around my neck and rubbed my cheek on the collar. I was so hopeful and happy that I was almost floating. Was it finally my turn for happiness?

As Morgan had said, the restaurant was superb, the food excellent, and the environment impressive. We fed each other juicy tender steak and buttery lobster and watched the ocean through big picture windows. When the sun set, brilliant pink and lavender ribbons painted the sky. I was having a wonderful time.

After we had finished the delicious meal and stood up, Morgan winced in pain. I was concerned and ran to his aid, "Morgan, what's wrong?" I asked.

Morgan told me that he had a bad back, but that he would be fine. "I should have known better than to pick you up," he said.

Morgan wanted to go into the bar and have a drink. He tipped the piano player and he played all of my favorite tunes, while Morgan and I talked for hours by candlelight at an intimate little table.

I found that Morgan was a difficult man to get to know; he preferred that I do most of the talking. As usual I was never at a loss for words, and he listened intently to everything I said.

Could it be that I had finally met the right man? I wasn't too sure, after what I had been through with Larry and his "bad back," finding out that Morgan had back trouble was a real turn off for me. But, Morgan was an entirely different person he probably had real back pain, not "convenient excuse" back pain, a totally different story. Could I overlook it? I was sure going to try; after all, nobody's perfect.

Morgan could only stay in the city for one day and then had to rush back home. He explained that he would be working on location in the desert for two weeks, filming a science fiction movie and asked if I would please be in L.A. waiting for him when he returned.

It wasn't easy for me to travel, never knowing when I might have a debilitating panic attack. I wanted Morgan to make the trip and come and see me again, but with his schedule it was impossible. It was clear that we would never get the chance to know each other if I didn't go to visit him.

Was I going to let my panic attacks destroy this opportunity? No! I decided that I was going to see Morgan no matter how bad the panic got. I had given up enough and had changed my whole life because of this disorder. I was determined not to let it rule my life anymore, I was going to fight it, and I did!

As it turned out, Morgan and I had started a great relationship. I had a wonderful time on the trip to L.A., and after that we wanted to see each other often. I was able to arrange my work schedule so that I could fly to L.A. every other week, for four days at a time. I fought the panic attacks and it was well worth it, Morgan never disappointed me. He took me out for extravagant dinners and we attended exotic parties hosted by the beautiful people. I went to work with Morgan and watched as my favorite stars worked on their latest films. Morgan lived a fascinating exciting life and he enjoyed sharing it with me.

Always the thoughtful gentleman, Morgan would have dozens of roses waiting for me at the jewelry store when I returned home to the small town. Each time there was a stream of interested acquaintances waiting for me there, all of them anxious to hear about my latest adventure, where I had gone, and who I had met. They wanted to see my new designer clothes and the other expensive gifts that Morgan had bought for me. I enjoyed telling them inside stories about the movie stars and what had happened on the set during filming. I liked getting all the special attention from the people in town; it was nice to be admired.

I had just walked in the door, returning home from one of my trips, and the phone was ringing off the hook. I dropped my bags on the floor and ran to answer it; it was Morgan, "Penelope, sorry to bother you so soon, but I just found out that I'm up for an award. Would you like to go to the show with me?"

Morgan was always very stoic, but I could tell that this truly excited him; I could hear it in his voice. "Of course I want to go." I loved the award shows, all of the incredible glamorous stars gathered in one place; and with Morgan up for an award, this one would be even more special.

"I'll be tied up and won't be able to take you shopping for a gown," Morgan told me. "I'll leave you my credit card. Be ready to go tomorrow, I'll call you back and let you know when your flight leaves."

After returning to L.A., I went shopping and found the most gorgeous gown that I had ever seen. It was made of silk and covered in sparkling sequins and shimmering pearls, with sleeves that were fashioned to look much like an angels wings. It was a flashy gown, but elegant, and I couldn't wait to wear it.

Morgan enjoyed dressing me up, in the past, he had always gone shopping with me and selected my wardrobe, so he knew what to expect. But this time, it would be a complete surprise. It was a special occasion for Morgan and I wanted to look fabulous for him. The hairdresser came to my hotel room and fixed my hair in a glamorous new style, and then helped me with a sexy Hollywood make-up. When we were finished, I slipped into my beautiful new gown and the fine jewelry that I had borrowed from the jewelry store, where I worked. Diamonds and rubies befitting a queen; they were the most expensive items in the store and I was thankful to Al, the owner, for letting me borrow them. When I was ready, there wasn't a part of me that didn't sparkle.

I stepped into the room, and when Morgan saw me he was breathless, "I'm afraid to even touch you," he said. "Please stand in the light and let me enjoy just looking at you."

"Come on, let's go, quit being so dramatic," I said. Morgan giggled, and then I grabbed his hand and we were on our way.

Being at the award show was magical. Everyone was looking their best; I had never seen so many diamonds and fabulous attire. I thoroughly enjoyed myself, chatting and flirting with the stars during commercial breaks.

When Morgan's category came up, we were disappointed; he didn't win that year. "It's just politics anyway," he told me. "But, as they say, 'It's an honor just to be nominated.'"

The show went on, and as exciting and fun as it was to be there, it was very long, and I was glad when it was finally over and it was time to go on to the party.

The doors of the big building opened, and the guests began to slowly walk out, leaving ample room between each couple as they exited and faced the cameras and the frantic fans. I could hear the screams rise to a high pitch and then die down as stars exited the building and then disappeared from sight.

When I got close enough to peek outside, I could see that the police had a barricade up. The wild crowd was pushing against it and waving signs and banners.

The couple ahead of us starred in a popular sitcom. When I watched them walk out, they acted as though they would have liked to climb into a hole. They quickly went down the steps and turned the corner, not looking in the direction of the crowd or acknowledging them in any way.

Then it was our turn, Morgan and I stepped out onto the platform and the crowd began to rage. I don't know who they thought we were, but the excitement was contagious. I didn't want to disappoint my "fans" so I waved my arm over my head, "I love you all!" I shouted. I threw kisses and smiled, posing for the cameras. Morgan was having a hard time keeping a straight face.

With me encouraging them, the crowd began to get out of control and they were trying to bust through the barricade to get at me. The police were beginning to have a hard time, so I cut the show short, but it was too late. A group of fanatics managed to break through and push past the officers. They were after me, and all I could think about was the expensive jewelry that I had borrowed from the jewelry store. I was responsible for it and couldn't let them get it away from me.

The group of crazed fans rushed up the stairs, and soon they were only a few feet away. I knew that Morgan was a complete zero when it came to anything physical and I couldn't depend on him to protect me, or the jewelry. I was hoping that the policemen would be able to keep them away, but the group was too fast for them. A wild-man at the head of the pack reached out to grab me from a few steps below. I hiked up my gorgeous gown, gave him a swift kick to the chest and sent him tumbling down the stairs, where the police grabbed him and pushed the whole bunch of them back behind the barricade. It was strange; in all the shoving and confusion none of the cameras had managed to get a shot of me kicking the guy. I was just lucky I guess.

After the incident, I was tense, I didn't know how Morgan would react. Had I embarrassed him or insulted his manhood? Apparently I hadn't, "You're incredible, sweetheart," was what he said.

At first, I was relieved that Morgan wasn't upset or angry with me, but in the car I had time to think about it. I wondered what would have happened if I hadn't been able to defend myself and the out of control fan had gotten hold of me. I was disappointed in Morgan; I didn't expect him to do a flip, spin around in some fierce Karate move and pulverize the guy. But, he could have at least stood in front of me or made an effort of some sort. Instead, he just stood there like a complete dork and did nothing, waiting for the police to intervene. The police; who were at the bottom of the stairs with no way to reach me in time. If I hadn't kicked the guy off me, by the time the cop could have gotten close enough to help, the man would have already knocked me down, or grabbed the jewels and run away. I didn't say anything about it to Morgan, but I think that he knew how I felt.

How important had this been? Was it okay that Morgan was a wimp and couldn't or wouldn't even try protect me? I wasn't sure.

On the trip home, I was still perplexed about the incident, but when the airport shuttle pulled up in front of my house, I found a fabulous new, red Porsche waiting for me in the driveway! I couldn't believe my eyes! I jumped out of the shuttle and read the note on the windshield, "Hope this makes up for everything, Love Morgan."

Well, it certainly did make up for everything, everything and anything! Maybe Morgan was a wimp and couldn't protect me, but I could watch out for myself anyway. "Nobody's perfect," I said, as I jumped in the flashy car. I took a long ride in the winding hills; sleek and fast, the Porsche handled beautifully. I was in love and happy to get rid of the old car that I had been driving since the accident.

When I returned to work, I found that everyone had seen me on television at the award show. I was the talk of the town and they all wanted a piece of me. I immediately found that my "admirer's" wanted to get into the movies and thought that I was their ticket in. It was actually a joke, as far as I was concerned. None of these people had ever studied acting or had any experience whatsoever; they were completely unqualified. I would never ask Morgan to put his reputation on the line for so foolish a favor. But, however foolish their request, when I didn't help them, they blamed me that they had never gotten their "big break" and planned to get back at me.

Now I had yet another kind of an enemy, not an enemy that stood and faced me. This enemy was much more sinister than that, the ultimate coward. Honey dripped from their lying tongues when they talked to me face to face, but they fought behind the scenes, sneakily undermining me. I suppose that I should have expected to encounter a bit of jealousy, but I was naïve and I hadn't. As long as no one had a knife to my throat or a gun to my head, I didn't think them dangerous. I wasn't about to concern myself with this petty nonsense, and I jumped on the plane to see Morgan, leaving my troubles behind.

On this visit, Morgan and I were invited to a going-away party for one of his friends, a movie producer who was moving to New York to work on a major project.

My experience with Morgan's friends, who worked in the movie industry, was quite different than most people might expect. We see so many stories on the news and in magazines about drugs and scandalous sex that I think the general public has a very warped view of what the truth really is. These people were not a group of sex-crazed, alcohol abusing, drug addicts; no, far from it, they were moral intelligent and creative. Hard working people, who were up well before dawn and working long hours late into the night. I met captivating people who talked about fascinating things. Maybe someone else would have a different experience than I did, but that's the way that I found it.

Truth is, in the beginning I was prepared to have a wild high-flying time at the Hollywood parties, but was surprised to find that I was always the wildest one there. Morgan's friends seemed to get a kick out of me, and I was usually the one who ended up doing most of the entertaining. I enjoyed the company of these interesting powerful people and their attention as well. Strangely enough, I felt as though I fit in, it was the first time in my life that I had ever felt that way and I was looking forward to another pleasant time at the director's going away party.

When I got off the plane in L.A., Morgan said that he wanted to show me off and he took me directly to a fashion designer to have new clothes made for me for the special party. This designer was very famous and designed clothes for the sexy, more flamboyant stars. He took my measurements and designed something special just for me.

The clothes turned out beautifully and everything was ready, right on time. Morgan dressed me up like his prize and we were on our way.

The party was held at a trendy nightclub that had been bought out exclusively for the party that night. By the time that Morgan and I arrived, the festive affair had already begun. We walked in the door and Morgan did something strange, he nodded hello to the other guests, but didn't stop and talk to anyone. He walked me right past them all and across the room to the table furthest away from everyone.

I had on very high heels and my short black, leather skirt was adorned with rows of dangling golden chains that swished back and forth and made a tinkling tiny bell sound when I walked. The chains were flashing in the spotlights as we crossed the floor. Morgan was smiling when everyone stopped what they were doing to watch me. After we sat down, Morgan looked at me intently and asked, "Do you know why I like being with you?"

"No, why?" I asked. This was an interesting question and I was eager to hear the answer. I was prepared to hear how much he adored me, but no, not even close.

He said, "Because if I were here by myself no one would pay any attention to me. I could sit here at this table all night long and no one would come and talk to me. But, because I'm here with you, it won't be long before the whole party will move to this end of the room."

"That's ridiculous," I said, "people think that you're interesting, you have a lot of friends."

It was strange, but somehow I felt pressured now; it was as though I had been told what my job description was and what was expected of me. What if I couldn't perform? What if no one came to our table as Morgan had predicted? What if everyone just let the two of us sit by ourselves all night? Would Morgan be disappointed in me?

I didn't have the time to get myself all worked up and uptight over it because minutes later, three men came walking up to our table to say hello and compliment me on my new outfit. After they sat down, a few more people came to join us as well. Soon, the whole party really had moved to our end of the room, Morgan was right! I sat there in amazement.

Well ya know, the whole bunch of 'em were kinda quiet and reserved, and I was a rough and rowdy cowgirl; I guess that that's what they needed at a party. One thing I can say about country people, we do know how to have a good time, and I did have a good time, I always did.

The party was fabulous; it was quite the sendoff for the producer and no expense was spared. The band that played that night, had the number one hit record at the time, and I danced and enjoyed every minute of it.

Later that evening, one of Morgan's friends arrived. He was the host of a popular talent show. He came to the party alone and then danced and joked with me, monopolizing most of my time. Luckily, it wasn't a chore for me as he had a great sense of humor and I liked him. When we returned to the table after one of our dances, he asked me to be the spokes model on his next show.

I immediately laughed and told him that he was crazy, thinking that it was a joke. When I found out that he was serious, I told him what I thought. "I'm not pretty enough, and besides that, I have a little tiny voice. How will I announce the acts?"

"That's what would be so cute, you have a darling voice," he said. "It's not often that you find the combination of both beauty and charm. You're a lot of fun, and we'd have a great time doing the show together. Think it over and get back to me. Morgan, you know how to reach me, try to get her to change her mind." We said our good-byes and he left the party.

After his friend was gone, Morgan asked me a question, "I really want to know why you think that you're not pretty enough. The only difference between you and the models on the show, is that you don't know that you're pretty. You're tall and willowy and have the most gorgeous set of long silky legs that I've ever seen. You're a rare beauty Penelope, and rare things are more valuable; why, I find your coloring alone an aphrodisiac." Morgan gently stroked my cheek and looked into my eyes, "dark green eyes and soft snow-white skin." Then he grabbed a handful of my hair and twisted it around his fist, "red hair, long tangled and wild!" He pulled me close to him by my hair, "but I have to say that my favorite thing about you are those cute little, Cupid's bow lips, they're so sweet and irresistible." Morgan kissed me, "You're a hard combination to beat honey, I'd put you up against any of them. You be a good girl and do the show for me."

No one had ever paid me such a complement and I was embarrassed. I wasn't quite sure how to respond, so I didn't. I didn't say a word, I just took it in. I knew that the boys had always liked me, but I thought that it was because I was a tomboy, and that we always had fun together. It had never occurred to me that it might mean more than that, that maybe it meant that I was pretty.

When I was on the sets with Morgan, I was occasionally offered small parts in some of the movies. I wasn't flattered or thought that I was special because of it. Actors aren't necessarily attractive, they come in all shapes and sizes. But this offer was different, it meant that I was pretty.

After being banged around so much of my life and having my nose broken, I never thought of myself as being pretty. I felt different about myself now, maybe I wasn't so bad after all. Maybe I really was pretty. Maybe I could be the spokes model!

I thought it through, but the idea of being in front of all those people and trying to talk and announce the acts ... no way! I gave Morgan a positive N. O. I wasn't going to stand up in front of the whole country and make a fool of myself. Besides that, I didn't have aspirations to be a model or an actress, there were plenty of glamorous women more qualified than I whom I thought could do a much better job. But the compliment had still changed the way I felt inside.

The whole night had been kind of a fairytale story. "I'll have a lot to tell my friends when I get home after this visit," I thought, but the night wasn't over yet. Morgan and I were slow dancing to a romantic love song and as we glided across the shiny floor, under the twinkling lights, he asked me to marry him.

The excitement overwhelmed me, I didn't love Morgan and I surprised myself when I said yes. "He's so kind and honorable, I'll grow to love him," I reasoned.

I was going through with it, and as soon I returned home, I gave notice at work and made arrangements to move to L.A.

All of my life I had sat on the sidelines, going to weddings and being happy for everyone else who had found happiness. But now, it was finally my turn to have a wonderful life with an incredible man. Who knows what fantastic thing might happen next? It was a magical time; I felt like Cinderella. I had to pinch myself to make sure that it wasn't just a dream. But, it wasn't a dream and it wasn't going to end, Morgan and I were planning to be married and this was going to be my life! A life of riches and excitement!

Later that week, I got my regular nightly call from Morgan; I was happy to hear from him and wanted to talk about the wedding arrangements. Morgan interrupted me and said that he had something important to tell me … and it was a bombshell! He told me that he was married, and that he had filed for divorce after I accepted his proposal!

I was silent and he went on, "My marriage was over long before I met you. Don't worry, all this will amount to is me writing a check twice a month."

"Why didn't you tell me that you were married?" I asked. "How could you lie to me, lie through our whole relationship!?"

"I knew that you wouldn't accept it, that you weren't that kind of a woman," he answered. "I was afraid that if I told you, you wouldn't have had anything to do with me and I wanted time for you to get to know me first. Remember what you said about, Michael, the night we met? If you wouldn't have anything to do with him, a famous rich and handsome man, because he was married, I knew that I didn't stand a chance."

There wasn't much that I could say to that, he was absolutely right and I wouldn't have had anything to do with him. But, because he had waited to tell me until after he had proposed didn't change that fact, it only made things worse. Our whole relationship had been a scandal and a lie.

I thought about all of the people that I had met while we were dating, surely they all must have known that he was married. Oh my, what they must have thought of me! He had disgraced himself and me as well! And his wife, that poor woman; did he do all of the wonderful things for her that he had done for me? Did he make her feel like she was the most valuable thing in his life, only to cheat on her and treat her this shabbily?

Suddenly, I felt nothing for Morgan but contempt, he had betrayed his wife, a woman, a sister. No matter what his reasons may have been for doing things the way he had, everything that he had done was done the wrong way, and I couldn't be a part of it. At this point I was innocent, but if I let it go on, I was as guilty as he was. I would be the home wrecker, the woman who had broken up a marriage.

I had overlooked the fact that Morgan was much older than me, that he wasn't sexy and that he often whined about his bad back. Even though he was a wimp and incapable of protecting me, I could still get past it because I believed that he was someone worthwhile, a kind and honorable man. But all my admiration was gone now; the only thing left was Morgan's money and I wouldn't sell myself. The decision was simple, if he cheated on one wife, he would cheat on another.

I wanted nothing more to do with him and I made a quick and cold comment, "You're a disgrace and I'm finished with you," then I hung up the phone. I wouldn't talk to Morgan, answer his letters or accept any of his gifts. He continued to send me dozens of roses every week, but it didn't matter to me, I felt betrayed and I could never trust him again. It was over, and I think that I actually hated him.

I was fortunate to get my job back at the jewelry store and I quickly got on with my life. I tried not to allow myself to miss the glamour and excitement that I had lost. It wouldn't have been right for me to marry a man that I didn't love anyway, I would have been compromising. I believed that it had all worked out for the best.

I tried to comfort myself, "I'm not that old yet, and I must still look pretty good, I'm sure that I'll get another chance for love and happiness."

When the girls at the shopping center, where I worked, found out that Morgan and I had broken up, I couldn't believe some of the things that they said to me. "You're crazy Penelope, it wouldn't bother me one bit if I found out that he was married, not if I was getting all that expensive stuff."

"Who cares about his stupid wife anyway, if she's not woman enough to hold him, that's her problem."

But, I think that the worst one was … "When you steal a man from another woman, it means that you're better than her."

These women were serious about the things that they were saying! Some of them even went on a campaign to try and get information from me about Morgan so that they could contact him and catch him for themselves. It was horrible, they were completely immoral; they didn't know the difference between right and wrong and they didn't care to.

It amazed me how brazen they were at the prospect of acquiring a few possessions. So much so, that it never even occurred to them that it might be dangerous. Finding out that a spouse is cheating could easily be a shock that could throw someone over the edge, or even drive them to murder! Even me, I would be afraid of what I might do, if I found out that another woman had invaded my territory!

But when it comes to greed, I regretfully learned that nothing else matters; strangely enough, I had never known that before.

I was completely disgusted with my co-workers, and the sad part was that I had to work with them every day.

And that wasn't the only thing that was hard on me, I had lost Pat. Shortly after I accepted Morgan's marriage proposal, Pat married Lance. Lance had an incredible business opportunity come his way, but it was out of state and he wouldn't leave without, Pat. Since I had already planned to live in L.A., Pat decided to accept his latest proposal. The good news was that Lance truly loved Pat; there was never any doubt, she would have a good life with him.

A year after the marriage, Pat had two big, strappin' boys and devoted all of her time to giving them a proper upbringing. The two of us still remained close; we talked regularly on the phone and visited whenever we could, but her life was full, and there wasn't much room left for me anymore. I wouldn't have had it any other way, Pat was doing the right thing, caring for her family full time. I guess that's what had taken her so long to finally marry Lance; she knew that she had to be ready to completely devote herself to marriage and to her family, and that's exactly what she did. I was proud of her and happy to be an Auntie.

INVISIBLE CAGE

I continued to work at the jewelry store, I was surrounded by beautiful shiny gold and sparkling jewels; but I had no satisfaction at the end of the day. Selling a piece of jewelry didn't leave me with a feeling of accomplishment. Although I appreciated the job and truly liked Al and his wife Victoria, the fact was, that I had advanced as far as I could and there was no chance for further opportunity. I was making just enough money to barely meet my obligations, but not enough to ever get ahead or to move out of the bad neighborhood, and that was never going to change. Every time that I had an added expense, it went on my credit cards and the balances continued to climb.

The Porsche frequently had electrical problems. It was crazy how much the mechanics charged for labor and even the simplest of parts on the foreign car. I realized that in my current situation, I could never work my way out and I was going further and further into debt.

Days turned into weeks, weeks into months, months into years. Sunday, Monday, Tuesday, Wednesday, Thursday, Friday, Saturday, over and over again, another week of my life wasted, a week that I would never get back. My life was quickly passing me by and I knew that I had to do something, but what? There weren't any better jobs in town and I was still in a continuing struggle with the panic attacks, and couldn't drive the freeway to find one someplace else. I was stuck; I felt as though I was locked in a cage and I couldn't find the key. There was no escape in sight, no guiding light, no direction, I was merely existing.

Through the years, all of the big ranches in the area had been sold off and vineyards were planted in their place. The Horse Center was shut down and the real cowboys were a thing of the past. The town had changed completely, and so had the people in it, it was more like a country club than an actual place to live. I found that I no longer fit in with the wannabe sophisticated crowd; they drank wine and ate grapes with brie cheese on hard crackers.

Unfortunately, I no longer fit in with my family anymore either; after Grandma and Grandpa Wells passed away, the family was scattered and fragmented. It was all over; the close caring family that I had grown up with was gone, there was no hint of the tight-knit clan that we had once been.

Except for Uncle Henry, all of the brothers had been divorced, including my father. He had left the state and remarried. It was tragic for me as his new wife was jealous of the close relationship that Daddy and I had. Every time that I traveled to visit him, she let me know that I wasn't welcome and caused serious problems. It placed Dad in the uncomfortable position of being in the middle, so I stayed away.

Dad came to see me whenever he was in town, but always with his vicious wife in tow. She made certain that she never allowed my father and me to have any quality time together. She was always a negative presence, ruining whatever moments that we could have shared. His new wife was a conniving woman and Dad was blind the hateful creature that he had married.

Mom became a party girl. She had married my father at a young age and now that she was single again, she wanted to play the field. There was no room in her new life for anyone who reminded her of the past. She had moved on and even her own children didn't know where she was living.

Most of my cousins, including Linda Lou, had moved away and the cousins that were still in town were all married and had homes and children of their own.

Husbands of married women usually don't like their wives going out with single women, and the husbands of my cousins were no exception. They made it nearly impossible for us to spend any time together and our visits were limited to brief afternoon encounters during the children's naptime. I must admit, that although I loved my baby cousins dearly, listening to their mother's unending conversations about dirty diapers, complaints of sleepless nights, and their husbands unwillingness to help them, I quit trying to nurture the relationships myself. I had better ways to spend the few days that I wasn't at work.

My cousins let me know that they were disappointed in me. They expected me to marry a local boy, have children, and get with the program, as they had done. But, it just wasn't in me; I wasn't like them and we had nothing in common anymore.

Trying to find a friend in the small town was useless as well, the locals didn't understand anyone who wasn't just like them and unfortunately, they hadn't been out of their own backyards … and I had. I couldn't find a friend that I could talk to about anything meaningful. Conversations were limited to the local gossip and the shows on television.

During this bleak time of my life, I briefly dated a few of the local men, but there wasn't much to choose from. My first attempt to date again was with a man named Fred. I wasn't attracted to him, but he had asked me out, so I decided to give it a chance.

With little else to do in the small town, we ended up going to a movie. By coincidence, the movie that night, was one that I had seen being filmed, during my time with Morgan. I had an interesting story to tell about the actors and some inside facts about the movie. I of course, thought that my date would be interested in hearing these little anecdotes, but I was wrong, it made him angry. He even went as far as to call me a liar.

In retrospect, I think that I must have made him feel small, which was not my intention; I was just trying to be interesting and make conversation. Needless to say, I never saw him again and decided that in the future, I wouldn't talk about my movie experiences.

Time dragged on, and I finally did meet a man that I found attractive, but after the first date he told me that he was afraid of me! I was shocked, it was the first time that I had ever heard such a thing! I came to the conclusion that he simply wasn't a real man, but I was distressed to find that after that incident, it became commonplace, and I actually came to expect it, every time that I tried to date someone new.

Having men tell me that I was intimidating and that they were afraid of me was strange; it made me feel like some sort of a monster. Was I really a scary person? And if I was, what could I do about it?

Later on, I tried to date some of the "bikers" in the area and it was a joke, I couldn't engage them at any level. I don't know why they just couldn't have been real and enjoyed riding their motorcycles together. That would have been great, but these guys walked around trying to act tough. I could never really understand what prompted all of the tough acting, there were no real threats of any kind in the little country club town. I supposed that because they rode Harley Davidson's they believed that it gave them some sort of status. But, I'll tell you one thing, they wouldn't have lasted a day on the streets in the city where I had gone to school. And the shame of it was, that there wasn't a biker in that city who wouldn't have loved to escape the constant threat of violence and the necessity of actually being tough … for real. They would have jumped at the opportunity to live in peace and enjoy the safety of the little country club town.

I finally came to the conclusion that there simply wasn't a man in the area that could handle me. I sadly realized that I would have to change my whole life in order to fit in and that just wasn't possible. I couldn't put on an act and pretend that I was in kindergarten again. And that's exactly what these people seemed like to me, immature kindergarteners, trying to tell me about life and how to live and act, when the most that they knew themselves was how to look both ways when crossing the street.

While it was true that I hadn't traveled the world or achieved greatness, I had lived a gritty untamed life. I had had experiences that the small-minded people in town could never begin to comprehend or understand. In Junior High, I had fought in a race war and experienced the pain and fear of battle as my friends and I fought side by side for our very lives. At the age of thirteen, I already knew the gurgling sound made by someone struggling to stay alive while breathing through a bloody gash in the throat.

I proudly rode with Chainsaw Charlie and the motorcycle gang, my protectors, who guarded and shielded me from the cruel unfair world that had been thrust upon me. And Parker, the man that I wanted to spend the rest of my life with, mercilessly killed on the cold barroom floor. I had suffered immense pain, pain that I hoped none of them would ever know, and I bore the scars.

During my years working for the private investigator, I had matched wits with thieves and dangerous sexual predators and I took them down. I enjoyed the satisfaction of knowing that I had helped to make the world a safer place; I had purpose and goals. Then there was Windsor, my sexy killer boyfriend and the intense unbridled passion that we had once shared in the bedroom. With Morgan, my Hollywood man, I had lived the high life and rubbed shoulders with the beautiful people.

When I looked back, I guessed that with all of my experiences I had become an intimidating woman, but that was the way it was and there was no going back, no way to change any of it; it had made me what and who I was.

Even though it didn't always look like it, to people on the outside looking in, I had never done anything to be ashamed of, and I refused make excuses for myself. I decided that I wasn't going to put on an act and pretend to be something that I wasn't. I would be myself, no matter what the cost.

As far as dating, I didn't want a mere boy for a partner; what I wanted was a real man, an experienced man who knew how to please a woman. One who could handle me and who wasn't afraid, someone with whom I could be free to be myself. I was tired of living in a box and struggling to fit into it. I had failed miserably at it anyway.

It was senseless to continue my search for happiness in the town and I gave up and resigned myself to being an outcast. No one knew who I really was, no one had respect or admiration for me and I received no acknowledgement for the things that I had been through or accomplished in the past.

What had happened to The Angel and the love and caring that she had experienced from Chainsaw Charlie? I wanted to feel precious, to be cherished again. I no longer enjoyed the caring or protection of anyone. I was on my own, a scary monster.

I was a stranger in my own home town. I no longer belonged there, but I was trapped with no way out. So I strapped my shoulders into the harness and began to pull the plow; it was my lot in life, one row, one senseless meaningless day after another in the barren field that was now my life.

Was I going to live the rest of my days unloved by a man, working an unfulfilling job and being the favorite subject of every vicious gossip in town?

I kept hoping that something would change, and one day it did.

This book was brought to you by:
GALVANIZED GROUP INC.

Move on with the adventure:

TROUBLE WITH A DREAM III

Thank you for buying our book
.
Like us on Facebook
Follow us on Twitter

Galvanized Group Inc.

We'd love to hear from you: galvanizedgroupinc@gmail.com

www.ingramcontent.com/pod-product-compliance
Lightning Source LLC
Chambersburg PA
CBHW070852120626
46556CB00002B/954